DIAMONDS
TEAK &
MURDER

Cover Design: Spellbinding Design
Editing: Amabel Daniels
Formatting: Tadpole Designs

To Mom

For giving me the idea.

And for saving my very first book, "TOM WIT OWT" (Tom Went Out), in all its stapled looseleaf and crayon stick-figure glory.

You made me believe I could.

CHAPTER ONE

Ty climbed the stairs to the deck of the vintage yacht to see if he could find out where the sound and light originated. Someone had to be aboard *The Sunset Lady*, and there were too many valuable art pieces on it for this to be something random. He called out. No response. Definitely someone who wasn't supposed to be aboard. After heading past the pilot house and into the main living room area and noting that nothing was out of place, he slipped down the stairs to the cabins below. Two cabins and a bathroom were to his left. Again, he saw all was in order. As he turned toward the crew cabins, something came swinging at his head. His attacker grunted, and Ty ducked out of the way just in time to see a figure dressed in black. Ty scrambled up the stairs. Who was this? His pursuer was hot on his heels as he tore through the living room and onto the deck of the bow. Ty turned around to see the dark form barreling straight at him. He paused a second too long, and the intruder ran directly into him, hitting him in the head with something hard and pushing him into the railing, banging his head against the metal so that he saw stars.

"What the hell?"

His attacker said nothing but regained his footing and crouched to attack again.

"What the hell are you doing here? Who the hell are you?" Ty yelled. The only response was a low rumbling sound from the throat of his pursuer who lunged again, this time, knocking him onto his back. This guy wasn't big, but he was strong and had the element of surprise on his side. His face was darkened with something, making him unrecognizable. Ty realized how close he was to the edge of the forward deck and decided to stop fucking around. This jackass needed to be tossed. He tried to get up, but his pursuer was pushing him toward the edge. As he scrambled to get his footing or a hand-hold on anything that would stop his progress, he began to panic when all he met were smooth surfaces designed for easy cleaning.

"Wait— Stop," he yelled as the person continued to grunt and push. "Stop!" He frantically grabbed at anything within reach. His hands found his assailant's hat and ripped it off. "What the...?" he whispered.

His attacker paused, giving him the chance to scramble to his feet. "You?"

With one last growl, the attacker spun backward and landed a powerful kick to Ty's chest. The look of surprise never left his face as he sailed over the side of the boat and landed in a crumpled heap on the dusty ground below.

CHAPTER TWO

Allie woke to the still-unfamiliar sound of the landline phone. It was pitch-black out and unnaturally still. She glanced at the clock. Three AM. Why on earth was anyone calling her at this time of night? No one knew her home number, and Ryan was asleep in his bedroom.

Ryan. She panicked at the thought that her brother had gotten out of the trailer somehow, and had run into some kind of trouble. She wrestled with the sheets until her feet hit the floor and stumbled around the coffee table. Five hurried steps to his room, but he was right where he should be, sleeping through the racket from the phone. The ringing stopped and then started again. She gently closed the door and sprinted back to the kitchen, hurrying around the counter to grab it.

"Hello?" Her voice cracked with sleep.

"Allie? I'm so sorry to bother you at this hour, but it's… It's Ty. I mean, this is Neil, but something has happened to

3

Ty…" Something had to be really wrong if her boss was calling about his son, the yard foreman, at this hour.

Still trying to get her bearings, she said, "Neil? What's happened?"

"He's had an accident. He fell off one of the boats in the yard." He paused. "He's… dead."

"What?" she said, still not comprehending.

"Ty is dead," he repeated, emphasizing each word. "The Sheriff's Department is here, and I need you to… I need you to come down to the yard."

Allie hesitated. What could she do about Ryan? She separated the blinds a bit so she could see the neighbor's trailer and saw with relief that her lights were on. Peg was a night owl and wouldn't hesitate to come over to keep an eye on things.

"I'll be there as soon as I can," she said and hung up.

PEG WALKED BRISKLY across the small space between their trailers, her knitting bag in tow. Despite her salt-and-pepper pixie cut, most people were surprised to learn she was in her early seventies. When she came through the door, she asked, "You don't mind if I watch the TV on low, do you? I'm in the middle of a program."

Allie nodded and said, "Sure, whatever you need." The white hair elastic she pulled from the pocket of her skinny jeans had a shocking number of strands of her long chestnut hair entwined around it, but there was no time to untangle the mess. She smoothed her hair as much as she could, pulled a ponytail through the elastic, and snatched her green hoodie from the back of the chair.

"Thank you so much for doing this. I still don't know what's going on, and I'm not sure how long I'll be. Ryan is still asleep."

"Not a problem, honey. You know we'll be just fine. You go do what you need to do." The fine features of Peg's face relaxed into a soft smile. "I used to do this for your parents from time to time. Of course, not in the middle of the night, but I don't mind at all. And Ryan and I get along great, you know that. He'll probably never know I was here," she reassured, her piercing pale-blue eyes twinkling. "It was Neil that called you?"

"Yes, he said his son Ty fell off one of the boats in the yard and is... dead... I just can't imagine... Boats are second nature to Ty." Allie remembered Ty's patience when he first took her clamming, showing her how to drag the rake in the sand and later teaching her how to use her toes to find the clams. She also remembered his quiet smile at her excitement each time she found one and dug it out herself.

"Sounds suspicious to me. The sheriff is there? Fill me in when you get back," Peg said, settling her petite frame into a recliner.

"I will," Allie promised absently as she grabbed her keys. She was still trying to wrap her brain around what she was going to walk into at the boatyard.

SHE HAD NEVER SEEN the yard like this, lights blazing in the middle of the night, with the gate wide open, and ten to fifteen people milling around. They were focused on the stately, polished-wood yacht called *The Sunset Lady*, twenty feet high in its braces, and she guessed that was where it had happened. Every step she took kicked up dust from the ground, and the blue lights from the cruisers swinging around the scene only added to the surreal quality of the picture. The frogs and insects that would normally be in full chorus were silent, fearing the humans who had invaded their space. The sailboats and pleasure cruisers perched on blocks, waiting their turns for repair along the perimeter of the yard, seemed to look on at the scene in the center. There, bright lights atop poles that seemed far too skinny to support their weight illuminated what looked like a pile of rags from this distance. A chill went through her as she realized that those "rags" were likely what was left of Ty Guthrie.

Avoiding the spectacle, she walked up the steps to the office and pulled on the door. The fluorescent lights overhead seemed harsher in the middle of the night, and it was quiet enough to hear their buzz over the hum of conversation from Neil's office. As she approached the open door to Neil's office, she could see him at his desk with his head in his hands, while his wife, Vicky, leaned on a dented file cabinet, looking at the plastic clock on the wall. Across from Neil sat Chief Detective Bishop from the Sheriff's Department. She hadn't seen him since April, when she'd had to identify the bodies of her parents.

"Neil," she started.

"Allie!" he said as his head snapped up. Chief Detective Bishop nodded to her briefly.

Vicky also turned to greet her with a slight glare, quickly masked. "Allie. We are so glad you are here."

"What happened?" Allie asked, gripping the back of the

chair. The grief on Neil's face, the quiet of the office, and the image of the "pile of rags" in the yard began to coalesce as the finality of Ty's death settled into her brain.

"We don't know," Neil said, glancing at Chief Detective Bishop. "To my knowledge, all the staff had left yesterday evening—it was Monday, right?—by about 5:30. The next thing I know, it's the middle of the night, and I get a call from the Sheriff's Department that our alarm company had called them when we didn't respond to the alarm going off. I guess the company called my cell phone, but I keep it on mute at night. Some deputies got here about an hour ago and called me on the landline when they found Ty." He put his hand to his forehead. Vicky placed a reassuring arm around his shoulders.

The gesture of comfort reminded Allie of happier times. Neil had been friends with her father, once upon a time, and it still struck her as odd. Even at the age of eleven, she could tell that her dad and Neil were very different people. Then, Neil had been a lanky, tan, preppy man with a shock of dark hair in contrast to her father's stocky body, fair complexion, and work boots. Nowadays, Neil was a little paunchy, a little pink, and had a head of mostly gray, wavy hair. He was nice enough, but when his temper took hold, his face turned bright red and his voice boomed. His second son, Zack, seemed to get him most riled, but anyone could set off that hair trigger, especially family. Ty had tried to stay in the yard as much as possible.

You could tell Neil had money, and always had, unlike his second wife, Vicky. His expensive clothes seemed like a second skin, but no matter how much jewelry dripped from her fingers, wrists, neck, and ears, you would never mistake Vicky for Old Southern Money. Maybe it was her constant expression of wariness, or the way she always stood slightly behind Neil. Maybe it was the dye job that never seemed to cover her darker roots, or the way her clothes from the expensive department store in town never looked quite right on her frame. She had married Neil eight years before Allie's family had moved to the area, but she still seemed uncomfortable with his wealth. And in spite of the money, she was a sour person, as if her life had not panned out the way she had hoped. Even though she would flash a smile and holler a "Hey, y'all!" in greeting, as expected, as soon as the formalities were over, her face fell naturally to a frown.

Allie realized Neil was speaking to her. "I need you to help the Chief Detective with whatever he needs," he said, gruffly.

She nodded, glancing at Bishop.

"And it's going to be pretty crazy around here for a while." He rubbed his forehead. "Between law enforcement, the press, and the boat owners..." He closed his eyes. "We'll just need you to keep things under control." He couldn't sit still, cradling his head in his hands one moment and straightening his back to look at the clock the next while Vicky chewed her lip and sighed. She was probably thinking about how her son Zack would be affected by all of this. Where was Zack, anyway?

"Does Zack know?" Allie asked.

Neil's gaze slid to Vicky. "We tried to call him but couldn't reach him," Vicky said, wringing her hands.

"We'll try again in a bit. I would hate for him to have to learn about his brother from someone else."

"Chief Detective?" Allie said, motioning to the outer office.

"Hey, Allie," he said, following her. "I know this is a shock. Are you doing all right?"

"I guess I'm okay," she said, her mind betraying her for a moment and remembering the young Ty, the one who had taken her clamming and flounder gigging when she was just a girl. Once they were out of earshot of Neil's office, she said, "I just don't understand how this could have happened."

Bishop made sure the back of his uniform polo was tucked into his crisp dark dress pants. His badge and gun hung off his belt, and his oxfords had been recently shined. He smiled at her. "I haven't talked to you in a while, since your parents' accident. How are you and Ryan making out? Have things settled down a little bit for you two?"

"I suppose so," she answered carefully, not wanting to drag up the memories. They were dangerously close anyway, with death in the air. "He's adjusting, and so am I. It'll take some time, I think."

"Of course, it will. Your lives have changed so much. Has he started talking again?"

"No, not yet. A word here and there, but the doctor says that's the grief, not the autism."

"And what about your grief?"

Allie blushed. "I haven't had time to grieve."

"If you need anything, anything at all, please call me," he said, putting his hand on her shoulder.

9

"You know I will, Chief Detective Bishop."

"Charlie, please. This ain't the big city here," he reminded her with his ready smile.

"Can I ask you something?"

"Of course," Charlie said.

"You've been here for at least an hour. And you've seen one boatyard, you've seen them all. Why did you tell Neil you needed my help?"

He puffed out his barrel chest as he lifted his waistband. "Well, I'm gonna let you in on a little something. The techs are out there with one of my detectives, and we're not sure this was an accident." His fingers traced his silver mustache that matched his close-cropped hair.

Allie let that sink in for a minute. It definitely made more sense than Ty falling off a boat. While Ty had been careful about his public persona, one to one, he could be less-than-charming, lighting into the yard crew over the tiniest of issues or ghosting a string of paramours. She became aware of Charlie watching her reactions to the news.

"It's a possibility," she said.

"I know you didn't deal with dead bodies as a fraud investigator in Chicago, but I thought you'd sense something wasn't quite right here. Of course, we have to wait for the autopsy, but we're looking at all possibilities, and one of them is that there was someone else here who caused him to fall. I assume Ty was living somewhere close by?"

"He's been living on his sailboat in the yard since this spring, just about our only live-aboard in the yard, I think," she answered carefully, reaching over the front of her desk to move some papers around.

"I wondered if that was the case. I had heard a bit about him and Barbie breaking up. Well, the first thing I'll need is a list of employees, and then…"

She handed him the employee roster.

The door swung open and Mike Gillikin walked in, concern on his face. He was the yard mechanic and looked out of place without his coveralls. Fully dressed in jeans and a rumpled, long-sleeved shirt, he stifled a yawn and ran a hand through his eye-length honey-blond hair. His dark-blue eyes had a difficult time staying open until they found Allie. He made right for her.

"Are you all right? What happened?" he asked, taking her hands in his. They felt rough, warm, and dry, and Allie didn't want to let go.

She said, "I'm fine, but Ty had some sort of accident and fell off the deck of *The Sunset Lady*. He's dead."

"Neil just said there was an accident in the yard and I needed to come in! I had no idea…" He looked at Charlie as if seeing him for the first time.

"Mike," Charlie said with a nod.

"Charlie." Mike dropped Allie's hands gently. He put one hand on her shoulder and said, "Are you sure you're okay?"

"Yeah, I'm fine," she said.

"Do I hear Mike out there? Mike?" Neil yelled from his office.

"Gotta go," Mike said. "I'll catch up with you before you leave."

"Okay," she said and smiled at him. Charlie cleared his throat when Mike turned to go into Neil's office.

"What?" she asked.

"Nothing," Charlie said, trying to hide a smile. Allie wondered if he had suspected her crush on Mike and was momentarily mortified. But then she remembered that Charlie was a trained law enforcement officer and more observant than most people, which calmed her a little. She hoped Mike had not seen on her face whatever giveaway had been so clear to Charlie.

"Are you sure you're up to this? The body ain't pretty," he said.

"Um, yeah, I'm pretty sure," she said. In fact, she wasn't at all sure. With the death of her parents being so recent, she wasn't exactly certain how her psyche would react upon seeing another dead body, but she thought it would be important to see what the detectives saw if she was going to be of any help.

CHAPTER THREE

Charlie Bishop and Allie went out to the crime scene. *The Sunset Lady*, a brand of yacht called a "Trumpy," was one of Allie's favorites in the yard, even though it belonged to such miserable people. It was a vintage yacht with loads of woodwork and hand-crafted details. Why had Ty Guthrie been anywhere near it after hours?

It was a clear, dry night, cool enough for her hoodie to be necessary. There would be no footprints left tonight. A detective and a few techs were squatting and kneeling around the body in the middle of the bright lights. They must be used to it, but Allie had to shield her eyes. One of the techs photographed the scene, while the other examined the body itself. The detective was taking measurements and jotting down notes in his pad.

As she and Charlie got closer, she could see the prone form of Ty Guthrie on the ground. His left arm was flung across his chest, and his neck twisted at an unnatural angle. His right leg was bent where it shouldn't, and one of his Keens lay a few feet from the body. She looked up at the bow of the yacht and calculated at least a twenty-five-foot drop. No one had closed his eyes, and they were clouded, meaning they had been open when his life left that inhospitable body. Allie wondered what those eyes had seen last. He was dressed in an old Guy Harvey T-shirt and flannel pajama bottoms. His signature ball cap was nowhere to be seen, and Allie absently thought he was about two weeks past due for a haircut. Dark smudges stained his hands and forearms. *Is that engine grease? Was he working on the boat before he fell?* Allie took stock of her feelings and realized she felt pity for this man, rather than any horror or revulsion. He had been kind to her, both when she was a girl and when she returned to Carteret County a few months ago. To others, he may have been charming, but never kind. She took a moment to recognize that rare kindness he had shown her and send a good thought to whatever higher power was up there. He was barely into his forties, knowledgeable about boats and yard work, and it had all ended this horribly. *Why?*

Charlie introduced her to Detective Lawson, and the techs, Barry and Sandi, and then knelt down next to the body and slipped on a pair of latex gloves. He picked up one of Ty's hands to get a closer look at the smudges.

"Doesn't look like oil," he said carefully. "Not sure what that is." He motioned for Allie to kneel down and take a peek.

"I don't think it's paint, either," she said. As she bent to look at his hands, she got a strong whiff of beer. She looked at Ty's face again, trying to remember their last conversation, and couldn't. Charlie was making note of some redness on his forearms, as well.

"What did you do, here, buddy?" he said under his breath. Allie sniffed the air, took in the normal scents of oil and gasoline, metal and water, but also that tang of malted alcohol.

"Do you smell the beer?" she asked Charlie.

"Yep. Of course, he was known to tie a few on, but we'll have to wait and see what the toxicology report says. He may have fallen if he was drunk."

Charlie asked the techs if they had cleared the boat yet, and one of them said that they had not. He hesitated and then asked Allie what she knew of the boat itself.

"The boat was built in 1937 and goes by the name of *The Sunset Lady*, although her name has changed several times since she was built. She is roughly sixty feet long and worth millions of dollars."

"And the owners?" Charlie asked.

"It's owned by Keith and Donna Briggs, who are staying at a condo in downtown Beaufort until the work is done. The captain and crew that brought her here left as soon as she was brought into the yard, about four months ago, and will return when she's ready to sail," Allie rattled off.

"Why is it worth so much?" Charlie asked, looking at the boat with raised eyebrows.

"It is a Trumpy yacht, which was extremely popular as a status symbol with the hoi polloi in the thirties, forties, and even fifties, and anyone who was anyone owned one. Firestones, Rockefellers, Chryslers. In fact, there was even a presidential Trumpy called the USS *Sequoia*. Now there are only about a hundred left."

Charlie let out a low whistle. "Would someone try to steal it?"

"No, not the boat itself. Only the yard workers know exactly what still needs to be repaired, and it would take several men and heavy equipment to move her into the Intracoastal anyway," Allie replied. "These boats often have very high-end art and accoutrements on board, but anything of real value was removed and is stored in the office safe for insurance purposes."

"Who would know about all that?" Charlie asked.

"Anyone who worked for the yard," Allie said, knowing this was not much help.

Charlie looked at the list she had given him as he pulled on some reading glasses. "So, we have a few regular yard laborers who worked under Ty, and just Holly who works in the office beside yourself," he said. "Anyone else?"

"Well, there are the subs who do the contract work on the boats, but they aren't here all the time. I don't think any have been hired for *The Sunset Lady* yet, but I can double-check tomorrow. There's also Zack, Vicky and Neil's son, who was Ty's half-brother. He works in the yard sometimes."

"When he's not wide open, causing trouble, you mean," Charlie mused.

"Yes," she agreed simply. "Barbie used to work in the office, until she and Ty separated."

"Ah, yes. Ty's soon-to-be ex-wife…" Charlie. "Probably had a reason to hurt him…"

"But not necessarily the opportunity," Allie said. "She doesn't work in the office anymore, plus she's just had foot surgery and is on one of those wheelie-things so she can get around."

"Good to know. Who else?"

"Any of the live-aboards or DIY owners—boat owners staying on their boats right now, if we have any, but I don't think so."

"Anyone beside those we've mentioned would not have access to the yard, correct?"

"Correct. But I thought the alarm company alerted you? Couldn't it have been someone from outside?" Allie asked.

"We don't think so. The alarm company *did* alert us. Someone set the alarm off in their hurry *to get out of* the yard. They either lost their key card, or left it behind, and somehow managed to shove the gate open in order to get out. That triggered the alarm, the company called the office and got no response, so they called us in."

"So, there should be a key card on the scene somewhere."

"Yes, there should, if that's how they got in, and that's if we're dealing with a homicide here, which we haven't determined. If we find it, it may be able to give us some more information."

Allie took Charlie around the yard so he could get his bearings and information on the various owners and tasks for which the yard workers, subs, and Ty himself would have been responsible. They circled the perimeter of the yard and watched the Medical Examiner's Office van collect the body. The scene techs wrapped up on the ground and moved on to process the boat.

Charlie's cell phone vibrated. He pulled it from its holder at his side to look at the screen. He hesitated, looked around, and answered, switching to speaker so Allie could also hear the conversation.

"Chief Detective Bishop," he said, then put his finger to his lips to signal Allie that he didn't want the caller to know she was listening, too.

"Charlie. It's Kat. Give me a status update," said a female voice that sounded tired but used to taking command in the middle of the night.

"Ty Guthrie is dead on the grounds of Guthrie's Marine. We've secured the yard and notified the family. Neil and Vicky are here. I have a detective and crime-scene techs gathering evidence as we speak, but whether or not a crime occurred remains to be seen," he reported.

"Well, I've just had a call from Neil Guthrie. I don't need to tell you we need to tread carefully here, Charlie. Neil's not only an old friend, but he also comes from a respected family. We will have no leaks and no public conjecture. We will not give any information to the press that could be embarrassing for the family. We'll wait for the facts and determine our course of action from there," she said.

"Of course," Charlie said, raising an eyebrow at Allie.

"But we treat this as an accident until we have proof otherwise. There is no need to bother the family unnecessarily, either."

"Yes, ma'am," Charlie said dutifully.

"All right. I'm going back to bed. Call me in the morning to let me know how everything is progressing."

"I will. Goodnight, ma'am," he said.

"Goodnight," she said and hung up.

Charlie put his phone away. "That was Katherine Matthews, the DA."

"I see," Allie said.

They headed back toward the office and Charlie said, "A deputy will be here in the morning to help with security of the scene, and we've already started trying to contact the owners of the yacht. Tomorrow, you can check on the status of the workers assigned to the boat, and keep track of who goes in and out of the yard. I'll bring a detective over mid-morning to search the boats, and then maybe you can bring Ryan over for supper tomorrow night? About 6:30? Sheila can whip up something for the four of us, and you can fill me in. What do you think?"

"All right," she said. "Charlie?"

"Yes, Allie?"

"I don't think Ty's death was an accident."

"You may be right on that. Time will tell." He stopped near the door to the office and smiled at her. "Thanks for your help. Your parents would be proud of you."

Allie smiled around the sudden lump in her throat and went back into the office. She approached Neil's office. If he was in a mood, she would steer clear and head home. If not, she wanted to catch Mike before she left. She caught the tail end of a conversation *without* raised voices and popped her head inside the door.

"I'm going to head home now, but I'll be back early in

the morning to start what needs to be done," she said to Neil, with a glance at Mike, who stood up.

"I think we're clear on what we need to do labor-wise," he said.

Neil said, "I'm trusting you both to handle all of this. I'm not sure when or if Vicky and I will be in... It's a lot. We're in the thick of hurricane season, and we definitely can't slack off here."

"I understand. We'll take care of things," Allie said.

They said their goodbyes, and Mike walked Allie to her car. Again, he put his hand on her shoulder, and she felt a thrill rise up from behind her belly button. Mike was a good guy, and if she were the type to make a move, she might have already. She'd had plenty of opportunities with their many lunch hours spent together on the Beaufort boardwalk over the past four months, but she could never find the words.

"You sure you're okay?" he asked again.

"Mike, I'm fine. It was a little tough tonight, but I'm a lot stronger than I look," Allie said.

"Oh, I know you are. But it's okay to not be so tough every once in a while," he said with a smile. "I'll see you in the morning, but call me if you need anything. You've got my number." He hopped into his truck and waved as she got into hers.

CHAPTER FOUR

"Whew," Allie said, dropping her purse and keys on the table and smiling at Peg.

"How was it?" Peg asked, looking up from her knitting.

"Not the easiest thing ever," Allie admitted. "I was a little worried about seeing a dead body, but I was actually okay. My brain kind of took over."

"What did the sheriff say?" Peg said, finishing her row and stashing her current project in her bag.

"Well, it was Charlie Bishop there tonight," Allie said.

"The same one who worked your parents' accident scene?" Peg's head snapped up.

Allie nodded.

Peg pursed her lips. "So, what do you think happened?"

"I'm not sure. Neither is Charlie. Ty could have gotten drunk and fallen off the boat. He reeked of beer," Allie said.

"But you don't think that, do you?"

"No. My gut tells me someone was involved in this.

The biggest clue is the alarm." Allie explained how the key card system worked and that someone must have left the scene without one. "It may still have been an accident, but someone knows something," Allie concluded.

"Hm." Peg rubbed her chin with her thumb and index finger. "Interesting."

"All of this has to stay between the two of us, Peg."

"I know, dear. Who would I tell?" Peg reassured her, smoothing out her pink scrubs. She still wore them along with her crocs because they were comfortable. "I live alone, only go to the senior center about twice a month. I have my doggies, a sister in Raleigh, you two—that's it!" Peg began to gather up her bag to get ready to go.

"Did you know my dad and Neil were friends?" Allie asked.

"That must have been a little before my time. Your parents never mentioned the Guthries to me, so whatever friendship they had probably cooled by the time I met them," Peg said.

"I mean, I remember hanging out with them when I was young, but then they just kind of fade from memory. Ty used to take me clamming and flounder gigging," Allie mused. "You know how you don't really understand things that happened when you were a kid until you're an adult? I'm not even sure I understand now." She looked around the trailer as if for the first time. Her parents had upgraded the details even if they had down-graded from a house. The carpet was soft, the vinyl was thick. The walls were painted a light, neutral color, and there were aqua and cream-colored accents throughout the space.

"Well, you didn't live here with your parents all that long, did you?"

"No, I think we moved to the area when I was about eleven, and Ryan was a toddler. Dad was stationed at Cherry Point, and then Ryan was diagnosed with autism, and they decided they needed to stay in one spot. I was doing really well in school—not having any distractions like friends will do that to you, I guess," Allie said. "Typical military brat—blend in, don't stand out, and all that. When everyone was focused on Ryan, I focused on my work and graduated early. I decided I wanted to go to college in Chicago where my Aunt Cheryl lived, so I went to live with her and that was that. I haven't really been back until this spring."

"You're a brave girl, Allie," Peg remarked.

Allie looked down at her hands. She didn't want Peg to see her get emotional.

"You were here only about five years, then," Peg figured.

"Yep, I didn't even learn to drive down here. I did that up north."

"Well, your parents must have moved into this trailer soon after you left because they needed to save money and didn't need the space in the house, and I moved in next door about the same time, when Ryan was about seven, so…"

"Something happened to their relationship with the Guthries before I left. Before 2003."

Peg did the math with her finger in the air. "Yes! I think you're right. Could you ask Neil about it?"

"I could. But it's awkward. I'm curious about what

happened between my dad and Neil. But right now, the priority is finding out what happened to Ty."

They sat in silence as each followed their own thoughts. Finally, Peg said, "Well, my dear, I need to head back to my little furry friends. They will need walking soon. The sun is almost up."

"Oh my gosh, Peg, I am so sorry to keep you up so late!" Allie said, realizing how late, or early, it had become.

"Oh, honey, don't worry! I'm an old woman who has nothing but time on her hands. I love to help you out, you know that. Now get some rest. You have to be back to work in a few hours. Make sure to nap sometime tomorrow if you can. I'll talk to you later!" Peg grabbed her things and hustled across the yard to her trailer.

BEFORE SMOOTHING the rumpled sheets back down on the couch, Allie slipped down the hall to Ryan's room and nudged the door open. Knowing he was asleep, she stepped into the room and leaned over him, brushing his hair with her fingertips. He was always so peaceful in his sleep. She sat down next to him, her eyes never leaving his face.

"One of the reasons I looked for an office job when I moved down here was so that I would have enough time for you," she murmured. "I didn't need the stress and the drama of tracking down bad guys on the internet to follow me here." Allie looked around his room, still not as familiar with his space and his things as she should be. She had missed a lot in her absence and started to second-guess herself, remembering Ryan's first meltdown after she had arrived. He had to have his toast made just the right way, and when she had messed it up, he had erupted into a yelling, stomping, fist-wielding rage. He hadn't hurt her—she had used some of her blocks and dodges from her boxing training. But there had been little warning, and when it was over ten minutes later, they were both shell-shocked.

She stroked his hair again and remembered the day the Guthries had taken her family to Shackleford Banks to see the wild ponies when Ryan was a toddler. When Neil had beached the boat, Ryan was the first out of the boat and onto the narrow beach, headed straight for the scrub to search for the ponies. He had had no fear, and Ty had been the one to take him by the hand and talk softly to him about the ponies, how they had been on a boat torn apart by a storm, and had swum to the island and survived on marsh grass and rain ever since. Ryan had listened when Ty had warned him to stay back because they were wild, and he attached himself to Ty for the rest of the day. For his part, Ty seemed to enjoy the attention from the little boy, much as he had taken to Allie. Someone had robbed that man of his life, and it left a hole in the fragile fabric of her memory.

As she thought about her neighbor Peg, Allie thanked the powers that be for the thousandth time for the help that little old lady provided. As much as she was pulled by the puzzle, Ty's death was a threat to her attempt at a calm adjustment to this new life. "Just breathe," she said aloud. She had to try to get some sleep for a couple of hours before getting Ryan ready for his day program.

Just what had happened in that boatyard?

CHAPTER FIVE

In the morning, Allie dressed in her workout gear and went to the shed behind the trailer, where her dad had rigged up a punching bag. She spent twenty minutes working up a sweat and going through three rounds, perfecting her stance and throwing combinations. She didn't do this enough, but she needed it today to shrug off the stress of the previous night. When she finished, Allie went back inside, showered, and dressed. Then she woke Ryan and fixed him some breakfast while he completed a word-find puzzle at the table.

"It's Tuesday, Ryan. Are you working on more folding and mailing at Station Club today?" she asked.

No response.

"Not sure, huh?"

"Not sure," he repeated.

"That's not too difficult to do, is it?"

Again, no response.

"But I bet you have to be careful of getting paper cuts, huh?"

"Yep," he said. Conversation was usually pretty one-sided like this, but she kept trying. He hadn't always been so nonverbal and could be quite chatty about his intense interests like pirates, video games, and cars. But since her parents' death, he hadn't spoken much and needed extra reassurance whenever anyone was leaving his presence that they would return. Another student being absent at the Station Club was often what triggered a meltdown these days.

Allie helped him brush his teeth, gave him directions to get dressed, letting him know what the weather was supposed to be like that day, and helped him gather his things. She drove him to his day program and said good-bye, to no response. As Ryan shut the car door, she rubbed her face with her hands. *Would this ever get any easier?*

She drove to work, still amazed at the amount of traffic in Morehead City, a "fringe rural" town with only one high school and a population 300 times smaller than Chicago. The large international port at the mouth of the Newport River loomed on her right as she went over the tall bridge spanning the Intracoastal Waterway, and she had a brief chance to appreciate the stunning view of the barrier islands and the cerulean vastness of the Atlantic Ocean beyond. She shifted her attention to the task ahead of her. After years of being the new kid at school because of her dad's military career, she had gotten proficient at blending in and reading other people's emotions and motives. Today, she had to manage her regular workload, plan for how to deal with any media attention that may come their way, and keep an eye on anyone coming and going from the yard. And if she had a chance, she had to figure out a way to satisfy her curiosity about what happened between Neil and her father all those years ago.

When Allie pulled in, she noticed there were no law enforcement vehicles in sight, even though Charlie had promised a deputy. She wondered if the owners of *The Sunset Lady* had even been reached last night. If they had, she knew they would be here bright and early, full of piss and vinegar. Neil's car was there, but she suspected it wouldn't be for very long. She braced herself as she opened the door and walked in.

The office was relatively small, and everything in it was beige, old, banged-up, and bought at an auction. Nothing was very efficient or comfortable, but it had been cheap. There was one window out to the yard and another that faced the small parking area.

She knocked on Neil's door, and he motioned for her to come in and sit down. "Thanks for your help last night. It's difficult to manage things when you're kin to a victim," he began.

"I have a great neighbor who popped over, so it was no problem," she said. "How are you doing?"

"As well as can be expected, I guess. He was my son, and I keep having to remind myself he's not coming back." His voice broke. He cleared his throat and sat up straight. "And then there's the business headache on top of it all— he was the best yard foreman around, and I've asked Mike to fill in for now. But we need to get somebody to replace him, which I just can't even begin to think about right now... It's overwhelming."

"Of course, it is. Mike and I will take care of things today. You need time to process it all."

"All right," he said, standing. "It wouldn't look good for me to be here today, anyway."

"Is there anything special you'd like me to do?"

"The Briggs will probably be in early today. Are you sure you can handle them?" he asked.

"They don't scare me," she said.

"Okay," he said. "Call me if they get too boisterous."

"I will."

"Make sure those statements get in the mail today, and be sure to charge late fees when necessary. Oh, and keep an eye on that invest that's off the coast of Africa, too. If that thing turns into a hurricane, haul-out will be a bitch," he said as he made his way out the door.

Allie had learned to watch the Weather Channel as religiously as the locals during hurricane season. An invest was a storm off the coast of Africa that had the possibility of turning into a hurricane, and was all the buzz in the area when one cropped up.

Allie watched Neil pull out of the small parking area and noticed a deputy had arrived as Charlie had promised. She sat down at her desk and took a deep breath in the quiet of the office, the calm before the storm. She thought about all her years at TransUnion in Chicago, investigating fraud and all of the hundreds of cases in which she had been involved. Interviewing witnesses and suspects was nothing new to her, nor was the research and surveillance. She was also quite used to working with law enforcement, although none as fatherly as Charlie Bishop. She had thought she'd left that life behind in the colder climes of the Midwest, but here she was, in the middle of it all again.

She took out a copy of the employee roster so she could make a mental note of who came in today. *Let's see, besides Mike, we should see Sammy today—I'm sure Mike will fill him in about what to work on, but will he take direction without Ty here to be on him? I don't think the subs are scheduled to come in yet for* The Sunset Lady. *I should check Neil's office for the valuables from the boat just in case, because I know the Briggs will be asking when they come in...* Allie continued to build her to-do list and prepare herself for the day.

With that completed, she went into her drawer, grabbed the file for *The Sunset Lady*, and ventured into Neil's office, heading for the closet. Reaching up, she pulled on the string to turn on the bulb and turned to the safe. She entered the combination, pulled the large handle, and looked inside, comparing the contents to her inventory list. "One Picasso in gilded frame, one Rodin statuette, one Persian rug, circa 1178, and one Tiffany lamp, circa 1930. Yep, all here," she said and closed up the safe. *That was it? There had to be more than that of value aboard the boat. Why wasn't everything put in the safe?* Allie idly wondered.

"Mornin', Allie!" Holly Mason called out, putting her large hobo-style purse on the desk closest to the door. Holly worked in the office part-time, answering phones, which always amazed Allie because she had a thick, Down East accent, difficult for anyone not from the area to understand. People from the formerly isolated areas in the far-eastern regions of the county still spoke with the distinctive short "i" sounds that turned into "ee's", long "i's" that turned into "oi's"—"high tide" became "hoi toid," and entire sentences could often run together as if speaking in cursive. To Allie's ear, it sounded like a brogue from the British Isles. Holly was thin, young, and beautiful with striking light-blue eyes and long blonde hair. She also wasn't very bright, which was why she did well with routine and scripts for the phone.

"Why's there a—" Holly began.

"You heard about—" Allie interrupted.

"No, what?" Holly said, her eyes searching Allie's as her brows knit together.

"Ty Guthrie apparently fell off *The Sunset Lady* early this morning and died," Allie said simply, watching for her reaction.

"No!" Holly gasped in shock as her hand flew to cover her mouth.

"Yes, unfortunately. That's why there's a sheriff's deputy out there. They're looking into it."

"I should hope so! He's the last person that'd ever tumble off a boat!" Holly said.

Allie asked her to handle the phones and told her what Neil wanted her to say if anyone from the media called for comment. "If anyone from the Sheriff's Department calls, please forward them to me."

The media had been largely quiet, probably due in large part to there being no real local TV stations and only one countywide newspaper. But apparently, someone had just tipped them off, because the phone began to ring off the hook. A suspicious death in Carteret County might be the story of the year. Holly began to field the calls, using her script as instructed. Allie felt sorry for her, and she helped field some calls herself when her invoicing was finished.

"Guthrie's Marine Center, this is Allie. Can I help you?"

"Yes, can I get a comment from you about the body found in your boatyard last evening?"

"The boatyard will be releasing a statement once the Sheriff's Department has released their findings. As of right now, we don't know anything and have no comment. Thank you, goodbye," she said as she hung up and pressed the button for another line.

Shortly afterward, a reporter and a cameraman showed up at the yard, and Allie had to go outside and tell them they were not permitted on the grounds. She reiterated the canned response and asked them to leave, which they did after the sheriff's deputy helped them find their way.

She scanned the road for more TV vans and headed inside. "I guess we have to close the gate, Holly," Allie suggested.

"All right, we can do that. Won't stop them from filming outside the gates, though."

"Not much we can do about that. But our owners won't like to see their vessels on the news tonight, either," Allie replied.

"Ya reckon'?" Holly asked with a smile.

Later, when the phones had died down a bit, Holly asked, "Did Ty's ex used to work here?"

"Barbie? Yes, she did. But when she and Ty split up, she quit. I hear it was quite a scene. That was before my time, though."

"It seems like they go through a lot of people in this yard. Made me think twice before taking the job here, but they seem like nice people…"

"Yeah, they're nice people." Allie paused. "Of course, Neil has his moments," she said, thinking of the angry outbursts she had witnessed already in her short tenure. "I think Barbie and Neil scared people out of the office, and Ty scares… scared people out of the yard. None of them are… were exactly easy to work for. Vicky tries to stay out of it, and Zack… well, Zack is just Zack."

"What is his deal, anyway?" Holly asked.

"He's spoiled. Has always thought his parents liked Ty more than him. Kind of a self-fulfilling prophecy with that kid," Allie said, although she was using words that were too big for Holly. "Because he was pissed at his parents because he thought they liked Ty more, he would do stupid stuff like get high and drunk, which would get him into trouble, and disappoint them—a never-ending cycle." Allie traced a circle in the air with her finger.

"Oh, I get it," Holly said, smiling. "Like makeup that makes you break out, which needs more makeup… right?"

"Exactly." Allie smiled. "I need to get back to work. The gate company rep should be here today, and I'm still expecting the Briggs to barge in soon. Chief Detective Bishop and Detective Lawson will also be here to search Ty's boat, and *The Sunset Lady*," she said, standing up to stretch before tackling the work that needed to be done. She looked outside at what was shaping up to be another beautiful, clear day, a sign of the high-pressure system that was currently parked over the southeastern states.

Checking the Weather Channel would be a good idea before

the boys get here, she thought, sitting at her desk again. Apparently, it was early days yet, but the invest was creeping toward the Caribbean and would certainly bear watching. A sound outside made her look up from the screen, and Allie felt her stomach muscles tighten, realizing she was about to be hit by a hurricane of a different sort.

"WHAT IN BLOODY 'ell is going on 'ere?!" Keith Briggs blew into the office moments later, with his wife Donna in tow. "Somebody gets shoved off our boat and no one decides to let us in on this bit of information?"

Keith Briggs was rounder than any other human being Allie had encountered. His stubby little teeth were one of the first things you noticed, and if he was upset, which was more often than not, you noticed the spittle flying everywhere, his face reddening while he screamed. He had very little hair, but what was there was grown out and combed over in an attempt that didn't fool anyone. Allie wondered absently if he used a product to get the few strands to stay put.

"Hello, Mr. Briggs. I'm glad you came in today. The Sheriff's Department did attempt to call you last evening but was unable to reach you. They have yet to clear *The Sunset Lady*, although it appears there was no damage done to the vessel. We will need you to see if anything is missing, of course, and we do apologize for the inconvenience. But you will need to wait until the Chief Detective is able to do a search of the vessel himself, and then they will give you access. I also hope you understand that the deceased person in question is Ty Guthrie, the yard foreman, and Mr. Guthrie's son," Allie said.

"I don't give a rat's arse who it was, someone should have called me before a bunch of coppers swarmed all over my million-dollar boat!"

Everyone had wondered why this portly, hot-headed meatball had enough money to buy and maintain a Trumpy when he sounded like a thug from East London. Allie noticed he wasn't too keen on law enforcement and made a mental note that his primary concern was the Sheriff's Department's presence on his boat.

"Too right!" Donna Briggs joined in. "And now how long'll it be before we can get back on the water?"

The inimitable Mrs. Briggs was a bawdy bottle-blonde who worked to maintain the body of a twenty-something. The shape of her body was at odds with her fifty-something face, which didn't mean she hadn't tried to fix that, too, but the results were less than stellar. She had plastic instead of cheekbones and a chin, and Botox instead of lips. Her eyebrows were painted on, and she looked more mannequin than anything else. Allie guessed a nose job was next.

"As of right now, our yard crew will be doing the necessary work as soon as they can, and until we can hire a replacement foreman. There should be very little disruption to our schedule," Allie said calmly.

"Where was the security the yard promised? How did these people get in? This is not acceptable, and I will be getting in touch with my solicitor today! You people were supposed to protect my boat and my assets!" Keith Briggs sputtered.

"Remember that the valuable items from *The Sunset Lady* were removed upon your arrival and placed in the office for safe-keeping."

"And are they still here?" he asked with a smirk.

"They are. They have not been disturbed in the least," Allie said.

"Well, no use standing here talking to you, as you don't know nuffink. We need to go look at 'er to see what they've nicked from us, Donna!"

"Lead the way, Keith!"

"Like I said, Mr. and Mrs. Briggs, they won't let you on yet!" Allie called after them as they stormed out of the office toward *The Sunset Lady*. Allie and Holly exchanged a look. She was sure that wasn't the last they would hear from them that day. Luckily, the deputy was there to protect and monitor the crime scene, and it was now his turn to deal with the pair.

CHAPTER SIX

Allie texted Neil to let him know that the Briggs had arrived, and they had been handled, at least for now. As soon as she set her phone down, the door swung open again and she braced herself for another assault from the Briggs, but it was just Mike.

Mike, a sweet guy who got along with just about everyone, didn't draw too much attention to himself and stayed under the radar of Neil Guthrie's notoriously hot temper. Mike, who treated "the office ladies" with respect and looked great in a pair of Wranglers. Mike, who had been so concerned for her last night and had held her hands in his . . .

"How are you doing?" he asked.

"I'm okay. You?" she asked, blushing slightly.

"All right. What do you think about this?"

"Nothing yet. It's suspicious, but I guess a lot rests on autopsy results."

"Ty wouldn't fall…"

"I know, it seems fishy, doesn't it?" Allie responded.

She was relieved to note that if Mike had anything to do with it, he wouldn't be pointing out that someone probably killed Ty.

"More than fishy," he said. "I can't believe it." He crossed his arms and shook his head slightly, turning to look out at the yard. "Ty was a dick, but no one deserves to die like that."

Allie didn't respond. She waited for him to explain, but as the seconds ticked by, she realized he might not. "I heard he treated you guys poorly sometimes," she said.

"More like every day," Mike said. "But he knew his way around a boat, and he was a good foreman. I just wish he didn't have to belittle people to get them to do the work."

"Did he do that to you?" She regarded his tall, slender frame, not for the first time. Mike was about her age but looked a little older due to working in the elements. He had the look of a lot of the men on the coast—tan skin and sun-bleached hair.

"No, I didn't need to be reminded to do the work," he said with a smile. "I just tried to stay out of his way."

"Hmm… Well, don't be surprised if the Sheriff's Department contacts you to ask you some questions."

"Oh yeah? So, they don't think it was an accident either," Mike surmised.

"I think they're investigating all possibilities," Allie said.

"Well, I don't have anything to hide. I had no reason to go after Ty. Like I said, I just tried to stay out of his way."

"I believe you." Allie winked. "The Briggs are on the warpath, so I'd stay out of their way for a bit, too. I've got a copy of the list Neil gave you of the other work that still needs to be done on the current projects in the yard. Will you be my point of contact and keep me posted on your progress?"

"Sure thing. I better go get some stuff ready. Oh, did that Aquacork decking get delivered for *The Lucy May II* yet?"

"Tracking says it should be here this afternoon," Allie said, checking the computer.

"Will you let us know when it comes in? Sammy will be doing the install on that as soon as it gets here," he said.

"Will do." She smiled.

"Wanna do our usual lunch sometime this week?" he asked, smiling back.

"Sure!" she said a little too brightly.

"Great! Thanks, Allie!" Mike said and headed out the door.

The phone rang. Neil cut off her phone greeting and asked, "Has anyone from the media called?"

"Yes, we had a few outlets make their presence known today, but we handled it," Allie said. "Were you able to reach Zack?"

"We haven't heard from him, and we're starting to worry. I went by his house, but it didn't look like anyone was home. If he shows up, will you please ask him to call us?"

This was not unusual for Zack. He was in his early twenties and seemed to be making the most of it, to his detriment. There were rumors of drug and alcohol abuse, and possibly other addictions. He went through money like water, and he was a continual source of worry for his parents, not to mention a point of contention. Neil had all but washed his hands of him, giving up hope that he would ever become a respectable human being capable of joining the family business, which Vicky resented, never giving up on her only child. Favorites were chosen and lines were drawn. Their marriage clearly suffered.

"Of course, Neil. Is there anything else you need?"

"Not right now. Text me if anything comes up."

Allie thought it was time to get to work, so she started to dig up the information Charlie needed for the investigation. She confirmed there weren't any live-aboards and only two DIY owners who weren't staying in the yard at that point in time, which she realized made sense. Anyone living in the yard would definitely have been awakened by anything happening in the yard last night, and if by nothing else than the law enforcement activity. There were a few subs contracted to start work on *The Sunset Lady*, but they hadn't started yet. There were some other boats that were being worked on in the yard, and a few subs on those. She made a list of the subs they used on a regular basis, anyway, just to cover all of her bases.

The door opened and Sammy came in. "Hey, Allie, what's going on? Why is the gate closed? And why is the Sheriff's Department here?" Sammy asked as he craned his neck to look back out at the yard.

She assessed him for a moment. Sammy was on the shorter side, but stocky, with a head full of reddish, wiry hair. He spoke with a thick Down East accent, like Holly, and it sometimes took Allie a second to process before she understood what he had said.

"Have you heard the news?" she asked.

"No—what's up?" Sammy asked.

"Ty had an accident last night. It looks like he fell from the Trumpy. He's dead."

He stilled for a moment. "Do what?" Sammy asked, using the regional phrase of incomprehension.

"Just what I said, he fell and died in the yard last night."

"That's a bunch of bull. Someone got fed up with him and pushed him, maybe, but he didn't fall."

"There was a strong smell of beer…" Allie mentioned, cautiously.

"Figures," he muttered.

"I've heard he wasn't the easiest guy to work with in the yard. Maybe someone did get fed up," Allie said.

"I wouldn't blame them if they did. The guy was an ass. Knew his job but made everyone else's life a living hell," Sammy said.

Allie noted he seemed surprised at the news, although he harbored a special hatred for Ty. She told him Mike was already in the yard and had the job list of what needed to be accomplished, and he went out the door.

"Also, there's an invest in the Atlantic, so keep your ears open!" she called after him.

The phone rang and Holly answered it. "Can I put you on hold for a minute?" she asked and then motioned to Allie that it was the Sheriff's Department.

"I'll take it in Neil's office," she said, getting up. She closed the door behind her and picked up the phone. "Hey, Charlie. So far, Mr. and Mrs. Briggs have been in, as well as all three yard guys. Neil was here for a bit and left, and then called and said he hasn't been able to reach Zack."

"Yeah, we've heard from the Briggs already, and there's a reason no one's been able to reach Zack…" Charlie said.

"What?" Allie asked.

"He was picked up last night, about three in the morning. He was drunk or high on something, and wandering down 101. Someone almost hit him with their truck and called 911. The responding officer found him incoherent and brought him in. He refused his phone call."

"Oh my God," Allie said. "Does Neil know?"

"I just called him. I'll be back down to the yard in a few minutes so we can check out those boats, okay?"

"Right. See you then," she said and hung up the phone, wondering what they might find on the boats where Ty Guthrie had lived and died.

CHAPTER SEVEN

A llie assessed the *Barbara Jean* as she, Charlie, and a deputy approached her in the yard. She was a thirty-foot sailboat currently on blocks in the yard, and she had been there for a while, having been Ty's home since he had split with Barbie in the spring. The boat's body was solid white with several navy-blue pinstripes near the top, now graying with exposure to the weather and dust of the yard. She looked naked and somehow pitiful without her sails.

"Why don't you come on up with us? See what you see," Charlie said.

"Are you sure?" she asked.

Charlie nodded.

First to climb the ladder and step foot on the deck, Allie paused to look back at *The Sunset Lady*, imagining Ty doing the same, but in the dark. *What got your attention over there?* With Charlie and the deputy behind her, she went below, the smell of stale, unwashed linens assaulting her nostrils. It seemed, for Ty, living as a bachelor didn't include doing his own laundry.

With the dated curtains closed, it was dim, and the deputy instinctively pulled out his Maglite to do the search. Allie crossed over to the front of the cabin and tugged the curtains open to allow more light in, and motes of dust filled the air. Bishop motioned for the deputy to put the beer bottles cluttering the table into evidence bags. *A few with lipstick near the top.* Ty's signature baseball cap was there too, old and forlorn without its owner. Allie glanced at Charlie, unsure of what could be touched or moved. Charlie looked back at her and smiled.

"The bachelor's life, huh?"

"I guess so," she murmured, surveying the place. "What is it we hope to find here, Charlie?"

"Not sure, Allie. Something out of the ordinary, something that's out of place. Or anything that might give us some information about Ty we didn't already know, or why someone might want to hurt him."

"That forward cabin will be a tight squeeze," the deputy remarked.

"Why don't you climb up in the berth?" Charlie said to Allie, handing her a pair of latex gloves.

Allie maneuvered around the two men and the table and peered into the forward cabin. She asked the deputy for his Maglite and she stepped into the space. With only enough room to turn around, she climbed onto the berth to get a closer look. She crawled over the rumpled bed linens and a pillow to inspect a short shelf on the left side.

Among the detritus of small items there, she found a small, cheaply framed photo of what must have been Ty as a child with his mother, Nancy. He was the smiling, chubby toddler on her lap. Nancy looked into the camera as she laughed and gripped Ty tightly in a backward hug. She had a long mane of chestnut hair and green eyes and was dressed in short shorts and a tank top. With a thought, Allie turned the small frame over and popped the back off to see if anything was written on the back. *Mom*, it said simply, in a young man's disjointed cursive.

A chink in the tough guy armor. Her death hit him hard. He was only about fifteen at the time, and he had been an only child. Southern boys and their mamas.

She tucked the photo frame into her pocket and looked again at the shelf to see if anything else was of interest. Nothing much to note. Receipts for takeout, beer, and gas, and notes about work needing to be done in the yard, beer caps, a few used drinking glasses. She called to Charlie to let him know she was coming out and backed out of the space.

"Did you find anything?" he asked.

"Only some receipts and notes, and a small photo of him with his real mother, Nancy, from when he was a toddler," she said as she handed everything to Charlie.

"She was a real nice lady," he said quietly, his thumb brushing over her face in the frame. "It was a right shame to lose her so young."

"How did she die?" Allie asked.

"Car accident on 101," Charlie said, looking away.

Yet another reason Ty had a soft spot for me. Allie pursed her lips, took a deep breath through her nose, and asked, "What did you find?"

"His laptop, which we'll bring back to the lab and have our techs look into, but really not much else," Charlie supplied.

"There has to be more here," Allie said. "There's no cell phone?"

"You would think so, but we haven't found one yet," Charlie said.

"I know he had one," Allie said, pulling out her own to call his number. Nothing. "I wonder if he rented a storage unit for the rest of his stuff when he moved out? I'll have to ask Barbie," she said.

"Good idea. There isn't a whole lotta room on a sailboat." Charlie chuckled.

THEY HEADED toward *The Sunset Lady* in the yard. She was a fine example of a Trumpy yacht whose owners were typically interested in preservation, and with the maintenance and upkeep required, you couldn't just take them anywhere. Guthrie's Marine had a growing reputation for being able to handle work orders for Trumpies, and when the Briggs had bought *The Sunset Lady* in the spring, they had brought her down to have the requisite work done before heading further down the Intracoastal for the winter.

Allie looked around the yard as she walked toward the yacht. It was creepy to think of someone being out there, ready to attack her. She stopped as she got close to examine the ground again where Ty had fallen. There was no real sign that anything sinister had happened there, but she paused for a moment anyway, because she had known Ty, had spoken with him on a regular basis, and he was a human being who was no longer a part of this world. His life had left his body right here in this space. It was sad and also angered her. Someone had either caused it, or knew something about it, and had remained silent.

Charlie started up the ladder to her deck and Allie followed. As she continued up the steps, she noticed *The Sunset Lady* didn't need any work on her underside—she was beautiful. Her sides were a cream white while her belly was a teal green with a thin border of navy blue between. She crossed a brass nameplate as she stepped onto the boat, bearing her name and the year she was built. In the cabin, plastic sheeting covered every inch of the cream high-pile carpet and the plush furniture, and the plastic looked askew in places. *Maybe there had been a scuffle on board...* A few valuable-looking pieces of art and rugs were still aboard, but she had been told that anything of real value had been removed to the office already. *Are these not worth anything, or is it all relative to people like the Briggs?*

"What are we looking for here?" she asked quietly.

"Same as the other. Anything out of place, anything the techs might have missed. I also like to see if I can re-create the crime in my head," Charlie answered.

"If there *was* a crime. There was so much beer on the *Barbara Jean*, I'm starting to think maybe he did just fall off the deck," Allie said.

"It's a possibility," Charlie admitted.

He turned to head below deck, and she followed, passing through the tiny galley kitchen—*granite countertops!*—to the living quarters. Turning to the aft, the staff quarters which hadn't been touched since the captain and mates had left in the spring looked spartan and undisturbed. But toward the bow, there had been some traffic recently. There were some slight marks on the walls, and the carpet was mussed. Did it look like that before? Her intuition was jabbing her, whispering that someone had been here.

She peeked her head into the heads and cabins but couldn't see anything out of place. Something was definitely off, though. Had the artwork been moved, or was that where the pieces in Neil's safe should hang? They headed back up to the pilot house and again saw nothing out of place, then went to the deck where Ty had likely spent his last moments alive. There were a few dirty smudges on the deck, but nothing discernible. Charlie perched against the railing of the bow.

"If he was attacked, this is where it ended. But there are no footprints or anything because it's been so dry. If it had just been a little rainy, we might have something to work with here," he said.

Allie walked to the front edge and looked down to where Ty's body had lain. "If he was pushed or attacked, there's nothing here to suggest it. Pretty much the only indication that he wasn't alone is the alarm going off at the gate, am I right?"

"At this point, yes," Charlie admitted.

"Not much to go on, unfortunately," Allie said.

"It's not hopeless yet, kiddo. You never know what turns up over the course of an investigation, you know that," Charlie said, standing. "Let's get you back to work. Then, I'll see you tonight for supper."

CHAPTER EIGHT

H olly and Allie ate their lunches at their desks, chatting about nothing in particular. Hearing a vehicle pull up, Holly stood to peek out the window. "The Briggs."

A moment later, the pair shoved the door open and began huffing and puffing. "We will now get aboard our very own boat, and there in't anyfink you can do about it, is there?" Keith Briggs said. He turned on his heel and waddled out the door, Donna Briggs marching out behind him with a glare for both of the girls.

Twenty minutes passed and they returned. "We are going back to our condo. My solicitor will be calling you shortly. It doesn't look as though anything has been disturbed on the boat, but I can't say for sure. Our insurance company will be sending out an investigator, and he has a complete inventory on file, and will be expecting to have a looky-loo with you," Keith Briggs proclaimed. "I would like assurances that no one will be able to get into the yard again, and that you have beefed up your security measures. Otherwise, I will be moving *The Sunset Lady* to a different yard."

"I will verify all of that with Mr. Guthrie and look forward to speaking with your solicitor and the insurance investigator. I do apologize for the inconvenience, Mr. Briggs," Allie said.

"Well, an apology ain't gonna cut it, is it?" Donna Briggs retorted, hands on hips. "We want our boat and all of our valuables safe, and so far, you just haven't done the job, have ye? In fact, ye've made a right pig's ear out of the whole mess!"

"We will strive to do our very best for you, both in terms of security and maintenance of *The Sunset Lady*. Please don't hesitate to call us if you need anything."

They stormed out of the office yet again. Holly exhaled loudly, blowing the air up and making her bangs dance. Allie rolled her eyes and immediately called Neil.

"The Briggs are pissed," she said. "They want 'assurances' that the yard is safe. Are we adding any more layers of security? Have you spoken with Tom?"

"I've called him, and he will be doubling up on the rounds they do overnight, and I've also called the gate security company who should be sending someone out today to reconfigure the key cards. That means you'll need to redistribute them to the staff."

"Not a problem. They also said their 'solicitor' would be calling and an insurance investigator would be coming to do a walkthrough with their inventory of insured items on *The Sunset Lady*. Do you have any problem with that?"

"I don't see any problem, but it might be good to get in touch with our attorney, just in case. His number is in my

Rolodex. Give him a call and ask him to call me. They're going to do an autopsy on Ty, and it will happen some-time this week," Neil added.

Not sure what to say, Allie made a noncommittal noise and waited for him to continue.

"We have to wait until they are done to begin making funeral plans, but once we do, you need to make sure everyone gets the information."

"Of course."

"And we've… er… heard from Zack. He was picked up by a sheriff's deputy last night. Intoxication and disturbing the peace…"

Again, she wasn't sure what to say. "Oh, wow," she mumbled.

He sighed. "When this has all blown over, I think Vicky and I will go away for a bit."

"Okay. Call me if you need anything else." Allie hung up the phone. She realized she hadn't even drunk her coffee yet today and headed to the little kitchenette in the corner of the office. She was warming it up in the microwave when she heard an unusual noise from outside. A split second before the door opened, she realized it was the sound of a wheeled contraption coming up the wooden ramp toward the door.

Barbara Guthrie, "Barbie" to her closest friends, maneuvered her knee scooter through the door. Her big blown-out, bleach-blonde hair was what Allie first saw when she rolled into the room.

"Well, hello, ladies!" she said, and Allie was unsur-prised to note that there was not a hint of sorrow in her greeting. Barbie was Ty's soon-to-be ex-wife, and while

Allie didn't know her well, theirs was a hotly contested divorce. Barbie swept further into the room and told Holly to bring her a chair. Once her large frame was settled, she asked, "So what's the word, hummingbird?"

Allie said, "I assume you've heard the news."

"You bet I have. What the hell happened?" Barbie answered, more like a curious spectator than someone who had once been married to the recently deceased. *Did she bring popcorn?* She searched Barbie's heavily made-up face for a hint of sorrow, but her expression was only one of extreme interest.

"He fell off a boat in the yard. That's all we know right now."

"But the Sheriff's Department was here, right? Do they think there was foul play?"

"I don't know," Allie said.

"Oh, come on, you know something..." Barbie pressured.

"Well, it is a little strange that Ty would fall off a boat, right? I mean, have you ever seen him so much as wobble out there in the yard?" Allie asked.

"There's always a first time," Barbie said. "And he did like to have a few beers before bed. But someone could have had a hand in it. Do they think it was intentional?"

"I don't know," Allie repeated.

"Huh," Barbie said. "What would he be doing on that yacht, anyway?"

"I don't think anyone knows that. We're all just as clueless as you," Allie said, wondering as she said it how Barbie would react to being called *clueless*. It seemed to go right over her head, which was unusual, as Barbie usually had a retort for everything.

"Well, as you know, it isn't easy for me to get around, but I thought I would come in and see how everyone was doing. I take it Neil and Vicky aren't here…" she said, craning her neck for a look into Neil's office.

"No."

"I didn't see their cars, so I figured. If you talk to them, pass along my condolences, would you? Even though Ty and I were getting a divorce, and I hated the sumbitch, no one deserves to bury their own son," Barbie said.

"That's thoughtful of you, Barbie," Allie said.

"Only a few more weeks and I can get out of this boot and back on my feet!" Barbie said excitedly.

"That's great!" There was an awkward silence. Barbie clearly was stalling. She wanted more information.

"Has Neil said anything about what will happen now, with the company?"

"No, I don't think he's even gotten to that thought yet, although Ty will be hard to replace in the yard, for sure," Allie said.

"He was a bastard, but he was good at his job," Barbie acknowledged. "Too bad he couldn't keep it in his pants."

Allie said nothing, noting Holly's cheeks flushed much like her own. Everyone knew Ty had a different girl on his arm every time you turned around, but she didn't need to know the sordid details. Then again, it was an opportunity to get more information.

"Was Ty seeing someone in particular?"

"Oh, who the hell knows. I don't keep tabs on his escapades. We were good together in the beginning, though. It would have been a lot easier on me and everyone else if he could have... Well, if he could have been less of a dick."

Barbie gathered herself together, preparing to leave. "Well, girls, it's been wonderful. Keep me in the loop, will you? Lord knows the papers aren't saying much, and I am interested in how this turns out, you know?"

Allie understood but made no offer to call her. "We'll see you!"

"Buh-bye!" Barbie said and rolled out the door.

ALLIE WORKED on writing her observations down for Charlie and coming up with a list of subs who work for the company. The insurance company called and scheduled an appointment with her for the next morning to do a walkthrough of *The Sunset Lady* with an investigator to look for any missing items. Just after lunch, the gate guy came to re-do the pass card configuration. He came into the office and handed Allie an envelope full of new ones to issue, and was ready to head out.

"Can I ask you a couple of questions?" she asked.

"Sure, I'll answer if I can," he said.

"So people need this to get into the gate here, and they cannot get in without it, correct?" she asked, holding up the beige, nondescript rectangle of plastic.

"That's correct, ma'am. I think your gate is normally open during the day, but closed at night, correct?"

"Yes, that's correct." Allie glanced at the embroidered name on his shirt that read *Alex*. "So anyone who would need to get in after the gate is closed would get a keycard for access. And the alarm goes off if someone tries to get in without one?"

"That's correct," Alex said.

"And it goes off if someone tries to get out without one?"

"Well, that's a little more complicated. It will go off if someone tries to open the gate without one from either side."

"Is there any way someone could pass through the gate either way without a card, and without setting off the alarm?" she asked.

"No, ma'am."

"Is there any way to trace a specific card's use?"

"No, ma'am. They all have the same encoding," he said.

"And do you have in your records when the last time the code was changed?"

"I don't have that here, ma'am, but I can have the company give you a call with that information."

"That would be great. Do the cards ever expire, as in get too old to work?" she asked.

"We've never come across that, ma'am."

"If we haven't changed our code in a while, there are actually quite a number of people who could access the yard?"

"That's correct, ma'am. That's why we encourage companies to do it at least once a year, like when you change the batteries in your smoke detectors," he explained.

"That's a good policy," she said. "Thank you so much for your time, and if you could make sure the company gets back to me with the date the last time was that we changed the code, it would help me a great deal."

"I'll give them a call as soon as I get back to the truck. Is there anything else, ma'am?"

"No, thank you."

He tipped his hat in thanks and was gone. She pulled out her employee list and realized she could have them return the old key card to get the new one, saving Charlie a step in his investigation. Anyone missing their old one might have been the one to leave it behind. After a quick search, she found the previous key card issue sheet, noting that the last one was dated several years ago. As she scanned the old document, she realized several people who no longer worked for the company were on the list. *Did they have to turn them in when they quit or were fired? Somehow, I doubt it.* Next time she spoke to Neil, she would have to ask about where the returned key cards might be, or if there was any record of previous employees returning them. In the meantime, current employees would need the cards, so she created a sign-in sheet and sent a mass text to those who would need them now, with a reminder to bring their old cards to turn in. Any live-aboards or DIY owners would probably have key cards, as well, and possibly all owners, and she would need to check with Neil and her predecessor in the office, Barbie, to see what the procedure was for owners.

MID-AFTERNOON, James, the UPS man who always came prepared with a joke, delivered a few packages containing supplies for the various repair and maintenance projects going on in the yard.

"How's my lovely Allie today?" he said.

"Could be better," she admitted.

"Saw something on the news about this place. Is everybody okay?" he asked.

"Ty Guthrie, the owner's son is dead. He fell off one of the boats," she explained.

"What? That's terrible! Was he a friend?"

"Kind of," she said. "It's a little complicated."

"I'm so sorry," James said, and she could tell it was heartfelt.

"Thanks, James. How many you got for me today?" She took the handheld he offered.

"Three. You know where to sign!" he said.

"Thanks." She smiled and handed it back to him.

She opened the packages and entered the supplies into inventory. Then she went out to the yard to find one of the boys.

"Hey, Allie," Sammy said from the deck of *The Lucy May II.*

"Hey, Sammy! The Aquacork is in, and there are some engine parts for the *Devil's Plaything*, and a jar of some kind of finishing paste which I think is for the *Swingtime III*," she said.

"Okay, thanks. You can leave the engine parts and paste in the office for now, but I'll be in shortly for the Aquacork," he said.

"Will do. Need anything else?" she asked.

"A winning lottery ticket." He smiled.

"Don't we all?" she asked and headed back inside.

BEFORE THE END of the day, Mike and Sammy came into the office to fill out paperwork for what they had done that day and mark their timecards. Then they stood at Allie's desk to get their new key cards. Only Mike had his old one to turn back in.

"I think mine's in my truck somewhere. I'll have to look for it," Sammy said.

"Okay, Sammy. Just bring it in when you find it. Thanks!" Allie called as Sammy left. *There's a suspect.* They started closing down the office for the day, and Mike leaned on a file cabinet to stay out of their way. Holly turned her card in and grabbed a new one, too.

"Go ahead, Holly. I'm going to call Neil real quick to check in and then I'll be right behind you," Allie said.

Mike cleared his throat behind her. "Do you mind if I hang out for a sec and talk to Neil when you're done? It's about an order for *The Lucy May II*. I can lock up. I have keys."

"Sure!" she said and dialed Neil's number. "How are you?" she asked Neil when he picked up.

"Okay. Anything big to report?" Neil asked.

"Not really. The gate guy came, so you'll need a new key card. I've been having everyone turn in their old one to get the new one, too. Do you know if that was done last time?"

"I'm not sure. It would have been Barbie who handled that…"

"Do DIY owners, live-aboards, and other owners get key cards?"

"Sometimes yes, and sometimes no. If they're staying overnights, we definitely give them cards. If they are just owners, generally we don't, but if they give us a hard time or are some VIP-type people, we'll give them to them. Barbie should have had a list somewhere. You could call and ask her. She might be willing to help, but I wouldn't count on it," Neil said.

"Maybe I will. She was in today, by the way, trying to get information."

"Real torn up, I bet, too, huh?" he said darkly.

"Not really, but she did offer her condolences. I told her I didn't know much, and she went away empty-handed. The Briggs' solicitor will be calling in the morning, so we'll handle that then, and I have an appointment with the insurance investigator tomorrow morning. If there isn't anything else, Mike is here waiting to talk to you, and I have to go get Ryan," Allie said.

"Before you go, have you been watching the weather reports?"

"Yes," she said. "It's still too early to tell where the invest will go."

"Put Mike on. I'll talk to you tomorrow," Neil said.

Allie handed the phone to Mike and hesitated a moment, unused to allowing someone else to lock up. She quickly chided herself for doubting him, even for a moment, and waved to him as she headed out the door to her truck.

CHAPTER NINE

Allie drove back over the bridge into Morehead City toward the Station Club to pick up Ryan from his vocational day program. *At least he's working. College wasn't an option only because they weren't equipped for him, not because he's dumb.* Allie braced herself for Ryan's reaction to the slight change in their routine tonight. His program exhausted him. By the end of the day, he was ready to curl up in his pajamas and call it a night. She had prepared him that tonight would be a little different and hoped it had been enough to avert a meltdown due to the change in schedule.

Ryan climbed into the truck, immediately pulling his Nintendo DS from his bag.

"Hey, bud!" Allie said. No response.

She looked at her younger brother as his attention focused immediately on his game. While her hair was a lighter chestnut, his was a darker black-brown. He had freckles, while she did not, though, and he had been the only one in the family with blue eyes. *What a gorgeous kid.*

Just looking at him, you'd never know he can't tie his own shoes. His tall frame barely fit in her pickup. Although his clothes hung off of him, he probably weighed less than Allie herself, and she was a good seven inches shorter.

"Did you have a good day today?"

A brief look, and then back to his game.

"Remember where we're going today?"

No response.

"We're going over to Chief Detective Bishop's house. Do you remember him and his wife Sheila?"

Another brief look, and a return to the game.

Allie could have sworn the look said, "Do you really think I'm that dumb? Of course, I remember." She checked herself. It was a natural response to someone who didn't communicate with you, she reasoned, but she should talk to him as the young adult he was.

"Chief Detective Bishop was the one who helped us after… after Mom and Dad died," she finished, uncertain if the mention of their parents would upset Ryan. She watched out of the corner of her eye as Ryan looked out the window briefly before returning back to the game. *Of course, it still hurts. I'm still hurting, too.*

"And his wife Sheila is the one who makes the really good lasagna you like so much," she added brightly. "Maybe she'll make that for supper tonight, too!"

A brief look, and then, "Maybe," he echoed, a smile playing on his lips.

The way to any boy's heart. Food.

"Ready to head that way, then?" she asked.

"Sure," he said.

A contented smile spread on her face as she turned

back to the road and drove toward Charlie's house. She rolled the windows down so they could enjoy the late afternoon sun and breezes along the scenic drive lined with trees and putting greens. She pulled the truck into the drive of an eighties-era colonial and cut the engine. "Ready to go in?" she asked.

Ryan looked at her, gripping his DS tightly, hand on the door handle.

"Yes, you can take it in, but no playing at the table, okay?" she said.

There was no response, but she knew Ryan consented to her terms because he was out of the truck and heading to the front door. If he had disagreed, he wouldn't have gotten out of the truck. He was already ringing the doorbell, a must at any house equipped with one in case they had dogs that would bark at the noise. He loved that they responded that way.

Sheila Bishop pulled the front door open as Allie joined Ryan on the porch. Sure enough, a small white dog behind Sheila had alerted the entire neighborhood to their arrival, and Ryan laughed and clapped his hands at Pepper's excitement.

"Come on in, you two!" Sheila said as she pushed the storm door open and stepped back for them to enter. They did, and Ryan made a beeline for the living room, Pepper following happily. Sheila and Allie watched them go and then turned to each other to exchange greetings.

"Come on in, sugar," Sheila repeated, leading the way into the living room and kitchen area.

"What can I help you with?" Allie offered.

"Oh, honey, what kind of hostess would I be if made

you work? It's almost done, anyway. We'll be eating shortly. You sit right there at the counter and tell me how you've been. I haven't seen you in ages!" Sheila said and returned to her small tasks in the kitchen.

"Well, I've been working at the boatyard for the past four months, and just basically adjusting to life down here again," Allie said.

"It has to be a big change from Chicago. You'd been there for almost eight years, right?"

"Just about. I worked for TransUnion and had a nice big apartment all to myself, with all my stuff," she said, almost wistfully. "I haven't unpacked a thing since I've moved in. Been sleeping on the couch, because well... taking their stuff out just doesn't seem right."

"Well, I can understand that," Sheila said softly. "Still, it will have to be done at some point. It's where you live now, and it won't feel permanent until you move in, both body and spirit."

"I know you're right. I also know I'm not ready yet," Allie said.

"And that is okay. No one knows the right time except for you."

"Hello, ladies!" Charlie entered the room, looking decidedly more like a regular person in jeans and a Hawaiian shirt. "Sorry I'm a little late. I was on the phone in the den, talking to my deputy about another case."

"We've only just gotten here," Allie said.

"Well, I hope you are both ready for some lasagna!" Charlie said, loud enough for Ryan to hear in the other room.

He dropped his game on the couch and bounced into

the dining room as if Sonic the Hedgehog was seated at the table. The adults chuckled at his enthusiasm, and they all joined him in the dining room, Sheila and Charlie bringing in the food. After supper, Ryan announced it was time for his favorite, *Wheel of Fortune* on TV. Sheila led him back into the living room to watch, and Allie and Charlie headed for the den.

"Okay, what did you find out?" he asked.

"The Briggs—the owners of the Trumpy—were upset that no one contacted them and that the department went aboard without notifying them first, so I will have to deal with their 'solicitor' tomorrow. Primarily, they want to make sure nothing has been stolen. Their valuables are still locked up in the safe in Neil's office. I verified that myself. Also, Keith Briggs has a particular antipathy toward law enforcement."

"Hmm... All right, what else?" Charlie asked, brow cocked.

"Holly was surprised at the news, and I doubt she's clever enough to hide any lurking emotions. I spoke with the yard laborers. Mike said he thought there was foul play, which leads me to believe he didn't have anything to do with it. Anyone who had pushed Ty off the boat certainly wouldn't want anyone to suspect it was murder."

"Sound judgment," Charlie commented.

"Besides, he said he stayed out of Ty's way even though he could be a jerk to others in the yard. He had no real motive. And he's a generally nice guy," Allie concluded.

"Sometimes they are the most deceiving," Charlie said, smiling with a wink.

Allie ignored the wink. Clearly, Charlie was teasing

her. "Sammy was a bit less diplomatic. He said he could understand why someone had killed him. He also had lost his key card."

"We still haven't found a key card on the scene, so we're not sure where to go with that," Charlie said. "Either the perpetrator left it somewhere we haven't looked, or they got into the yard some other way. Maybe Ty let him in." Charlie sat back in thought.

"Wow. That's an idea," Allie said.

"What else?" Charlie asked.

"Barbie. She wheeled herself in showing no hint of sadness at the news, but full of questions."

"What did she want to know?"

"She wanted to know what Ty was doing on *The Sunset Lady*, and if your department thought it was murder. She also asked what Neil's plans were for the business. I played dumb. She mentioned Ty's infidelities, and I asked her about it, but she brushed it off."

"So she's trying to get information. That's interesting," Charlie said.

"That was about it. Mike and Holly were the only ones to return their old gate keys, and I'll have to ask Barbie what happened when she issued the last batch of key cards. Who knows if I'll get any help from her, though. I've got the insurance walkthrough tomorrow, and I put together a list of subs that are contracted by the company, although none were working on the Trumpy yet. And there are no live-aboards and only a couple of DIY owners who aren't staying in the yard right now either."

"This helps a great deal, Allie. Thank you."

"I was wondering," Allie said. "Do you think I could

help on the case? I realized today that my mind is already in overdrive, analyzing body language, reviewing timelines, and sifting through evidence. It's difficult for me to sit back on this."

Charlie leaned forward and folded his hands. "I'll be honest, I considered asking you. And I let you on the boats with us to see what you'd come up with. But I wasn't sure if you were up to it. You've been through a lot this year."

Allie sighed. "I know I have. And I know I have a lot on my plate with Ryan and adjusting to everything here. But Ty didn't deserve this." She paused. "Did you know that when my parents died, he told me that his mom's death was the hardest thing he'd ever been through, and said if I ever needed to talk, he was there for me?"

Charlie shook his head.

"He may have been a jerk generally, but I think inside, he was a scared boy trying to deal with what life had handed him. Much like Ryan. And I think I can help. I'm in the office, dealing with these people every day. If Ty was murdered, it's likely somebody we've already spoken to."

Charlie nodded. "Well, I don't think I can bring you on in any official sense. We can't share everything with you, of course, but we may need some of your insights. You're a bright girl, Allie, with a strong background in investigations, even if they were of a different sort. We have a whole county to protect, and fewer and fewer people to do it. We'll take any help we can get. But you need to be sure about this."

Allie nodded.

"I don't want to put you in an uncomfortable position at work, either. I know Neil is your boss, and the Guthries are old family friends."

Allie shook her head. "Not for years. I think I can handle it."

"The DA won't like it, but in this case, it may be better to ask pardon than permission. If she gets word, I'll explain your qualifications and that you are consulting on the case. I have the authority to do so, but we'll cross that bridge if and when we get to it," he said.

Allie smiled. "All right then. What's next?"

"Detective Lawson found a ring of keys in Ty's truck, so we'll go through those and see if we find anything. And we should get an autopsy report soon, or at least an update from the medical examiner. Let me know how the insurance examiner appointment goes, and we'll go from there."

Relaxing back in his chair, he said, "Okay, now how are you and Ryan doing?" Charlie said,

"All right, I guess."

"Is he talking yet?"

"No, although he comprehends so much of what's going on around him," Allie said.

"And you? Are you still sleeping on the couch?"

Allie hesitated and picked at a hangnail on her thumb. "I just don't want to get rid of their stuff. It's too permanent, you know?"

"I understand, Allie," Charlie said. "When the time comes, you be sure to call me if you need some help."

"I will. I'm just not there yet," she said, then smiled. "Ryan seems to be doing well in his day program."

"Excellent. Are you starting to get to know him a little bit?"

"It's tough. I know the exterior stuff like his obsessions and his routines. I'm starting to be able to read his looks, a little," she said. "At least I think I can understand them."

"It's a start. It'll just take some time. He has to get to know you again. You've been away for almost half his life," he said.

"I know. I carry a lot of guilt for that," she said.

"You shouldn't. That's just life. You had no idea your parents would have an accident, and you had every right to pursue your dreams." Charlie patted her shoulder.

But was I pursuing my dreams, or running away from the messier parts of my life?

"Maybe you should consider counseling for you, and for Ryan," he said quietly. "It couldn't hurt."

"Maybe," she responded, unwilling to commit. There were so many times in the past four months that she just had no idea what to do. It was unsettling.

Sensing her anxiety, Charlie changed the subject. "Are you keeping an eye on the Atlantic? There's a few invests out there that may turn into something. It *is* hurricane season!"

"I've got the Weather Channel on my desktop at work and I'm checking it just about hourly." She laughed.

He laughed with her and said, "Come on. Let's join Sheila and Ryan. Up for a movie on the Disney Channel?"

"Sounds like a plan," Allie said, following him out to the living room.

CHAPTER TEN

Mike was waiting for them when they arrived home, arms crossed, leaning against his truck in the fading sunlight. When Allie pulled in, she and Ryan got out.

"Hey, Ryan!" Mike said.

Ryan responded with what could have been "Hey" and a brief flicker of eye contact. He remembered Mike and rocked on his feet, clapping his hands softly.

"How ya doin', buddy? I brought you something," Mike said, handing Ryan a big book of logic puzzles from the dollar store. "And I was thinking you and I should take your sister to MacDaddy's next Wednesday night for some bowling and video games. What do you think?"

"Yes!" Ryan exclaimed, beginning to hop from one foot to the other.

Seeing his excitement, Allie gave Ryan the house keys so he could let himself in. She knew he would be more comfortable flapping his hands and making guttural noises inside. To anyone else, it was nothing more than some strange movements and noises. But for Ryan, it was the stim he used to communicate his happiness. She turned to Mike.

"A smooth move. Now I can't say no," she said with a wry smile.

He shrugged, laughing. "A man's gotta do what a man's gotta do."

"What brings you here, anyway?" It was her turn to lean on her truck and fold her arms.

"I really just dropped by to bring you your wallet. You left it at work today. I saw it on your desk as I was heading out, and I thought I'd bring it by," he said, handing it over.

"Wow. Oops. I guess this thing with Ty has me preoccupied." She fumbled with the wallet, cramming it back into her purse and blushing. "Thanks! You didn't have to do that!"

"I know. But ever since last night, I've been worried about you. I know it can't have been easy for you, with your parents' deaths so recent…" A slight blush rose in his cheeks, and he shoved his hands into his pockets.

"I'm tougher than I look." Allie eyed him.

"So you've said, but you've got a lot going on, a lot to deal with." He gestured toward the trailer, Ryan's excited sounds just audible from inside. "I just want to make sure you're really okay with all of this. You don't have to be strong all the time."

Allie suddenly envisioned her mom locking herself in her parents' room at the old house when it got to be too much. Her dad would simply take over, knowing she needed time and space. Allie could feel the weight of it all on her shoulders and felt her lower lip quiver. She looked at Mike.

"Thanks," she said simply.

"My mom died when I was in my teens, and now my dad's not doing so great, so I get it," he said quietly. "Lean on me if you need to, okay?"

"Okay. Thanks, Mike," she said, lowering her gaze. "Want to go for a walk?"

"I'd love to," he said, smiling.

"Let me get Ryan," she said and headed inside. "Ryan, Mike and I are going for a quick walk. Want to go?"

"Yes!" he said. He clearly liked Mike.

Ryan bounded out of the house and began walking around the drive of the trailer park, not waiting for the two of them. They laughed and followed him.

"So, how's it going, filling in for Ty?" she asked.

"Okay, I guess. There's a lot more to think about than just being a mechanic. Now I have to worry about everyone else getting their work done, too." He smiled.

"But, it's temporary, right? Or do you want to do this from now on?" she asked.

"I hope it's only temporary. Engines are my thing. Figuring out the problem and then figuring out the best solution. This other stuff keeps me up at night," he admitted.

Briefly, Allie imagined a shirtless Mike in bed, arms folded behind his head and staring at the ceiling.

"You doing okay?" he asked, reaching out to grab her hand briefly. Her hand warmed in his, and her insides began to go a little squishy at his touch.

"Uh, yeah. I'm good," she said. "There's lots to do."

"I know Neil can be demanding, but you have to take care of yourself and Ryan. That's most important."

"I know. I'm still learning how to be a single parent," she said.

The sun was beginning to set behind the trees, and the clouds took on the colors of sherbet as they rounded the last bend of the roadway. Ryan was already stomping up the steps and into the trailer, and they chuckled at his obvious good mood.

"Well, hey, thanks for going for a walk with 'us'!" she said, turning to Mike in the driveway. She was close enough to realize he smelled as good as he looked, and he seemed to lean in for a moment. She closed her eyes, willing him to put a hand to her shoulder or to touch her in some way, but nothing happened.

She opened her eyes again, and he stepped back and dug his keys out of his pocket. "Anytime." He laughed, opening the door of his truck and giving her a mock salute. "I gotta run. I'll see you in the morning, okay?"

"Okay. See you tomorrow." Allie watched as he pulled out and down the drive of the trailer park, turning toward the house only when Mike was out of sight.

ALLIE WAS DRIVING *the truck and Ryan was in the seat next to her. She wasn't sure where she was going, but she felt an urgent need to find a particular person. She didn't know the person's name or even gender, but had a nebulous feeling that she would know when she found them. She looked across the seat at Ryan, who was not playing his DS for once.*

"What?" he said, returning her look.

"Nothing," she said. "But we really have to go faster."

"Well, you're the one driving," he said with a smile on his face. Confused at her brother's speech, something on the road pulled her attention away from her brother, and when she saw it, she slammed on the brakes. The pavement was still wet from a recent storm, and she lost control of the truck, slamming the passenger's side door into a pine tree. When she relaxed her shoulders and turned to look, Ryan was gone.

ALLIE WOKE SUDDENLY, the nightmare vivid in her mind. She lay still for a moment, listening for a sound, any sound in the trailer. Hearing none, she carefully sat up and looked around the living room, trying to calm her erratic breathing. She stood then hurried down the short hall to Ryan's room, and carefully opened the door. The bedroom light was on, as it usually was when he slept, and he was right where he was supposed to be, sprawled out on his bed that was also crowded with video games and toys. She watched his chest rise and fall for a few moments, and satisfied that he was very much here and fine, she quietly closed the door and returned to the living room.

Needing comfort from something, anything, if only for a moment, she padded to the other end of the trailer and opened the door to what had been her parents' bedroom. She turned the bedside lamp on and stood there, discovering that she had been holding her breath. This was still a sacred space, and she didn't want to defile it, but she needed to feel her parents here, if only for a moment. She turned back to the door and then sat cross-legged in the doorway.

"I still need you," she said to the empty room. "I dreamt that I lost Ryan, too. Do you think I'm putting him in danger?" She wasn't expecting an answer, but she waited anyway. She closed her eyes and let her thoughts drift back to the times when the four of them were happiest together, living in the old house. She remembered playing with Ryan with sidewalk chalk on the driveway shortly after moving in. Some neighborhood kids had come over to investigate the new kids on the block and watched from the side of the driveway as little Ryan had stood and spun in circles in front of them.

"What is he, *retarded?*" the big one with the small, mean eyes had said. She had slowly come to her feet, dropped her chalk, and folded her arms.

"Who the hell are you?" she had said. "You don't know me, and you don't know my brother. No, he's not retarded, and that's not a nice word, anyway."

"He's a spaz!" the kid said.

"Get the hell off my lawn, asshole," she growled and started toward the mean kid. Surprisingly, he backed away, and the kids left, whispering and laughing to each other.

Allie had shaken her arms out, relieving them of the tension of clenching them through the short conversation, and was still shocked at the language she had used—she never cussed! She opened her hands to find little crescent-shaped indentations along the tops of her palms. She glanced at Ryan and then turned to look at the house to see if her parents had overheard her bad language. The

75

living room curtain flickered, and she had expected a talking-to that evening, but it had never come. Although now that she thought about it, her dad had bought her some boxing gloves a few weeks later.

"That's why you taught me to fight, Daddy?" Allie asked, putting it together for the first time. "So I could protect myself, and Ryan, too." Allie thought about how her parents had encouraged her to speak her mind, to be educated, to have a deep love and respect for them and for Ryan, and to fight for what she believed in. She took a deep breath and relaxed her shoulders. Somehow, her parents had given her comfort from across the great divide and had reminded her of her own strength. Even if she was scared, she was doing the right thing.

CHAPTER ELEVEN

Wednesday morning, Mr. Leicester from the Briggs' insurance company arrived on time and greeted her. He was middle-aged and balding, wearing a pale-brown suit and large, scuffed oxfords. Large round glasses, which he pushed up often, dominated his face, along with warm eyes and a soft-spoken voice. He carefully laid his jacket over the back of a chair and retrieved a clipboard from his aging brown leather briefcase.

Allie stood. "I'm ready," With her camera in hand, she led the way to the yard.

Once aboard, Mr. Leicester referenced his list and began.

"All right. In the main living room, just behind the pilot house, there should be a clear crystal vase with a swirl around it by Thuret, worth around $800…"

"There it is," she said, snapping a picture. *Why in the hell is that not in the safe, as well?*

"There should be a cobalt-blue crystal ashtray, worth around $300…"

"Yes, there," Allie responded, pointing, again amazed at the value.

"There should be a brass and marble table clock, worth around $700…"

"That is over here," she said, spinning around to face it.

She continued with Mr. Leicester in this vein for quite a while, astounded at the figures she was hearing. On the lower deck, Leicester was a few steps behind her, saying, "…a small oval bas-relief of a vestal virgin between the two portholes in the bathroom worth $17,000…"

"Uh… no, there is a small portrait of a man in a kilt…" Allie said staring between the portholes.

"That painting should be in the space above the staircase…" Leicester replied, anxiety in his voice, flipping pages of his inventory on his clipboard.

Allie squeezed around him, ran back up the stairs, and turned around. "No, there is a small portrait of a man with a cane…"

"*That* should be between the portholes in the *other* bathroom…" he was saying, trying to follow her and look at his list at the same time, panic raising the pitch of his voice.

Allie ran back down to the bathroom they had not yet gone through. "There nothing on the wall there, only a small Waterford crystal figurine shaped like a turtle on the counter," Allie called, remembering how something had seemed out of place only a few minutes before.

"That's a problem," Leicester said, sitting heavily on one of the plastic-covered plush chairs as Allie came back upstairs.

"I agree. Did you say $17,000? Why was the bas-relief not on the list to go into the safe?"

Mr. Leicester raised his eyebrows. "Of course, we advised them to secure their property, but Mr. and Mrs. Briggs felt confident that no one would consider it that valuable, whereas the more recognizable artworks, like the Picasso and the Tiffany lamp would immediately draw a thief's eye," Leicester said simply.

"Should we check the rest of the boat?" Allie said.

"Let's do it quickly, and then we will both need to make some phone calls," Leicester said.

WHEN ALLIE RETURNED to the office, she called Charlie right away.

"Charlie, there are some really valuable items missing from *The Sunset Lady*," she said a little breathlessly.

"I'm on my way," he said and hung up.

About fifteen minutes later, he pushed open the glass door and said, "Show me."

They went out to the boat, the pictures of the missing items, which Leicester had emailed to her immediately, in Allie's hand.

"We did the tour of the boat, and Leicester read off the descriptions as we went. I took photos of each item just to cover my own ass. When we got to the master bathroom, we realized that someone had switched the bas-relief that was there with a painting on the staircase, and had switched some items around. The painting that was supposed to be here on the staircase was put in the bathroom, and the painting that was in the other bathroom was put on the staircase. When we realized there was nothing in the other bathroom where there was definitely supposed to be something, we knew someone had gone to a lot of trouble to hide their handiwork."

"They figured as long as everything was recognized as a piece of art that was supposed to be on the boat, they wouldn't miss one or two things. What all was taken?"

"The missing bas-relief was worth $17,000—"

"Do what?" he asked in shock, slipping into the local vernacular. "Why wasn't that in the safe?"

"I asked that, too. Apparently, the Briggs thought that they were safe to assume no one would know it was worth anything."

"Hmmm..." Bishop seemed to consider that thought.

"Also, a small bulldog figurine of black quartz with a diamond collar, and a small mouse figurine, also fitted with diamonds and gold."

"All told, worth how much?"

"About $30,000 all told," Allie replied.

"Enough to make a big enough payday, but nothing noteworthy enough to raise any eyebrows when trying to fence," Bishop commented. "Well, we'll add this to the report, and we may have our motive for Ty Guthrie's murder."

"Was it definitely murder, then?"

"Still waiting on the autopsy, but it's looking more and more like it," Bishop replied.

"Ty caught someone on *The Sunset Lady*, and he or she made sure he wouldn't turn them in," Allie said, half to herself.

"Allie, don't share this development. Let's see what shakes out on this one," Bishop said.

"Holly may have heard me call you…"

"Ask her not to tell anyone. Not even Neil."

"Charlie, we need to tell Neil! Mr. Leicester is going to call The Briggs, and either they'll be here demanding satisfaction or their attorney will be calling. There's no getting around notifying Neil," Allie explained.

"You're right, you're right." Charlie shook his head. "Do me a favor and call him now. Put him on speaker, so I can hear his reaction. Then I have to get back to the office to start working on this."

Allie pulled out her cell phone and did as Charlie asked.

"Allie?" Neil answered. "What's up?"

"Neil, the Briggs' insurance investigator was here and determined there were some things missing from the boat," she said.

"What?" Neil yelled. "How in the hell did that happen? Not only is my son dead, but now there's been a theft? What was taken, for Christ's sake?"

Allie explained what had gone missing and the values of each item.

"I can't believe this. Somebody really screwed up here. Allie, you need to get to the bottom of this key card thing. We need to know who's behind this. We'll lose so much business if this gets out! No one will believe our yard is safe, and if customers can't trust us, we'll lose everything. This is unacceptable. I need to call my attorney. Contact Tom from security and have him call me *immediately*," Neil roared.

The line went dead, and Allie realized she was still wincing from the volume level of Neil's tirade. She looked at Charlie.

"So now he knows," Charlie said, blowing out the breath he'd been holding. "Time for us to get to work. But before I go, I spoke with the DA again today."

"Oh?" Allie knew this woman was not to be crossed.

"Yes, I didn't tell her you were helping us, but as I said, she may catch wind of it. If she does, she may approach you. Katherine Matthews likes to be in control, and when she's not, she can come off as a little... intimidating," Charlie said.

A frown tugged at the corner of Allie's mouth. She didn't need enemies here.

"I just wanted to give you a little background in case she seeks you out. Ms. Matthews comes from old money around here. Her daddy was a judge, and as such, pretty much led the Good Ol' Boy network when it still existed. Sheriff Tate came in in the nineties, and he cleaned up a lot of that nonsense, but Kat still holds on to the old ways, protecting the 'haves' in our community, sometimes to the detriment of the 'have-nots,'" he said. "That's why she's held the position for so long. The 'haves' make sure she's elected. It's like insurance for them."

"I see."

"Depending on how this case progresses, she may become more involved, and I just wanted you to know her probable intentions," he said.

"I'll watch my back," Allie said. Southerners were known for their charm, but "who you're kin to" still carried high importance, and not being a local meant she wasn't to be trusted, fully. Being a young, capable woman, she was probably at odds with the Good Ol' Boy network.

Charlie said goodbye and jumped into his cruiser.

Back in the office, Allie relayed Charlie's request to keep things quiet on the theft to Holly, who looked utterly confused but agreed. Allie went back to her desk and repeated Neil's message to Tom in security. As the phones had quieted down, and she was still waiting for the key card company to call her back, she decided to spend the afternoon doing a little digging.

"I need to go into Neil's office for a bit and look for some files," she said.

Holly looked up from painting her nails and smiled. "Okay!"

Allie went into Neil's office and opened the top file cabinet drawer. She glanced through the file tabs. "Insurance, personnel, legal, advertising…" The middle two drawers were full of client files. When she got to the bottom drawer, she found several unmarked, red, file-sized envelopes secured with string and button. These didn't seem to be for public consumption. She glanced around before opening the first one. It contained a single file folder labeled, *personal correspondence*.

Maybe there's something in here about why my parents and the Guthries split so suddenly. She decided to flip through, looking for her dad's name, but resolved not to pry too much further. She couldn't help noticing several handwritten notes signed *Your Kitten*. Allie was mortified to think that these may be from a lover of Neil's, and after not seeing anything from her dad, she quickly shut the file and replaced the envelope in the drawer.

Pulling out the next, she found a single file folder again, this time marked *contracts* and noted this was different than the regular client file folders she was familiar with that contained current agreements with boat owners for repair work. *What's in here?* She pulled it out and took it back to her desk.

She flipped through the contents slowly, reading through the various legal documents and news clippings as she went. Apparently, Neil liked to invest in outside businesses with the profits from the boat company. About three-quarters of the way through the file, she caught her breath when she saw her dad's name. It was a news clipping from 2000, an article about the opening of a new vintage engine restoration service, a partnership between Neil and Allie's dad.

A new partnership has sprung up out of the fertile economic environment that is Carteret County. With Diamond Lady Restoration, Jack Fox and Neil Guthrie have joined forces to offer antique marine engine restoration services to local boaters, as well as those who stop here on their way south via the Intracoastal Waterway. Interested clients can have their engines restored on the grounds of Guthrie's Marine Center, located in Beaufort off of Highway 101. 'It's something that you just can't find anywhere else in the area. You'd probably have to go as far as Myrtle Beach to find the kind of quality restoration we're offering right here in Carteret County. Jack brings years of engine experience to the table, and I can offer the space and great customer service that Guthrie's Marine has continued to offer area boaters for generations,' says Neil Guthrie. The pair have already begun several projects, they say, and look forward to an excellent boating season. You can contact Diamond Lady Restoration at (252)...

How had she not known about this? She copied the article and the accompanying legal documents and stuffed them into her purse before returning the file to the red envelope, and then that envelope back to the bottom drawer in the cabinet in Neil's office. She noted that there were several more red string and button envelopes that remained unexplored. Snooping on her boss was not something she would normally do, but she found herself bargaining with her inner investigator who was quite intrigued by the red files. She might have to come back and take another peek.

ROLAND JAMES, Esquire, the Briggs's solicitor, called and threatened litigation, and Allie referred him to the Guthrie's attorney. "Let the games begin," she muttered as she hung up. No sooner had the receiver hit the cradle than it rang again. Allie looked at the number to make sure it wasn't the Briggs' attorney still on the line. Seeing a local number, she picked up the receiver.

"Guthrie's Marine, this is Allie. How can I help you?"

"Allie, this is District Attorney Katherine Matthews. How are you today?"

"All right and you?"

"Fine, thanks. Listen. Neil Guthrie is an old friend, and apparently not only was there a death in the yard, but now there has been a theft aboard one of the boats. Are you aware of this?"

"Yes. I was the one who took the insurance investigator aboard *The Sunset Lady*," she explained.

"I see. Well, I'm sure Charlie Bishop has impressed this upon you, but the media does not need to be alerted to this unnecessarily. There will be no leaks from law enforcement, so if the media catches on to this, I will know where they got their information. Do you understand?"

"Yes, ma'am," Allie said. *Charlie wasn't kidding when he said she could be intimidating. This woman is used to getting her way.*

"The Guthries have been through enough and don't need to worry about their employees selling them out for five minutes of fame," Matthews continued.

"I would never do that," Allie said. *It's one thing to make sure no one's leaking information, but she's getting close to insulting me.*

"Just so you think real hard about whose team you're on, okay, honey?"

"Okay," Allie said. Matthews was clearly using that term of endearment to put her in her place, and her jaw clenched in response.

"Just so we're clear," Matthews said.

"Yes, we are," Allie said, working hard to stay civil.

"Good to talk to you, honey," Matthews said.

"And to you. Have a great day," Allie said.

"Bye, bye," Matthews said in a sing-song lilt, and then the line was dead. Allie noticed her hand was shaking as she hung up the phone. The DA had just threatened her.

CHAPTER TWELVE

"Okay, Holly, I'm long overdue for my lunch," Allie said. "I'm going to head downtown for a bite to eat. Do you want anything?"

"No, I brought my lunch today," Holly said. "But thanks!"

Allie grabbed a burger from The Spot and drove to the waterfront to eat. After parking the truck, she fed the meter and found a spot on a bench across from Clawson's. She dug out her cell phone from her purse and found the contact she was looking for.

"Hey, Barbie, it's Allie. How are you?"

"Fine, sugar. What's up?"

"Did Ty have a cell phone?"

"Doesn't everyone these days?" Barbie asked.

"It hasn't been found yet. I've been looking all over the office. What kind did he have?"

"Well, last I knew, he had one of those Samsung Galaxy models, but it's been quite a few months, and I have no idea if he still had it," Barbie said.

"Any idea where it might have gone?"

"How the hell would I know?" Barbie asked. "It wasn't on the *Barbara Jean*?"

"No. Is there some other place he kept his things?"

"Oh, like an apartment or something? Maybe a place he could meet all of his conquests, you mean?" Barbie asked.

"Well, that isn't quite what I meant…"

"It's a possibility, but then I would be the last to know about it, wouldn't I?"

"I suppose so," Allie said.

"Why don't you call around to the real estate companies and see if he held any rentals with them?"

"I guess that would be the next step. Also, Charlie didn't find many personal belongings on the *Barbara Jean*. Would you happen to know if Ty had a storage unit somewhere?"

"Probably. He took all of his stuff when he left. He didn't have much, but he did have some, including a couple of pieces of furniture which I doubt made it to the boat. I have no idea where, though. I guess you could call around to those places, too. Or check with Neil, as a few of those pieces came from Ty's mom, Nancy."

"Well, thanks, Barbie. You've been a big help," Allie said.

She laughed. "I don't think so, but at least now you know what I don't know, right?"

"Pretty much. Thanks again."

"Anytime."

When Allie returned, Holly gave her the message that the key card company had called back, and the last time the code had been changed was in 2012. *That's quite a while*, Allie thought. *Wonder how many employees have left the company since then. Wonder how many had a problem with Ty...*

Later that afternoon, Neil came in. He waved at Allie and Holly, who were both on the phone, and headed for his office. When Allie had finished her call, she approached the office and didn't hear him in conversation. She knocked lightly on the door frame.

"Neil? How is everything?" she asked softly.

"It's fine," he said with a sigh, not looking up. "Have you seen the paper?"

"No," she said.

"Front page news," he said, holding it up for her to see. A picture of the law enforcement vehicles with their lights ablaze in front of the yard to the entrance took up most of the space above the fold.

"They didn't get any information from us," Allie said.

"I know, but they didn't have to. The basics are a matter of public record," he said, shaking his head. "And the rest they can fill in with 'testimonials' about Ty's character. This won't be good for business."

Worried about business more than Ty. "I'm not sure if Charlie has spoken to you, but I don't think they've found Ty's cell phone yet, and they were also wondering if Ty had a storage unit somewhere," she said.

Neil gave her a calculating look. "I've been avoiding their calls. Ty's cell phone is here in my desk drawer," he said calmly, opening the drawer and pulling out a sizeable phone and charger. "He was charging it here in the office the day he died and must have forgotten it here. Something about it taking too long with the generators on the boat."

Why wouldn't he have offered the phone the night they found Ty? She asked, "Do you want me to call Charlie and tell him you have it?"

Another calculating look, and Neil said, "Sure," then went back to reading his paper.

"And the storage unit?"

"Oh, uh, I'm pretty sure he had a unit at All Seasons on Lennoxville Road, where he kept some of his mother's furniture, but as for a key, I have no idea."

"Okay," Allie said. "Is there anything else you need from me right now?"

"No, I think you've got it all handled," he said. *Was he smirking?*

"Thanks, Neil," she said and returned to her desk. *Does he know why I'm asking? Am I about to get fired?*

She picked up the phone to call Charlie, and Neil came out of the office with the paper under his arm. "I'm trying to avoid him," he said, pointing to her phone, "so I'm heading out. Not sure when I'll be back in, but text or call if you need any more... information."

"Uh, will do," she said, watching him walk out the door.

Deciding to text Charlie instead, she pulled out her own cell phone and looked at Holly, who was apparently confused about Neil's manner, as well.

Neil was just in and out, worried about the newspaper

article and how it would affect business, she texted. *And he's had Ty's phone in his desk this whole time... He just left*

Be there in a minute, Charlie texted back.

WHEN CHARLIE CAME into the office, he pulled an evidence bag and gloves out of his back pocket, and Allie rose to meet him. "It's in here on his desk," she said. They went into Neil's office and Charlie slipped the phone into the plastic bag, marking the exterior with the date, time, and location of collection in Sharpie.

"We'll get some techs on this right away," he said. "Interesting that he didn't say anything about this on Monday night."

"My thoughts exactly. And he kind of smirked at me when I asked him about it, like he knew I was asking questions for you," she added. "Gave me the creeps."

"I wouldn't worry too much about Neil. He just likes to do things his own way," Charlie said. "Hope we can get something from this."

"Me too," Allie said. "What do you think about his reaction? Like he cared more for the business than for Ty?"

"Maybe he does. He doesn't have a reputation for warm fuzzies, Allie."

"He said he thought Ty might have a storage unit at All Seasons on Lennoxville Road," Allie said.

"Okay," Charlie said. "We did get that ring of keys from his truck, so maybe the key is on there and we won't have to get the bolt cutters—" Charlie stopped mid-sentence when his phone rang. "Hold that thought," he said, dragging his finger across the screen of his phone to answer.

"Darius," he said. "What have you got?"

Allie watched his face for a reaction. His eyes opened a bit wider, and he held up his finger as if the person on the other end could see him. "Hold on a minute, can I put you on speaker? I have Allie Fox here, helping on the case, and I'd like her to hear this." He pulled the phone away from his face and scrunched up his eyes to locate the speaker function on the screen. Having pressed it, he said, "Darius Walker, county medical examiner, please meet Allie Fox, my investigative consultant on the Guthrie case. Go ahead, Darius."

"Can you hear me?" A deep voice came from the phone.

"Yes," they both replied simultaneously.

"Good. The pathologist has just about finished the autopsy and found something that might be of interest to the case—almost missed it, in fact. I thought you would want to know right away, rather than wait for the full report," Walker said.

"Okay, shoot," Charlie said.

"There was a contusion on the victim's left temple, indicating there was some sort of physical altercation before his death."

"Okay," Charlie said. "Is that it?"

"No. Besides the usual bruise pattern from being struck with something hefty, there was something embedded in the wound."

"Would you just spit it out, Darius? What was it?" Charlie was getting exasperated.

"Diamonds, Charlie. There were tiny diamonds in the man's temple," Walker said.

After a moment, Charlie said, "Well, that's not something you see every day."

"No, it isn't. That's why I thought it might have some bearing on your case," Walker said. "Listen, I have to go. There's much more to do here."

"Of course, of course," Charlie said, rubbing his beard absently.

"Thank you, Dr. Walker," Allie said.

"Yes, thanks, Darius," Charlie said.

"Anytime," Walker said, and the phone beeped to indicate he had hung up.

Charlie slipped his phone back into its holster and looked at Allie. "Weren't there some little diamond-encrusted knickknacks on that list of stolen items?"

"There were," Allie said, looking at the list. "He interrupted the theft."

"That's the most likely explanation," Charlie said.

CHAPTER THIRTEEN

When she and Ryan settled in at home later that evening, Allie pulled the documents about her dad's partnership with Neil from her purse. There was really no more information there than in the news clipping she had already read, although the legal documents spelled out that it was a fifty-fifty partnership. She was amazed at how much her dad had invested in the company and wondered what had happened. She would have to do some internet research on the weekend and possibly go through her parents' things. She checked the time and decided to see if Peg wanted to come over for supper and an update on the case. She knocked on Ryan's door and told him she was going to run across to Peg's for a minute but she would be right back. Ryan looked at her and gave a slight nod. She closed the door and headed for Peg's.

"Knock knock!" she called out through the screen door.

"Allie!" Peg said coming to the door. "How are ya darlin'?"

"Good, good," Allie reassured her. "Can't stay long. Just wanted to see if you wanted to come over for supper and some gossip tonight."

"I'd love to!" Peg said, obviously pleased. "You know me, old women never have plans that can't be postponed. I'd love to see how the case is going!"

"Great. How about seven?"

"Fantastic. I'll pop over and bring something sweet for dessert, okay?"

"Fantastic," she echoed and went back to her trailer.

There were very few foods Ryan would eat, so if she wanted him to come to the table, Allie had to make sure he was served something he liked. That meant spaghetti or lasagna, pizza, pork chops, or fish sticks. *We haven't had fish sticks in a while, so those will do.* Once that was settled, she slipped into some workout clothes and went to the shed for a half hour of shadowboxing, mulling through all she had learned that day in her head as she jabbed, feinted, and blocked. Ryan found her there a half hour later, asking, "Time for supper?"

"Sure, kiddo," she said, smiling. "Let me just clean up, and we'll pop some fish sticks in the oven!"

When supper was almost ready, she knocked on Ryan's door again and said, "Hey, Ryan, supper's almost ready, and we have smiley fries to eat, too. Peg is coming over to eat with us. Would you mind running over there and letting her know it's almost ready?"

Ryan said nothing but walked quickly next door, flapping hands in his excitement. "Fish sticks!" he said when Peg opened her door. He ran back to their trailer, leaving Peg to giggle at his enthusiasm. Peg followed him in the door with a half a gallon of ice cream, and said, "Smells good!"

Ryan was already at the table, and with some gentle encouragement from Peg, he got up to set the table for everyone as Allie finished up. She plated up the food for the three of them, and everyone sat at the table as Ryan hopped up to turn on *Wheel of Fortune*. Allie decided the gossip part of the evening was probably better for after supper when Ryan didn't have to hear about murder. She let Peg know with a nod in his direction to stick to safer topics throughout the meal.

When they were finished and the table was cleared, Peg brought out the half gallon of strawberry ice cream, Ryan's favorite. Everyone got their scoops, and Ryan stood with his bowl, looking at Allie.

"Yes, you can take it to your room, but don't spill, and bring your bowl and spoon back out when you're finished," she said.

"Before you go, kiddo!" Peg called to Ryan. "I've got a riddle for you, and you let me know when you figure it out, okay?"

"Okay!" he said, standing stock still, waiting for it.

"Are you ready? Here it is: What is the word, the first two letters of which stand for a man, the first three for a woman, the first four for a brave man, and the whole for a brave woman?" She paused for a moment. "Got it?"

"Got it!" he said, and he bounced off to his room, ice cream in hand.

"So, fill me in," Peg said, pulling her legs up under her in the recliner.

Allie told her everything that had happened so far at the yard.

"Are they sure it was murder?" Peg asked when she had finished.

"They're waiting on the results of the autopsy, but Charlie is pretty sure, especially now that they have a strong motive," Allie said.

"But anyone could have taken those things, even before the night of the murder, if that's what it was," Peg said. "Just playing devil's advocate here."

"That's a good point," Allie said. "But the Briggs have been there just about every day, and would most likely have noticed if something was gone."

"But you said yourself that the thief took great pains to confuse things," Peg said. "And they didn't even really realize the stuff was gone until their insurance guy came out."

"It's something worth considering."

"Who are your suspects?" Peg asked.

"Well, from my perspective, there are two yard laborers, the Briggs themselves, me and Holly, Neil and Vicky, Zack, and Barbie," Allie said. "And apparently, everyone who has worked for the Guthrie's since 2012."

"Did Barbie have access to the yard?"

"I don't know, but probably. She was in charge of issuing the key cards the last time around, and probably never turned hers in when she quit."

"Would any of them have any interest in stealing the stuff from the boat? Would they even know it was there?"

"The laborers would know it was there, and might have a financial motive, but maybe not the means to sell the stuff. I don't think Holly knows much of anything at all, really. Neil and Vicky don't really need to steal from anyone because they have plenty of money. Zack might know about the valuables still on the boat and would definitely have a financial motive, too. But again, I don't know if he'd have a clue about getting rid of the stuff. Same thing for Barbie. And the Briggs? I don't know why they would steal from themselves…"

"Stranger things have been known to happen," Peg said. "Are you helping Charlie out? Are you supposed to sleuth some more?"

"I'm keeping my ears open, for sure," Allie said. "And the DA doesn't want me involved, but Charlie says he can handle her."

"Be careful with her. People say she is a career politician with a heart of ice. Did you find anything out about your dad and Neil?"

"Funny you should mention that. I just did some digging today, knowing Neil wouldn't be in again. They started a company together in 2000."

"Interesting. Is it still running?"

"I don't know. I have to do some internet research this weekend."

"Good thinking. When friends do business deals, sometimes things turn sour, which is why you probably never heard anything about it," Peg said.

"I had the same thought," Allie said.

Just after dishes were done, and Peg was gathering

herself to go, Ryan came hopping out from his room. "Peg!" he said.

"What is it, Ryan?" Peg asked, concern on her face.

"Here," he said, shoving a piece of torn paper at her and beaming with pride. She took the paper and opened it up. In his careful handwriting, Ryan had written the answer to her riddle, *He. Her. Hero. Heroine.*

CHAPTER FOURTEEN

Thursday morning, Allie's cell phone vibrated on her desk and she saw that Charlie was calling. She picked up her phone and headed for the small bathroom in the front corner of the office. Once inside with the door locked, she answered, "Hey, what's up?"

"I'm just about to head over to the county morgue and speak with Dr. Walker again. He says he's got the full report from the pathologist, and I thought you may be interested in coming along."

"Is that allowed? I mean for me to be there?"

"Look, you don't have an official role, but if anyone questions me, you are consulting on this case. You have the background to pass for it, and no one will ask anyway. I'm one of the only investigators in the county, and if I want you there, you get to be there," Charlie explained. "Now, I understand if you don't want to go to the morgue, honey. Don't feel like you have to. But it sounds like he has something important for us, and I thought I'd offer."

Allie understood immediately what he meant. She

hadn't been to the morgue since she had to perform the tortuous task of identifying her parents' bodies. That was one of the hardest things she had ever had to do, and going back there was not her first choice for how to spend her lunch break. But on the other hand, being there for the autopsy results in person would be infinitely better than hearing about it second hand.

"Yep, I can be there. What time?"

"One o'clock. I'll meet you in the parking lot," Charlie said.

"Did forensics ever get you anything on those beer bottles we found on the *Barbara Jean*? The ones with lipstick?"

"Well, not a whole lot to work with. They said most of them weren't very recently emptied, and there's no use trying to get any DNA from them until we have a suspect to compare with. They did tell me that the brand name of the lipstick was something called Burberry Kisses and the shade was Union Red, Number 113, whatever that means... Does that mean anything to you, Allie?"

"Unfortunately not, Charlie. I'm not a makeup user. But hey," she said with a sudden thought. "I know someone who is. Let me see what I can find out, and I'll let you know if I come up with anything on it."

"Sounds great, Allie. It helps to have a woman's perspective on this one." Charlie laughed.

"HOLLY, I need your help with something..." Allie began and then hesitated. She was fairly certain that Holly had nothing to do with Ty's death, but was she sure enough to share information about the case?

"What's up, Allie?" Holly said, bright-eyed, clearly not used to being asked for help.

"I know you are our resident makeup expert."

"Oh, does this have to do with the case?" Holly's voice went up several pitches as she bounced in her seat.

"Nah, I just had someone recommend some lipstick to me, and because I obviously know nothing about makeup, I thought I'd ask you," Allie said.

"Okay, shoot!" Holly said, relishing her moment of expertise.

"What can you tell me about Burberry Kisses?"

"Burberry is a British brand. You probably know them from the plaid that was popular a decade ago. A few years ago, they branched out into makeup, and they have a whole line. It's a bit pricey for this area, but they do carry it at Sephora, and they have stores in Greenville and Wilmington. Did your mystery friend recommend a shade, too?" She waggled her eyebrows up at Allie.

"Sure, but can I ask why?"

"People say you can tell a lot about a woman based on the shade of lipstick they wear." Holly shrugged. "Maybe it will suit you, and maybe it won't."

"It was Union Red, Number 113."

"Okay, let's look it up," Holly said, turning to her computer. Within seconds, she had found a listing for the lipstick brand in question, and a whole palette of colors. "Union Red, you said?"

"Yep," Allie said.

"They say those who wear red are passionate and

ambitious. This isn't the most vibrant red ever, but it does take some guts to wear a shade like that."

"You said it was pricey—how much?" Allie asked, peering at the computer screen.

"Thirty-three dollars a tube." Holly giggled.

"What? People pay that for lipstick?" Allie asked, flabbergasted.

"Every day. Sometimes, even more."

"So, do you think Union Red is the one for me?"

"I don't know, Allie. Honestly, it's a little too diva for you, and you don't seem the type to travel that far or pay that much for lipstick—you have bigger things on your plate," Holly said.

"That's quite a bit from some lipstick on a bottle..." Allie said under her breath. "Well, thanks for your input, Holly. I think I may pass on this stuff. Maybe someone like Barbie could pull it off, but not me."

"You're welcome," Holly twinkled, seemingly excited that she could show off her expertise a bit.

CHARLIE AND ALLIE walked in together, discussing the M.E., who was relatively new to the area and a huge asset to the county. "He has the credentials, but more than that, he picks up on things that no one else does. It makes our jobs a lot easier."

"Sounds like quite a find for a county like this one," Allie said.

They passed through the door to the Medical Examiner's Office and signed in at the front desk. The Medical Examiner, Dr. Darius Walker, motioned them through the next set of doors through the window. He led them back to his office and they sat in the little-used chairs in front of his desk.

"Darius, this is Allie Fox, a former fraud investigator from the Chicago area, and she's consulting on the case," Charlie said.

"Nice to meet you in person, Miss Fox," Walker said, shaking her hand with a firm grip.

"Nice to meet you, too, Dr. Walker," she responded.

"Call me Darius," he said. He was about six-two with a dark, sleek fade, and black-rimmed glasses that gave him a bit of a retro look. He didn't smile easily, which gave him a serious air, but had a mellow, soothing voice that caught Allie's attention.

"What did the pathologist find, Darius?" Charlie asked.

"Well, the obvious broken bones and contusions you could see at the crime scene. His neck was broken, and his death would have been instantaneous when he hit the ground..."

"Would have?"

"That isn't what caused him to die, Charlie," Walker explained, leaning over the manila folder on his desk to emphasize the point.

"Are you saying he died on the boat and was pushed off?" Allie asked.

"Not exactly," Walker continued. "He suffered chest compressions that damaged his solar plexus and caused a heart attack—the real cause of death in this case."

Quiet fell on the small office as Allie and Charlie absorbed what Darius had told them.

"How do you know that the chest compressions

weren't from the fall?" Charlie asked. "I know from experience that there is a lot of internal damage from falls."

"It's the *type* of damage that's occurred here. When you are hit from the front in the chest, there can be damage to the aorta at three different fixed points. You don't have that when you have suffered blunt force trauma to the back," Walker explained. "From the crime scene, and the way he landed, we can determine that he landed on his back, therefore…"

"Something or someone hit his chest hard enough to make his heart stop beating before he hit the ground, is what you're telling us," Charlie said.

"Yes, that's about right," Walker replied.

"Would it have been possible for him to fall on something with that much force? Maybe during a struggle?" Allie asked, running through of the various equipment and fixtures on the deck of *The Sunset Lady* in her mind.

"No, I don't think so, unless he was running into something at thirty-five miles per hour," Walker supplied.

"What?" Allie and Charlie said simultaneously.

"The amount of force needed to cause chest compressions to stop someone's heart is equivalent to being hit by a car."

"I'm having a little trouble understanding. He got hit by something like a car?" Charlie asked.

"No, but someone somehow struck him in the chest with that much force," Walker said patiently. "In other words, your death just officially became a homicide."

Silence filled the room again while they felt the shift from the weight of that information.

"Do you have any idea how someone could do that to someone else?" Charlie asked.

"I have a few ideas," Walker said with a slight smile. "Comotio Cordis, the technical term for this, is actually pretty common in young adults playing sports. An injury like this causing cardiac arrest can be caused by fifty joules of impact energy. To give you an idea, a hockey puck impact can be as high as 180 joules, a karate punch 450, and a punch delivered by a professional boxer can be as high as 1028."

"Does the site of the injury give us any clues about what caused the impact? A bruise pattern, perhaps?" Charlie asked.

"There's not much to go by. There is a mark that is triangular but rounded, that is several inches across its widest part, see," Walker said, opening the manila folder on his desk and spinning the glossy photo inside, pointing to the mark on Ty's chest.

"So, it's murder, but we have no idea what kind of weapon we're looking for." Charlie sighed.

"But we do know the killer is relatively athletic to be able to wield something with enough force to make that kind of impact. Would that be safe to say?" Allie asked.

"I think that's a fair assessment," Walker said, looking at her with interest.

"Well, at least that's something," Charlie said.

"We'll keep looking at the contusion on his chest to see if any kind of implement matches that mark, and we'll notify you if and when we come up with anything," Walker said. "Of course, we'll have to release the body to the family before too long."

"I understand," Charlie said. "Time to let the family know, and re-evaluate our suspects," he said, turning to Allie.

"And time for me to get back to work," Allie added.

AS THEY WALKED OUT TOGETHER, Allie told Charlie about Holly's assessment of the lipstick, that the wearer went to great lengths to purchase the expensive stuff, and her profile of the mystery woman as a "diva."

"It *is* possible that Ty let this mystery person into the yard," Allie said.

"We can't rule it out. It's obvious he was in the habit of entertaining on the *Barbara Jean* after yard hours. He wouldn't have women there drinking beer during the day, would he?" Charlie asked.

"Absolutely not. He worked hard when he was on the clock. Besides, I think if Neil heard about anything like that, he'd put a stop to it right quick. That wasn't Ty's style, anyway. He never broadcasted his love life. It was always kind of a mystery and he liked it that way. Having a lady friend show up after hours sounds much more like him. Of course, it could have been someone entirely different."

"Well, let's say for a moment that he did let someone in. It would explain why we never found a key card."

"Yes, and it would increase our possible suspects ten-fold. In fact, it really could be anybody. Beer bottles aside, he could have let anyone in for any reason at all."

She sat for a moment, thinking about the enormity of that possibility.

"Needles and haystacks come to mind," Allie said, blowing out a sigh.

"Nevertheless, it's something we have to consider and investigate," Charlie said, rubbing his neck in irritation. "I'll see if forensics picked up any prints on *The Sunset Lady*, and we may have to have them out to the *Barbara Jean*, as well. Even if we find some, it may not help us until we have a suspect, but it could make the haystack a bit smaller."

CHAPTER FIFTEEN

Thinking about what Barbie had said about Ty and his extracurricular activities, and about possible needles in the haystack, Allie decided to do a little Facebook creeping to see what she could find out about who Ty might have let into the yard willingly. She doubted the Sheriff's Department had had much time to follow up on this all-important research tool yet. She had taken over control of the boatyard's social media presence when she began work at Guthrie's, convincing both Neil and Ty that it couldn't hurt business and had the potential to bring new clients in. They had set up business accounts and profiles on all of the major platforms, including Facebook, where it was set up as a managed page under Ty Guthrie's personal account. Because she actually managed the page, Allie had access and logged in now, going directly to Ty's profile. She scanned the "about" tab and didn't find much useful, then traveled over to his newsfeed. The last thing he had posted was a picture of one of the boats they had renovated in the yard. She scanned down the page at older posts and saw that he had been tagged in some pictures. She opened them and noted some of the names of others who had been tagged in the pictures. There were several younger women, and she pulled over a pad of post-it notes to start a list. Most were not names she recognized, but she started in surprise when she saw a picture with Holly in it. She and Ty looked a little cozy in it, and Allie realized she had not had any idea that they had seen each other outside of work. When Ty had come into the office, he had all but ignored Holly. This was interesting information, and Allie began to think of ways to get Holly to talk. And when Gemma Piner, Sammy's sister, popped up in another picture, she began to understand why Sammy hated Ty so much. As she scrolled down the feed, she also noticed a few mentions about a woman named "Rose," but she wasn't tagged in the posts—maybe she didn't have a Facebook page? It was curious, and Allie wondered if it was a real name or a nickname. Interesting.

Chief Detective Charlie called a bit later, and Allie took the call in Neil's office, briefly wondering when he might return to work.

"What's up?" Allie asked.

"Just checking in," he said. "Anything new?"

"I've found some interesting things on Ty's Facebook feed," Allie offered.

"Oh yeah? We've been so busy out in the field, I haven't had the time to assign anybody to the social media stuff yet. What'd you find?"

"First, I want to make sure that it's okay with you that

I'm still helping. I don't want to get in your way or jeopardize your investigations at all," Allie said.

"Don't you think I would have told you already if I thought you would do that?"

"Yes, but, I'm not a deputy, and I don't know. Will any of this be permissible evidence?"

"Of course, it will. What you're doing is no different than if I had stationed a deputy in your office to question people. You're just saving us some time by teasing out the most important aspects of the case," he said.

"All right. As long as you're sure," she said.

"I am. Seems like you're enjoying yourself anyway," he added.

"It's like a puzzle that needs solving, and you know Ryan and I both love of puzzles," she said, smiling.

"Right," he said, laughing. He paused and then said, "The DA told me she had spoken with you. I think she knows you're helping on the case, but she hasn't outright asked me. You're on her radar, though."

"Great," Allie said. "She pretty much threatened me on the phone. Do I need to be worried?"

"Let me worry about Kat Matthews," Charlie growled.

"Anyway, I have a list of names of some women Ty seems to have been associated with, including Holly," she said, quietly so that Holly wouldn't hear her name in the conversation.

"Interesting," Charlie said.

Allie gave him the list of names and then added, "And there are a few mentions from a couple months back of someone named Rose—I'm not sure if that's her real name or a nickname. And it wasn't a tag so I don't think this person has a Facebook page," Allie said.

"You'll have to explain that to me a little more in detail," Charlie said. "I'm not too familiar with how all those social media sites work."

Allie explained the basics of tagging and pages to him. "So if it was a nickname, or if she doesn't have a Facebook page, she may not have known he was posting about her, or maybe he was being secretive on purpose. Maybe she's married!" Allie said when the thought caught up with her.

"Hmm," Charlie said. "You might think about bringing Rose up in conversation with some of the people in the yard to see if anyone knows what you're talking about," he said. "Gauge their reactions, at least."

"Good idea," she said. "I will, although Ty was pretty secretive about who he was seeing. Do you have any idea where the thief might have tried to sell the stolen goods from *The Sunset Lady*?" Allie asked, remembering her list of questions from the morning.

"Probably some antique dealers, maybe outside of the county, say in New Bern or Wilmington. Somewhere higher-end goods might be sold and appreciated," Charlie said. "We've got some deputies on it, but if you want to check around yourself, you can definitely work on it," Charlie said.

"I've got some ideas about how to spend my weekend," she said.

"Well, I can tell you that the techs have looked at the phone Neil gave us, and said there are surprisingly few text messages and emails on it. There aren't even that many pictures, and the few that are, are only of boats. None of people."

"Isn't that weird, Charlie?" Allie asked, bewildered.

"I reckon," he said. "Especially in light of all of these flings he had with these women. How did he even contact them if not with this phone?"

"I checked his messages on Facebook, but there wasn't much there. I'm thinking he had another phone."

"I s'pose it's possible, although we had a hard enough time locating this one, thanks to Neil," Charlie said. "I guess we chalk this up to a dead end."

"I guess so. I'll keep poking, but speaking of Neil, I think I have to be more discreet around him," she said.

"Like I said, I wouldn't worry too much about him, but whatever you need to do," Charlie said.

"I'll talk to you later," she said.

"Right," he said and hung up.

<hr/>

ALLIE WORKED on some invoicing while Holly handled the phones and some filing. Neil always wanted her to inflate the charges to the customers, and she hated it. It was dishonest and smarmy, and she struggled with her conscience every time she had to do it, wondering why in the world her father had ever been friends with Neil. Right after lunch, the door swung open, and in walked Zack Guthrie.

"Hey," he said.

"Hey." Both Holly and Allie returned his greeting.

"How's it going?" he asked with seemingly no particular interest in the answer.

"Fine," Allie said. "How about you?"

She watched as he swept his hand through his styled hair. He looked tired. Most kids who grew up with money in the area tended toward the preppy end of the spectrum, wearing high-end variations of khaki shorts, Sperry Topsiders, and crisp cotton button-downs. Zack, on the other hand, in true rebellious fashion, had befriended kids from the less savory trailer parks in town and fancied himself more of a DJ-hip hop icon, wearing sagging oversized jeans, heavily embellished t-shirts that were much too large, expensive kicks, and the obligatory white sunglasses.

"As good as can be expected," he said. "I still can't believe it about Ty."

"None of us can," Allie said.

"I've been told I'm a suspect," Zack said.

"I hadn't heard," Allie said.

"I guess I had a little too much to drink that night and ended up getting picked up by the sheriff. I don't really remember where I was before I got picked up, so I have no alibi. Like I'd kill my own brother," he said as he sat in an office chair, shaking his head.

Allie didn't know how to respond, so she didn't, choosing instead to listen to what he might have to say.

"Growing up with Ty wasn't easy, ya know," he said. "He was always so good at everything he touched. Mom resented him because he always outdid me, and Neil always reminded me of how much better Ty was than me. I don't know why I'm sharing all of this, but anyone could see it," he said. "It was no secret. Ty was always going to be the one to take over this place, and I had no idea what I would do then. How did I fit in the plan? No one ever shared that with me." He paused. "Now that Ty's gone... Now what?"

Allie glanced at Holly, who only widened her eyes in response. "Have you talked to your dad?"

"Not much. He probably thinks it should have been me, not Ty."

"You really have no idea where you were that night?" Allie asked.

"I know I started at Backstreet Pub in Beaufort. Not sure after that."

"Who were you with?"

"Loreli and a few of my friends who hang out there," he said.

"Where is Loreli, anyway?" Allie asked. Loreli and Zack usually traveled everywhere together, attached at the hip.

"She's mad at me. I guess I left her at the pub that night, and when I got picked up, she said she wasn't going to bail me out again," Zack said, looking miserable.

"Have you tried to talk to her?" Allie asked.

"Only every hour. She won't pick up. I think she's blocking my calls now."

"Give her some time, Zack. Cool it on the phone calls for now," Allie suggested.

"Ya think?"

"I know," she said.

"Well, my dad asked me to come by and pick up a new key card. I think the old one is in my car, but I'll have to look for it. Then sometime soon, we're supposed to have 'a talk,' probably about my future," Zack said.

"It seems to me you're taking it seriously, which is a good sign," Allie said.

"Kinda hard not to take it seriously when your brother is dead," Zack said.

"Good point," Allie said.

Zack took the card Allie handed him, signed the page saying he was in receipt, and looked at her with eyes that could only be described as sad. "Thanks for letting me vent. I've had no one to talk to about all this."

"Anytime, Zack," Allie said, almost feeling pity for the kid.

CHAPTER SIXTEEN

The beefy form of Keith Briggs darkened the doorway for only a second before the door swung as far back as it could on the hinges, sucking air out of the office. Allie and Holly both turned in surprise and then bore the full brunt of his mood.

"Just wanted to make sure I am *allowed* on my own damned boat," he said loudly and sarcastically.

"Of course, you are, Mr. Briggs. Chief Detective Bishop has cleared the vessel for your use."

"Well, it's my bloody boat, in't it? Along with all the stuff you allowed a thief to steal from it, right under your noses! I'd like to see for myself what was nicked from us, how much damage the coppers did to it, and look around to see the general state of things, and there in't anyfink you can do about it, is there?"

"Of course, Mr. Briggs. Whatever you'd like." As he huffed out of the office again, Allie called after him, "Mind the stairs."

Allie barely had time to cock an eyebrow at Holly before Donna Briggs made her entrance.

"So the coppers are done with our property, and now we find some valuables were stolen. We do have rights, you know!"

"Yes, Mrs. Briggs. Mr. Briggs is just ahead of you and is now headed toward *The Sunset Lady* himself."

"All right then!" she said with a glare. "Say, did I hear that the bloke who fell off the boat was actually murdered?" she asked.

"Yes, the pathologist and medical examiner have determined so."

"Huh. Have they figured out why?" she asked, a little softer this time.

"No, I believe they are still investigating the matter," Allie said.

"'At's a rough way to go, I s'pect. Poor bloke," she said and then turned to follow in her husband's footsteps.

Another cocked eyebrow exchanged with Holly, and a quick look out the window to make sure no one else was prepared to surprise them, and Allie added, "Well, that was an interesting reaction."

"You reckon?" Holly agreed. "Turned into a regular teddy bear there for a minute."

"Yeah," Allie said, thinking.

About a half hour later, Charlie entered the office.

"Hello, ladies! Might the Briggs be here somewhere?"

"You know they are. You saw their Cadillac in the lot, Charlie." Allie shot him a look. His face broke into a wide grin.

"Well, how about if I just wait for them in Neil's office, then?"

"Sure. Should we tell them you're here?"

"Let's let it be a surprise, okay?"

Allie grinned at Charlie, and he winked back.

About fifteen minutes later, Mr. and Mrs. Briggs came back into the office.

"Well, I s'pose there isn't too much that's noticeable in the way of damage to the boat. But Leicester was right about the stolen property—I can't believe you people allowed that to happen!"

"The incident that occurred here is highly irregular, and—"

"Listen to you, always ready with an excuse. I don't know about you, Donna, but I'm pretty sure we'll be finding another yard to do any work for us in the future. This one 'ere has allowed a bloke to be killed on it, allowed thieves to steal from us, and can't even guarantee she'll be ready to go when we need to," he said with a sneer.

"Yes, Keith, I think we're done here," she said with teeth bared at Allie.

"But not before I get a detailed list of what has yet to be done on 'er!" Keith bellowed.

"Mr. and Mrs. Briggs, I'm so glad you could come in to speak with me today!" Charlie purred as he stepped out of Neil's office, surprising them.

"Who're you?" Keith Briggs said, eyes narrowing.

"I'm Chief Detective Bishop, in charge of the investigation into Ty Guthrie's murder, as well as the theft of the items from your boat, as it seems the two events are tied together," Charlie said, offering his hand.

Keith Briggs stared at it as if it were a slug and said, "I wasn't comin' in to speak wif you. I was comin' in to see when this bloody boatyard might have our boat ready so we could get sailing again."

"Well, now that you're here, you won't mind me asking a few questions. You'll have to wait until we're through with the crime scene before they can even touch it for repairs. So, let's see if we can get some answers about your stolen property," Charlie said, smoothly retracting his offered hand and putting it back into his pocket.

"Well, I'm not sure what we can tell ya. We don't know nuffink, right, Keith?" Donna said, folding her arms over her chest.

"Why don't we have a seat in Mr. Guthrie's office?" Charlie offered.

"That chap is never here!" Keith Briggs remarked as the couple reluctantly went in and took seats.

"Well, he has had a death in the family," Charlie said quietly, losing the charming smile for a moment.

"Of course," Donna said, actually looking embarrassed.

"Well, we've lost, too, haven't we? About 20,000 quid!" Keith said.

"Yes, that's what we're here to discuss. You've reviewed the items missing with your insurance company?"

"Yes, we have a detailed report at the condo," Donna said.

"Have you gone over the contents of the boat yourself, and do you agree with the report about the missing items?" Charlie asked.

"We have, and it is spot on," Keith said.

"And are you sure the items went missing the night of the murder?" Charlie asked.

"Wot do you mean?" Keith asked, volume rising.

"Is it possible that the items could have gone missing earlier? The thief did take some pains to confuse the location of the stolen items, and make them less noticeable…"

"I think we would have noticed that, don't you, Keith? We're here just about every day!" Donna said, shocked.

"No, it is not possible. Not in the least," Keith said, obstinate. "They were taken that night, absolutely."

"But you didn't notice before the insurance investigator alerted you, did you?"

The pair exchanged a brief look before Donna said, "I knew something was off, but I couldn't put my finger on it."

"And do you have any idea who might have known about the value of the items left on the boat? Most people would assume the valuables had already been placed in the safe here in this office."

"It must have been someone who worked here, saw the stuff, and took the chance to nick it."

"Do you think a boatyard worker would recognize the value in the stolen items?"

"How should I know what the stupid employees know or don't know? They see a yacht and recognize that just about everything on it is valuable," Keith countered.

"Can I ask why you didn't put these items in the safe?"

"We assumed no one would think anything aboard was valuable," Donna said.

Charlie paused a moment and then seized. "But, Mr.

Briggs, you just said that the employees would assume anything on a yacht was valuable."

No one spoke for a moment.

"Well, I guess we were wrong about that, weren't we?" He rose and indicated to Donna to do the same. "We are done here, Chief Detective. We have nuffink else to tell you except that we are the victims here, and we trust you will stop wasting time asking us stupid questions and work on catching the crook."

As the pair marched out of the office, Charlie said, "Well, they left pretty abruptly after only a little challenge. That's interesting."

"And they didn't even ask me about the progress on the boat, which was their original reason for coming in. You got them flustered, Charlie," Allie said.

"About what, though?" he mused.

CHARLIE'S CELL PHONE RANG, and he pulled it from its holster. "Bishop," he answered. "Uh, huh. Uh, huh. Okay, thanks," he said and hung up. "That was one of my detectives. They were able to use the storage unit key we found on a unit at All Seasons on Lennoxville. Mostly furniture, and nothing that really pertains to the case. There was another key on the ring, though."

"Really?"

"Yeah, to a safe-deposit box."

Allie raised her eyebrows.

"You'll never guess what we found in it," Charlie said.

"What?" Allie asked.

"Cash. About $20 grand. Safe but relatively untraceable. Question is, where'd he get it? And why was he hiding it?"

"What is it with this family and money?" Allie asked.

"What do you think this does to our suspect list?" Charlie asked.

"It's an interesting wrinkle. Of course, as you said, the source of that amount of money is the big question."

"You're right," Allie said. "Then again, this wasn't common knowledge, so maybe it has no impact on our suspect list, except to give us a reason to look more closely at the victim," Allie said.

"We'll have to think about this," Charlie said. "Also, there's a QuickBooks file on his laptop, which would save us from having to go through Neil. Would you have or be able to get the password for that?" Charlie asked.

"Yeah, I have it for keeping the books. I'll text it to you," Allie said.

"Maybe we can find some answers about this big wad of cash there," Charlie said.

"Somehow, I doubt it," Allie said.

CHAPTER SEVENTEEN

Friday morning, Charlie was ready for business as he came through the door to the office and asked, "Are Neil and Mike both in today?"

"Yes," Allie said.

"Okay. I need to ask Neil a few questions first, and then I'd like to ask Mike a few questions. Hopefully, I can do both in Neil's office, and hopefully, he'll let me keep the door open so you can hear what's said," Charlie said, the last part under his breath. He winked at her and went straight for Neil's office.

"Neil," he said as he went in.

"Charlie," she could hear Neil's wary reply.

"I need to ask you a few questions, purely routine," Charlie started.

"Okay. I'm not here long today. I have personal matters to attend to, as I'm sure you can understand."

"Completely. As I explained on the phone yesterday, in light of the pathologist's report, we are considering this a homicide now," he began.

"Well," Neil said and stopped. "I had hoped it was an accident, but I thought this might be coming."

"What can you tell me about Ty? Did he have any enemies?"

"Enemies? He was a boatyard foreman. How would he have enemies?"

"Anyone who might want to do him harm. You understand, Neil. We just want to bring the murderer to justice."

"I get it, Charlie, but he was my son. He may have had a harsh word with the guys in the yard from time to time, but nothing that would make someone want to kill him."

"He's been living on the *Barbara Jean* for a while now?"

"Since he filed for divorce from Barbie. A few months."

"How did he feel about that?"

"Free. That marriage was a mistake from the minute it happened."

"Would Barbie be considered an enemy?"

"Despite the fighting, I think she still loved Ty, although the feeling wasn't mutual. I don't think she'd hurt a hair on his head, either, because she was hoping to get some major alimony in the divorce, not that she necessarily would have."

"Is she still in his will?"

"I think a change to that was probably included in the very same appointment he made to file for divorce," Neil said.

"I see. So you can't think of anyone who might have wanted to hurt Ty?"

"No, I really can't."

"Zack still doesn't have an alibi for the night in question..."

"No, I suppose he doesn't, but do you really think he'd kill his brother?"

"Maybe not while in his right mind, but he was pretty messed up, Neil."

"Zack didn't do it. Wouldn't the murderer have to plan this a bit? Do you really think Zack was up to all of that, especially while 'messed up,' as you say?" Neil was getting hot now.

"I do have to follow all leads, Neil. It's the job."

"Zack is not a lead. He's the only son I have left, and he wasn't capable of this. Look elsewhere."

"Okay, Neil. Calm down," Charlie said. "Do you think it would be possible to ask your employees to volunteer to be printed? Inevitably, we'll find their prints in the evidence from the yard, and it will help our investigation a great deal."

"Or it might implicate them, huh? I guess I can ask," Neil said with an edge to his voice.

"Where were you on the night Ty died?"

Allie didn't hear anything for a minute and could imagine the stare down Charlie was getting from Neil.

"At home. With my wife."

"Okay. We'll need to talk to Vicky pretty soon, too."

"I think we're done here."

"Neil, this is just routine. Don't take it personally. I have to do it, and you know it."

"I said we're done here."

"I need to use your office to ask a few more questions, is that all right?"

"Sure. I was just leaving anyway."

Allie heard Neil snatch up his jacket, and a moment

later saw him storm out of the office on his way out the door. She had seen his face that angry before, but had never seen him restrain it. Usually an employee would be getting the full blunt force of his rage by now, but he had reined it in for Charlie, being as he was a law enforcement officer, she guessed.

CHARLIE POPPED his head out of the office. "Whew!" he said and smiled.

"He was pretty angry," Allie said.

"Can't be helped. Murder is the great equalizer. I have to ask everyone the same things regardless of income." He winked. "Can you call out to Mike and ask him to come in, please?"

"Sure thing."

———

"OKAY IF WE keep the door open, Mike? That way there are no allegations of misconduct on either of our parts…"

"No problem."

"Michael Gillikin is your legal name?"

"Yes, sir."

"And you've worked for Guthrie's Marine Center for…"

"Since 2007."

"And what is it you do here?"   ·

"I'm a marine mechanic."

Allie nodded. Mike was answering Charlie's questions

with a clear voice and no hesitations. He was doing well, and she realized she was nervous for him.

"And you went to school for that?"

"Yes, in Ormond Beach, Florida. At Wyotech Daytona."

"That's a good school."

"Yes, it is."

"And before that?"

"I'm from Pamlico County. When I finished up high school, I went to Florida for school and came back because my dad started to get sick." Allie heard Mike's voice break on the last word.

"I'm sorry to hear that."

"It's life."

"You must like working here, as you've been here a while," Charlie commented.

"It's a good, steady job, and I'm allowed to do what I do without too much drama," Mike said.

There was a pause, and Allie heard a chair creak as she guessed Charlie leaned back. "Did you get along with Ty Guthrie?"

"I kinda stayed out of his way. He was pretty rough on the guys, but as long as I did what needed to be done, we worked okay together."

"The medical examiner has determined that Ty's death was not accidental."

"Wow, really?" Mike sounded surprised.

"Yes. So, I need to ask a few more questions. Did you ever think about the fact that you would take over as yard foreman if something happened to Ty?"

"Uh, no. I've been here the longest of any of the regulars, so it makes sense, but I never thought about it until Neil spoke to me the night of the, um, murder." Mike stumbled over his words. Allie thought he sounded nervous.

"That's quite an increase in pay, isn't it?"

"I guess so. I didn't ask. I don't think it's permanent, anyway," Mike said.

"I need to know your whereabouts on the night he died."

"I was at home, alone. And then Neil called me to come in and help, so I came as soon as I could." The clear, steady voice had returned, Allie noted.

"Where do you live?"

"Country Club Apartments over by West Carteret High School."

"Okay. Can any neighbors vouch for your presence that night? Anyone see you go into your apartment?"

"I have no idea. I don't remember seeing anyone in particular, but it's possible."

"Okay. This is just routine, Mike. We have to ask questions."

"I know you do."

"Is there anything else you can think of that might be pertinent to our investigation?"

"I don't think so, not off the top of my head. I mean, you all know what an ass he could be sometimes, but that wasn't a reason to die, and I just can't imagine who hated him enough to do this," Mike said.

"All right, well, if you think of anything else, give me a call. Thanks for your time."

She heard Mike get up and saw him come out a

moment later. He gave her a nervous smile and headed out to the yard.

ALLIE SAW Barbie's Bronco pull up in the lot about twenty minutes later. There still hadn't been any rain, so the simple action of a vehicle pulling in stirred up the dry dirt into a cloud that drifted toward the yard. She watched as Barbie put one leg out of the vehicle and slid out to bear her weight on that leg while keeping the other bent behind her. She hopped to the rear door and bent into the Bronco to wrangle the scooter out of the backseat. She turned around and put the scooter on the ground, popped the steering mechanism into place, and rested her knee on the cushion. She set her shoulders back and began maneuvering up the ramp to the door.

Allie was there to get the door this time.

"Thanks, honey!" Barbie said. She was perfectly coiffed and seemed almost excited to be back in the office with the promise of more information, even if she had to go through questioning to get it. "Where do I go?"

"Neil's office," Allie said, unnecessarily gesturing the way. Barbie smiled at her and wheeled her way in.

"Hello, Ms. Guthrie!" Allie could hear Charlie get up from his seat when Barbie entered. "Is there anything I can get you?"

"Nah, I'm fine. But thank you, Chief Detective Bishop!"

"Please, call me Charlie,"

"Okay, Charlie." Allie could hear the flirty lilt on Charlie's name.

"We've gotten the results from the medical examiner's office, and we are ruling Ty's death a homicide."

"Dad-gum!" Barbie gasped, using a Southern substitution for a curse. "Okay."

"At this point, we have to question everyone. You understand, right?"

"Of course, of course."

"You probably knew Ty better than anyone…"

"Well, that's debatable!"

Charlie ignored the comment for now and went on. "Did Ty have any enemies?"

"Ty was not a nice man. I don't mean to speak ill of the dead, and I know I wasn't his favorite person either, but he did not treat anyone well."

"Can you give me some examples?"

"The yard workers. They were verbally abused at every turn. It didn't matter who you were or what you were doing, but you were wrong and worthy of being chewed out at any time. I know I heard fighting in the yard and threats being made before."

"Who else crossed paths with him?"

"Well, Charlie, you know as well as I do that he couldn't keep it in his pants. He didn't limit himself to single girls, so there are probably quite a few jealous husbands out there that wanted to see him dead, too."

"Okay. Anyone else?"

"Well, I wasn't sure if I should mention it before, but now that you know this really was a murder… Ty was mixed up in some bad stuff."

"What do you mean 'bad stuff'?"

"Like, not organized crime or anything, but he had some secret dealings with people. I don't have any details, but there were hushed phone calls, and private meetings... I don't know, exactly, but it always seemed shady to me."

"Do you have any idea who might have been involved in this shady stuff with him?"

"I had the feeling he was doing it alone."

There was a pause in the conversation.

"All right. Anything else you can tell us?"

"He didn't get along all that well with his family. He always resented Vicky and Zack, and they were always at odds. With Neil's temper thrown in, I've seen some knock-down-drag-out screaming matches, even in this office."

"Okay. Anyone else who might have wanted to hurt Ty?" Allie could hear the exasperation in Charlie's voice. It was subtle, but unmistakable.

"No, I don't think so. It's a pretty small community, really."

"Yes, it is at that," Charlie said, and Allie could hear the unspoken end of that statement: "And you just implicated everyone in it." She couldn't help but smile.

"All right, Ms. Guthrie. I have to ask. Where were you the night Ty was killed?"

"Let's see, what night was that? Sunday? I had physical therapy in Jacksonville, and then I headed home. I was probably out like a light by then. I go to bed rather early."

"Can anyone vouch for your alibi?"

"Probably not, Charlie. Unlike Ty, I don't sleep around."

"Okay. Just routine questions. Not like you're exactly mobile right now, anyway." Charlie chuckled.

"I can't wait to be done with this thing. It's a workout just to get out of my Bronco!"

After she left, Allie had a thought and ran out to catch Barbie before she left. She had just gotten herself into the driver's seat when Allie caught up with her.

"Barbie! Would you be able to help me with something?"

"Sure, sugar, what do you need?"

"I need to ask you some questions about key cards, and also what you might know about my parents and the Guthries."

"Ah… Okay. Yeah, I could probably fill you in on that. I have to run to PT in Jacksonville right now, but why don't we have supper at my place tomorrow night? I'll text you and we'll set it up."

"Sounds great. Thanks, Barbie!" Allie said. She watched Barbie drive out of the yard, throwing up gravel as she went, and wondered how much she would be able to get out of her.

When she came back inside the office, Charlie motioned her into Neil's office.

"A couple of things. I have a deputy coming out to take fingerprints from willing employees at the end of the day. You also need to know that Kat and I had it out over your involvement in the case," he said, perched on the corner of Neil's desk.

Allie paused to shut the door and then sat in one of the chairs facing the desk. "Okay, so what does that mean?"

"It means someone told her about you helping us, and she was not happy. Mostly at me for not telling her, and she said it could hurt our chain of evidence," he said.

"That's what I've been worried about, Charlie," Allie complained.

"I told you to let me worry about Kat. She's just trying to protect the Guthries and sees you as an outsider, a threat, an unknown quantity over which she has no control. It's uncomfortable for her. It's a good thing for her to experience, I think," he said with a glint in his eye.

"What can I expect her to do about this?" Allie asked, feeling acutely threatened. "Remember, she called me the other day just to threaten me to keep quiet about the theft."

"I doubt she'll do anything at all. I'm the Chief Detective, after all, and this is my case. You are a qualified consultant. What *can* she do?"

"I'd rather not find out," Allie said.

CHAPTER EIGHTEEN

Allie picked up Ryan later that afternoon, and she could tell he was excited for the weekend. He loved weekends because he didn't have to wake up quite so early and could create his own agenda, which quite often involved spending hours perfecting a single drawing and playing video games for the better part of the day. He also liked to take long walks outside, so she didn't begrudge him of his video game-playing too much. *He needs a break after a long week of work.* Autistic kids and adults worked twice as hard as everyone else, she knew, doing regular work, and then learning to be socially appropriate when it was such a foreign language to them. They needed and deserved their downtime, probably more than anyone else. *Time to just be themselves.* Allie patted his knee and he patted her hand. She wanted to get together with Peg again that night to rehash what had happened in the investigation, so she suggested pizza to Ryan—his all-time favorite food. He gave her a big smile, and she took that as agreement to the plan.

When they got home, she stopped at Peg's door as Ryan hopped up the steps to their trailer and let himself in. "Up for some pizza tonight?" Allie asked when Peg came to the door.

"As long as it comes with a side of gossip about the case!" Peg laughed. "Let me get my knitting and I'll be right over."

Allie dropped her things inside the door and went to her room to change. She ordered the pizza and came into the living room to find Peg already in the recliner, unwinding her skein and getting to work. She also found Ryan in the living room, for a change. He had his hand-held gaming system and was at the end of the couch, already in his jammies, ready for the weekend to start.

"What's new in the case?" Peg prompted.

Allie sat at the opposite end of the couch from Ryan and tucked her feet under her legs, getting comfortable. "It was definitely murder," she said, glancing at Ryan, not entirely sure he should hear this.

"Oh, he's all right," Peg admonished. "He's not as fragile as you think."

"He had a broken neck and some broken bones from the fall, but also some bruising from before the fall, and one right on his chest that was triangular in nature—does that mean he was hit with something?" Allie asked, voice lowered.

"I'm not so familiar with inflicted injuries, having worked in hospice care when I was a nurse," Peg said. "But it sounds like it. I'll have to think on that a bit," she said.

"He also had diamonds embedded in a bruise on his

head, which leads us to think one of the stolen statuettes was used to hit him, and also means he probably interrupted the theft in progress."

"Interesting," Peg said. "But why was he on the boat in the first place?"

"Good question. It's not as if he knew it was going to happen, right?"

"Maybe, maybe not."

"Why would he try to stop it if he was in on it?" Allie asked.

"Right," Peg said. "He must have woken up for some reason. Do they still think it was someone with a key card?"

"I think so, although they haven't found one at the scene. The alarm was only triggered when they left, meaning they didn't have it then. Wonder where it went?"

"Good question," Peg said. "What else have you found out?"

"I've got a list of Ty's conquests," Allie said. "I creeped him on Facebook yesterday."

"Any surprises?"

"Not a whole lot of names I knew, but Holly was one of them," she said.

"Oh, really?" Peg said, raising an eyebrow.

"I had the same reaction. Also some mysterious woman he referred to as Rose about a month back, but I think that was a nickname," Allie said.

"Meaning he had to hide her identity for some reason," Peg assumed.

"Maybe she was married?" Allie ventured.

"Or famous?" Peg countered.

"Are there any famous people in Carteret County?" Allie laughed.

"It's all relative." Peg laughed too.

"Also, Sammy's sister, Gemma," Allie added.

"Who is Sammy again?" Peg asked.

"One of the yard workers who wasn't very fond of Ty's motivational methods in the yard," Allie said.

"Oh, jeez," Peg said. "I wonder if he knew Ty was shagging his sister, too. If so, that's a great motive..." Peg said.

"I know," Allie said. "Sammy also said he couldn't find his expired key card."

"Sounds like a leading suspect," Peg said.

"He jumped to the top of my list when I found his sister's picture on Ty's Facebook feed, that's for sure," Allie said.

After the pizza came, Peg suggested they sit at the table and write out everything they knew.

"Great idea," Allie said.

They spread out some blank sheets of computer paper on the table. Peg said, "Let's write out all of the suspects and their motives."

"Okay, we have Barbie, the soon-to-be ex-wife. Her motive would be revenge and possibly money, but let's add a note that she couldn't have gotten up the steps," Allie said. "She had some kind of foot surgery at Carteret General about a month ago," Allie said.

"That kind of rules her out, huh?" Peg said, sounding disappointed.

"Yes, strong motive, but no opportunity," Allie said.

"Who's next?"

"Zack has no alibi, so he has opportunity, but the motive would be a little less clear. He did have a long-standing rivalry with Ty for Neil's approval," Allie said.

"Okay, so that makes him a suspect," Peg said. Allie noticed Ryan had gone to his room and come back with his box of colored pencils. He made a space at the table right next to them, selected a piece of blank paper from the few they had spread out on the table, and began to draw.

"Yes. Mike works in the yard but says he never really had a problem with Ty and stayed out of his way. He also turned in his key card," Allie said.

"I'd say he's still a suspect, but not a strong one," Peg said. "Next?"

"Sammy. As I said, he had a problem with Ty in the yard, maybe knew his sister had slept with him, and couldn't find his key card to turn in," Allie said.

"That all makes him a very strong suspect. Who else?"

"I suppose the Briggs and Neil and Vicky are probably suspects as well, but I'm not sure about their motives at all," Allie said.

"Agreed," Peg said. We'll put them at the bottom of the list. "Anyone else?"

"I guess Holly, now that we know she had some relationship with Ty, and this mysterious Rose," Allie said. "I'm not sure that having a relationship with him provides a motive, but Ty never treated anyone very well, and people do get a little crazy when they are infatuated."

"We know Holly probably had access, but until we find

out who Rose is, she's really a big question mark, isn't she?" Peg asked.

"Yes, agreed," Allie said. She looked at Ryan, who had taken a break from drawing and was now pacing the living room. He did that when he was thinking or anxious. She hoped it was the former. If he was anxious about something, it could escalate into a meltdown. Peg noticed her worried expression and suggested they turn on a Disney movie for Ryan.

"Good idea," Allie said. "Ryan, do you want to watch *Peter Pan?*"

Ryan stopped pacing and smiled. "Captain Hook!" he exclaimed and went over to the DVD shelf to dig it out. "We'll set this aside for later," Allie said, wondering what had set Ryan off. Had he heard something they had said that had bothered him?

LATER, after tucking Ryan in for the night, Allie headed back out to the family room and made up the couch for the night. Then she slipped into an old T-shirt and some yoga pants in the bathroom, unplugged her laptop from the charger, and plopped down for the night. As the computer hummed to life, she thought about her parents for the first time that day. The three of them had been close, even after Ryan had been born. By the time he was two, though, Maggie and Jack had gotten quite busy carting the toddler from doctor to specialist, and then from speech therapist to occupational therapist once he had been diagnosed. Sometimes they took turns, so that Allie could be picked up at school, or taken to a dentist appointment, but the focus clearly had to be on Ryan. Even as a self-absorbed pre-teen, Allie had understood the necessity of it. Not that she liked it, and didn't secretly revel in the guilty look on her parents' faces when they had to miss another parent-teacher conference or chorus concert. And she loved Ryan, but wasn't involved in all of the therapies, flashcard games, and behavior training at home, and always felt in the way. And when the frequent meltdowns occurred, she was off on her bike as quick as she could get away. That was part of the reason, early on, she had decided to try to graduate early and head up north to live with her aunt. There she could concentrate and alleviate some of her parents' guilt, or so she had always told herself.

Allie checked the bank account. She didn't let on to anyone, but she and Ryan had a little money for at least a little while, thanks to an accidental death insurance policy her parents had taken out, probably around the time of Ryan's diagnosis. They hadn't ever discussed with her what should happen if they were to die, but when the call came, Allie knew there was only one thing to do, and that was to take care of her brother. The amount from the insurance wasn't enough to live extravagantly, and even though she had some savings from her job in Chicago, she definitely still had to work. But it allowed her to take a less demanding and lower-paying job to focus on Ryan and his needs, at least for now. As she checked the account register, making sure there wasn't anything out of the ordinary, Allie thought about her father's career in the military. He had most certainly put in his twenty years.

Even with what they spent on Ryan's care, there should be plenty here. I wonder where all that money went? Maybe Dad lost a bundle to Neil Guthrie. I need to find out more. And maybe get some help with the money we do have. This won't support us for too long, and then what will we do?

CHAPTER NINETEEN

S aturday morning, still in her pajamas, Allie wandered into the kitchen to make herself some tea, noting that Ryan was still dead to the world. He often slept late on the weekend, and she would have to keep an eye on the clock so that he wouldn't upset his routine too much. It could be difficult to wake him on Monday mornings if he slept as long as he'd liked on the weekend. But for now, it was quiet in the trailer, and she looked forward to having some alone time to do some of the internet research she had promised herself.

With her tea made and a bagel to go with it, she sat on the couch and fired up her laptop. Where should she start? She knew Neil and her dad had started a business in 2000 and decided they would have had to have registered the name with the Secretary of State, so she researched there. It looked like the name had only been registered for two years, but not after that. "Only open for a couple of years, or maybe the name changed?"

Next, she did a simple Google search. People didn't

realize that very little dies on the internet. Old websites still appeared in search engines because people rarely took the time to take things down. Sure enough, a website popped up for the business, and when she clicked on it, there was her dad's smiling face, beaming at her from her computer. She returned to the Google search page to look for news articles about the business. On page four of her Google search, she found what had been looking for: an article in the local paper announcing a name change for the company in late 2002. *Diamond Lady Restoration* was now to be known as *Guthrie Restoration*. The article didn't say the reason for the name change, but Allie could guess. Neil had probably bought her dad out. Ryan had turned seven in 2002 and had been diagnosed the previous year. Autism therapies were not covered by insurance in the state of North Carolina then, so her mom and dad had probably needed money to continue them, and Neil had bought her dad out so they could have the cash they needed. But why would this have created bad blood, or something to hide?

Allie knew she was closer to an answer but wouldn't find it online. Maybe there would be a clue in her parents' things. But that meant she'd have to go through them, which she hadn't done yet. She checked on Ryan, knowing she would have to get him up in about a half an hour. Then, she headed toward her parents' room, opened the door, and stopped. The dust motes swirled in the muted sunlight of the room, disturbed by the motion of the door. She looked over the darkened room, the bed, the wardrobe, the side tables—everything just as it had been the day they had died. Allie felt her heart begin to race and could hear the blood pounding in her ears. She pulled the door closed. *I'm so not ready for this. Maybe I'll try again tomorrow.*

Allie went out to the shed to rid herself of the tension and anxieties of the past few days. Tasking herself with three two-minute rounds, she began throwing combinations and moving around the bag, first left to right, then right to left. *Jab-jab-cross. Jab-cross-hook-cross*. Feinting away from punches from her imaginary opponent, moving her feet across the plywood floor of the shed, she slowly worked the tension out of her body. When she was finished, she locked the shed door and went back inside to shower.

Ryan was still agitated about something when he woke up, choosing to pace outside instead of reaching for his handheld game right away. When he got like this, she had to be extra sensitive to his needs. Anything could escalate into a meltdown. When he was younger, her parents could subdue a meltdown by applying pressure, sometimes with their full bodies, or calm Ryan before it escalated by putting him in a tubful of water. Now that he was nineteen, he was bigger than Allie, and neither of those options were in her power. She just had to ride it out if it happened and hope to hell it happened inside the trailer and not in public where at the very least people would stare, and he might even hurt himself or others. Luckily, Charlie knew the situation so that if law enforcement were ever called, she was fairly certain he could intervene on Ryan's behalf, but she still worried. People just had no idea.

Allie turned on the TV and checked the Weather

Channel for a report on the invest to see how it was progressing. It was turning into a tropical storm and was about to hit the Caribbean. The conditions seemed to be right for it to intensify and could possibly threaten the US coastline, but they didn't know where yet.

Peg stopped over, with her doggies in tow, and asked, "Should I try to catch up to him and see if he'll help me walk them?"

"That's a great idea, Peg. He loves the dogs!" Allie said, relieved. She realized she had been holding her breath a bit, anxious about what Ryan's mood might turn into. He would jump at the chance to spend time with Peg's dogs, which would calm him.

"Great!" Peg said, and off she went.

Allie thought again about needing to look in her parents' things. "Maybe if I just get the little suitcase with all of the pictures," she said to herself. *Can I handle that, or will it be too much? Could Ryan handle seeing pictures of them?* She didn't know. Maybe she did need to call a counselor. They probably both needed help with this process.

Her phone chirped then, and Allie looked to see who had texted her. It was Barbie, asking if seven was okay for supper that night. She replied it was and asked for an address. With a date for supper, Allie thought she might see if she could set up a lunch date with another suspect.

"HOLLY! Do you want to go out to lunch today?" They didn't really socialize outside of work, but Allie wanted to see how serious Holly and Ty had been, and figured that she might be able to find out something useful.

"Uh, okay! Where did you want to go?" Holly asked.

"How about Panera?"

"Okay, I'll meet you there about 12:30?"

"Sounds great!"

Allie asked Peg to keep an eye on Ryan while she was out and let Ryan know she'd be gone for about an hour or so. "Okay," he said and gave her a quick smile before turning back to his game. Apparently, hanging out with Peg's doggies earlier had averted anything catastrophic, because he was back to his old routines.

"If you get hungry, you can make yourself a sandwich, or there's some easy mac in the cupboard," she said. He didn't respond, but she knew he had heard her. She wanted to arrive at Panera before Holly, so she grabbed her keys and headed to the truck.

Holly arrived shortly after she had, and Allie waved when she saw her. She noted Holly's wary expression. Allie could tell she was still wondering why she had called her but was careful to cover her true emotions like any good southerner. "Hey, Allie!" she said as she approached the table.

"I've already ordered," Allie said. "You go ahead."

"All right!" Holly said and went back to the line.

Allie watched her in line and thought about what she knew of Holly. She was local, from Marshallberg, and in her early twenties. She hadn't gone to more than community college, but that wasn't unusual for this area. She had probably gotten an associate's in secretarial work. Working in the boatyard office had to be one of her first full-time jobs. She wasn't very bright, but she could perform menial and repetitive tasks like answering phones and filing, which were the bulk of her job. She was attractive, and Allie saw now that Holly seemed to fit Ty's type. She wondered how she should approach Holly with her questions.

As they both finally settled at the table with their plates, Holly got right to the point. "What's up?" she asked.

"Thanks for coming out," Allie said, pausing to munch on her crusty bread. "I really needed a break from the tension at work. This thing with Ty is wearing me out."

Holly took a moment. "Ty wasn't as bad as everyone made him out to be. He didn't treat people very well, but everyone kind of knew that about him, so you expected it."

"How well did you know him?" Allie asked, hoping it came off more nonchalant than it sounded.

"Well, no one really knows this, but we were kind of a thing for a few weeks," Holly said. "Ty said to keep it on the down-low because, well, because people gossip, and he just didn't want to hear it from anyone."

"Wow, really?" Allie said acting surprised. "When was this?"

"We had just decided to end it about a month ago," Holly said.

"Who ended it?" Allie asked.

"It was a mutual decision," Holly said.

Meaning Ty had broken up with Holly. "Were you upset?" Allie asked.

"You mean did I want to kill him?" Holly laughed nervously. "No, like I said, it was mutual. He was too old for me, really. And he could be a right shit sometimes. There are better guys out there. So there were no hard feelings on my part," she assured Allie.

"Was there someone else?" Allie asked, hoping she wasn't crossing a line.

"Knowing Ty, he probably had someone on the side," Holly said. "But I'm telling you, I didn't really care. It was a fling, and I was over him. It's a shame he died, because he could be a nice guy, too. But he just wasn't right for me."

"Gotcha," Allie said.

They finished their lunch, chatting about other topics. Holly didn't seem to mind Allie's questions, and didn't seem to be all that upset at either the breakup or Ty's death. *Besides, Holly probably wouldn't even know how to give someone a contusion, and would probably just have fled if discovered on* The Sunset Lady, *Allie thought. And she had turned in her key card.*

Holly is probably not the culprit.

CHAPTER TWENTY

When Allie returned home, she went to Ryan's room to see what he was up to and found him drawing, continuing the picture he had started the night before. Something was clearly on his mind, but at least he was calmer now, coping with it in the best way he could. He would never show Allie any of his drawings until they were complete, and he was such a perfectionist, very few made the cut in his own eyes, but she loved to see them. They gave her a peek inside her brother that words just couldn't. But everyone needed some fresh air, and she was beginning to feel bad about leaving Ryan so much.

"I'm thinking a trip to the park might be in order. What do you say?" she asked gently as she sat next to him on the bed.

He looked at her after completing some minuscule adjustment to his work. "Right now?"

"How about ten minutes? I'll set the timer. Okay?"

"Okay," he said and resumed his work. Ryan, like most on the spectrum, got very engrossed in whatever he was doing, and often had difficulty transitioning from one thing to the next. It meant that he needed an amount of time, a buffer, to come out of one thing and be able to move on to the next.

When they got to the park, Allie said, "I'll be right here on the tennis courts if you need me. Go have fun!"

Ryan took off, "stimming." Allie knew that meant he was happy. She didn't care if other people stared or didn't understand why Ryan was running, flapping his hands, and making the guttural noises that both produced and expressed his joy at this moment in time. She smiled to herself and shook out the jump rope she had brought with her. They were probably staring at her, too, a chick in her late twenties jump roping by herself on the tennis courts, but her training calmed her and helped her process her thoughts, too. Maybe she and Ryan were more alike than she thought.

As she continued her routine and watched Ryan happily stimming, she became aware of a large black SUV pulling into the parking lot. It had tinted windows and sat with the motor running for several minutes. She was just about ready to pack it up, grab Ryan, and head to the truck when the driver cut the engine and stepped out. Allie was surprised to see a petite woman impeccably dressed in an expensive suit appear from behind the closing door. She looked to be in her late forties or early fifties with shoulder-length, dark-brown hair and sunglasses that hid most of her tanned face. The woman walked purposefully toward her, and Allie paused her routine, transferring both handles of the rope to her left hand.

"Allie Fox?" the woman asked, extending her right hand.

"Yes," Allie said, reserving hers until the woman revealed her name and purpose.

"Katherine Matthews," she said. "We've spoken on the phone."

Allie reached to shake her hand, remembering her threats, as DA Matthews removed her sunglasses with her other hand. "Can we walk a little?" Matthews asked, gesturing toward Ryan.

"I just have to keep him in sight," Allie explained.

"How are things going for you and Ryan?" Matthews asked as they started toward the sidewalk that circled the park.

Katherine Matthews has done her homework and is using my brother's name to unnerve me. It's working, Allie thought.

"As well as can be expected. He kind of retreated into himself when our parents died, but he has been more and more responsive since I've been here," Allie said, surprising herself by sharing so much.

"That has to be incredibly tough. Is he ever violent with you?" Matthews asked, eyeing Ryan.

"No, he's not," Allie said. A tingle went up her spine. *What is she implying, anyway?* "What can I help you with, Kat?" Allie asked, using the nickname to show that she wasn't the only one who did her homework.

"I wanted to meet you face to face. And I wanted to reiterate to you the delicacy of this case. You are not a law enforcement officer, as much as Charlie Bishop would like you to be a part of his team. I see your involvement as an unnecessary risk not only to the case, but to the

Guthrie family," Matthews said. She stopped on the sidewalk to face Allie. "I'll be frank with you, Allie. I don't like it at all. And I'm here because I feel like I need to remind you that you have much more important things to worry about than this case." Matthews gestured toward Ryan again. "The smart thing to do would be to step back and let the professionals handle it."

Allie paused, searching the DA's' face for a moment. She was a proud, arrogant woman, for sure, but there was some other emotion there, even though she was doing a masterful job of hiding it. Kat looked down at her watch and adjusted it to avoid Allie's direct gaze. She was nervous about something.

"From what I understand, Charlie Bishop has the authority to use consultants at his own discretion, which means that my involvement in the case is really not under your purview," Allie said calmly. "And I will thank you to leave my brother out of this. He has no involvement whatsoever."

DA Matthews seemed to regain some of her composure and smiled a haughty smile. "I see. Well, you do what you think is right, Allie. But some people in this community may disagree with you, and may find the neglect of your brother while you go off half-cocked chasing bad guys worth a phone call to child protective services. As I said before, you need to think about which team you're on, honey," she said, carefully returning her oversized sunglasses to her face. "You have a blessed day!" she sang as she strode back to her SUV, leaving Allie in stunned silence behind her.

ALLIE PULLED up to Barbie's house in Blair Farms and was a little shocked at the size of the thing. It looked like a mini-mansion, probably built in the housing boom of the nineties when people wanted more rooms than they knew what to do with, even if they couldn't furnish them. Of course, Barbie was still married into the Guthrie clan back then, and they certainly had more money than they knew what to do with. It was still light out, with a warm breeze, but the lights along the stone path to the door were just starting to come on, and Allie noted the tailored landscaping. As she placed her keys in her purse and followed the path to the front door, Allie noticed a weathered bench with decorative crab pots on either side on the porch. A large whelk and a piece of coral were perfectly situated on top. *Right out of* Southern Living.

Barbie opened the door with a loud but warm welcome and expertly maneuvered her scooter to allow Allie to come in. She followed her past the large carpeted staircase into the updated kitchen. Stainless steel appliances punctuated dark granite countertops and oak cabinets, and blue wine bottles lined the wall all the way to the white porcelain farm sink, their labels removed, and almost all of the corks replaced. *Barbie apparently likes wine.* The blue from the bottles was picked up in the French country tiles of the backsplash behind the six-burner stove, and in the blue stripe in the white tea towels on the stove handle. Every other accent was in copper, including the pots and pans hanging from the pot rack above the island. *There is a lot of Guthrie money in this kitchen. And something smells amazing.*

"I'm making chicken and dumplings. Is that okay?" Barbie asked.

"Sounds great. I don't think I've ever had it before, but I know it's a southern specialty."

"You bet it is. You're going to love it."

"Can I help with anything?"

"I'll grab a fresh bottle of wine from the fridge if you'll open it for me," Barbie said, handing her a corkscrew.

"Save this, right?" Allie asked, holding up the cork.

"Yes! I'm planning to use these things for some sort of project. I have a whole Pinterest board with ideas, but I think they look good as part of the decor right now, don't you?"

"I do. This is a beautiful kitchen."

"Thank you, honey! When you marry into the Guthrie family, you get used to having nice things," she said with a wry smile.

"What kind of wine is this?" Allie asked, trying to read the label, which was in what she thought was German. She poured out two glasses.

"It's a Riesling. Just about the only kind I drink. Growing up, it was grape Kool Aid and Orange Crush if we had a little more money that week. I've never lost my sweet tooth, so this is a good adult version." She laughed.

Allie laughed and took a sip. "It's good!" she said.

"Told you!" Barbie laughed. "The food's just about done, so I'll plate it up and we can take it into the living room. Do you want to watch a movie, too?"

"Nah, I can't stay too late. Ryan is with the neighbor and I can't leave him for too long, if that's okay."

"Sure, honey!"

They got their food, and Allie helped Barbie get hers to the living room. She propped her foot up on the couch, and there was still plenty of room for Allie on the other end.

"So key cards," Barbie started.

"Yes," Allie said. "How did that work? Did you keep a record of to whom they were issued, and did you collect the old ones when you did that?"

"Uh, let's see. I think there should be some record of who they were issued to. It may be on the computer. I don't think we saw any need to collect the old ones... Why? Is this important to the case?"

"I have no idea. We had to change the passcode, and I wanted to follow up with you so that we could stay consistent," Allie said. She hoped Barbie would believe this half-truth.

"I see. Check some of the older files on the computer. It should be an Excel file named *Key Cards* or it might be under the name of the security company. It may even be in the file labeled *Personnel*. I think they only changed the passcode a few times while I worked there," Barbie said.

"Okay, I'll do that. Thanks," Allie said. "Did you turn in your key card when you left?" she tried to ask nonchalantly

"I'm pretty sure I did," Barbie said. "Knowing me, I probably threw it at them on my way out!" She laughed.

"This chicken is fantastic!" Allie said.

"Thanks, honey. Vicky always thought I didn't know

how to cook for Ty, but that is one thing I do know how to do!"

"Also, what do you know about a partnership between my dad and Neil?"

Barbie put down her plate and picked up her wine glass. She took a sip, and then looked at Allie. "So you know they were partners in a small startup?"

"Yes, I found that out through a little research."

"Your dad had some money he had saved through his career. Neil encouraged him to invest his money in a company they would start together."

"Okay, but what happened?"

"When your parents got Ryan's diagnosis, that's when they decided they would stay long term, and that he would need the best care, the best therapies, all of that. And it would take money."

"Yeah, that's why they sold the house and moved into a trailer after I went up north."

"Neil offered to buy your dad out of the company they started."

"Okay, but what went wrong?"

"Your dad had invested almost everything, somewhere around a hundred thousand dollars. Neil knew he needed the money, so…" Barbie put down her wine glass. "He took advantage. He undercut Jack by close to fifty thousand dollars."

"Wow," was all Allie could manage to get out. The chicken and dumplings turned to sawdust in her mouth. She reached for her wine glass and took a rather large gulp to swallow it down.

"Obviously, the friendship ended. That's the way the

Guthries are. Everything is about money. It's the one thing they value more than anything else."

They sat quietly for a minute.

Barbie cleared her throat. "That had to be hard to take in. I know you remembered the good times."

"To be honest, I don't remember a whole lot except Ty taking me clamming and flounder gigging. I was just a kid, and it was a relief to get out of the house. Back then, he was like an older brother to me. But after I turned eleven, it stopped, and my interests turned to school and graduating early."

"Ty always had a soft spot for you. You reminded him of his mom, Nancy," Barbie said quietly.

Allie's mind flashed back to the picture she had found on the Barbara Jean. Thick, dark hair and green eyes, smiling at the camera. It clicked. *He must have loved and missed her so much.*

"Unfortunately, Neil and Vicky were never fond of me!" Barbie said with a bark of a laugh, breaking Allie's reverie. "It turned out okay, though. They are not nice people, as you are finding out now," Barbie said.

Allie said nothing, still processing what Barbie had told her about Neil and her dad.

"I didn't outright tell Chief Detective Bishop, but Ty actually blackmailed people."

"What?" Allie almost choked on her dumpling.

"Yep. He had a little black book he carried with him everywhere. That's where he kept all of his information on people. I told you. Not nice." She took a sip of her wine. "So when I said there were plenty of people who would want to see him dead, I wasn't lying!"

"Did you know any details?"

"Of course not. Those were his little 'pet projects.'"

"How did you know he was blackmailing people?"

"I overheard him on the phone one night, demanding more money from someone. I have no idea who it was, but I put two and two together."

"Wow. You're right, Barbie. Not nice."

"Can you see what I've been dealing with for years?"

"I see now."

"Anyway. Let's talk about happier things. How are you adjusting to North Carolina?"

Allie smiled and chatted with Barbie until it was time to go, but alarm bells were going off in her head the whole time.

She had to find that little black book.

CHAPTER TWENTY-ONE

Early Sunday morning, a light fog was visible in the large, open spaces of the marine park. Allie pulled into her normal spot at Guthrie's Marine Center and retrieved her key card from her bag.

"Invest 94-L has turned into a tropical storm and is now threatening the leeward Caribbean islands..." Public Radio East was reporting as she cut the engine off. She went to the gate and swiped her card, and the chain link fence creaked to life, rolling back to allow her entrance. She paused and looked around to be sure she was alone. The only sounds she could hear were from the waterfowl along the Intracoastal, so she pulled the latex gloves from her back pocket and walked toward the *Barbara Jean*.

When she had called Charlie late the night before and summarized her conversations with Barbie and Holly, she didn't need to explain the need to find the black book. He gave her permission to access Ty's boat and give it a more thorough going-over to see if she could find it, with the admonition to wear latex gloves so as not to disturb any evidence they may yet need to collect, although they hadn't found much in the previous search.

The trick now was to figure out where Ty would have hidden this notebook on his thirty-foot sailboat. Allie climbed the ladder, stepping over the yellow crime scene tape, and looked toward both the bow and the stern before entering the cabin. No obvious places on the deck, and it would be much more exposed to the elements out here, so logically, the notebook was in the cabin somewhere. Entering the living space, she again recoiled a bit at the smell of stale linens and clothing. It was slightly messier than before, owing to their own rooting around for possible evidence during the last search. *Ty would keep a notebook like that close to his person, if it did indeed contain information about whom he was blackmailing*, she thought. *I'll check the bed loft first.* Again, she crawled into the space with a little difficulty and looked over the small shelf where she had found the picture of Nancy, Ty's mom. *Nothing of any importance there.* She lifted up pillows and pulled sheets off the mattress-like cushion, but found nothing in the bedclothes or underneath. She exited the area, a little sweaty from the exertion, and looked around the rest of the cabin.

The table was still covered in a few beer bottles, water rings left by the ones the deputy had collected, and little else. Allie knelt down to look underneath, searching for drawers or compartments under the table or the benches. There were a couple of storage bins, so she sat cross-legged on the floor and pulled them out. One was full of sunscreen, towels, hats, and other odds and ends you might need on a day trip to Shack or the Cape. The other was full of manuals and documentation for the vessel, but no small black notebook. Closing the bin, she then stood up, this time focusing on the cushions of the bench. Sometimes they hid storage behind benches in boats, and Allie found the *Barbara Jean* was no exception, but behind the navy-blue vinyl cushions on each bench were rounded cut-out holes with only life vests and ropes. She pulled out her small dollar-store flashlight to double-check the corners of each cubby hole, but no luck. The pressboard cupboards of the small kitchenette only held dusty canned goods. The head had very little room to hide anything and warranted only a cursory look. She ventured up to the control panel and looked underneath, thinking there may be a hidden compartment behind the electronics, having heard of people smuggling drugs and arms that way from a friend in the Coast Guard when she worked in Chicago. But there were only wires and circuits behind the electronics. Lifting the seat cushions on every seat on the deck revealed no hidden compartments there either.

Have I missed it somewhere? She wasn't sure she had the energy to re-search the boat. Sitting for a minute, Allie closed her eyes and tried to channel Ty to see if she could imagine where he might hide something of importance. *The one thing that seemed most important to him on this boat was his beer, so maybe he kept his notebook near his beer? The fridge!* She hustled back to the kitchenette and opened the small refrigerator, but it was fairly empty, containing only a few condiment packets and an aging Chinese takeout container, and the tiny freezer space was absolutely bare. Allie rubbed her face in her hands and stared at the floor, at a loss for what to do. She had turned the boat inside out. She doubted anything like a notebook would be hidden in the engine compartment or near the bilges, as it would get wet or damaged, which was exactly the opposite of what Ty would have wanted.

As her mind turned over various possibilities, she noticed that the rug on the floor didn't quite lie flat. *One thing you need on a boat is even decking, so that if you run into rough weather, you don't have both rolling waves and a trip hazard to deal with*. Bending down to investigate, she pulled back the rug. One of the floorboards looked quite a bit shorter than the others… She hustled back on deck to grab the small tool kit she had run across there and pulled out a flat-head screwdriver. Finding the odd floorboard, Allie jammed the screwdriver between the end of it and the next board. She wiggled and pulled until the board popped out, revealing a small compartment containing an even smaller black notebook, and a nondescript black flip phone. The phone was turned off, and she thought it would be better for the technicians to mess with it, so she set it aside for now. She cleared a small space on the table, placed the notebook there, and then opened the cover. She couldn't read a word of it. It was all in code.

CHAPTER TWENTY-TWO

Allie dropped her purse in one of the chairs around the dining table and plopped into another. Charlie seemed excited on the phone about her find and would be there soon to pick up the notebook and phone. She heard a noise behind her and whirled around to see Ryan in his pajamas on the couch, looking at her.

"Hey, buddy," she said tiredly.

"Hey," he said. He picked up his iPad next to him and pressed play on whatever YouTube video he was watching. She could hear it, but just barely because Ryan knew to keep the volume low when he didn't want to use his headphones.

Allie pulled out the notebook and set it on the table. *Might as well work on it while I have the chance,* she thought. She went to the printer to get some blank paper and pulled a pen out of her purse. Then she opened the notebook and stared at the nonsense on the first page of the book.

She knew enough to look for combinations of letters

of three that could be "the" or single letters that could be "a" or "I," but these didn't seem to be in sentence format. They looked more like names and dates with some notes, which wasn't very helpful to someone trying to break the code. She also knew enough that some small key to a basic alphabetic switch code might be somewhere in the notebook to remind the code writer of the formula to the code he created. She flipped through the notebook several times, shook it, and then gave up and put her head in her hands.

She felt his presence next to her and then felt his hand on her shoulder.

"Puzzles?" Ryan asked.

"Yes, bud, I'm trying to figure this one out and it's quite tricky."

He sat next to her and put his hand out for the pen. He started working possible formulas for the code in front of them on the blank sheets of paper, while Allie sat back, amazed. She stole a look at her brother who was focused and content, working away. She watched him work for a bit, and then dug her phone out of her purse.

"I'm going to call Charlie real quick, okay, bud?" She didn't wait for a response and stepped outside.

"Charlie, it's Allie."

"Are you okay?"

"Yes, I wanted to see if I could work on the code a bit, but you'll never guess what's happening…"

"What?"

"Ryan is working on it."

Charlie was silent for a minute. "Really?" he asked.

"Yes. I'm going to see where this leads, but I have a

feeling he may just have it cracked before the end of the day," Allie said. "Word puzzles are kind of his thing, you know."

"Dad-gum! That would be fantastic. Allie, tell Ryan I'm proud of him, and keep me posted."

"Will do," she said and hung up.

Allie stepped back inside and looked over Ryan's shoulder at what he was working on. It didn't make sense yet but she could almost see his mind working, turning this puzzle over and over in his mind.

"How do you know how to do this, Ryan?"

"Puzzles!" he said and giggled, taking a moment to steal a glance at her and give a short flap with his hands, and then he was back to work.

Allie remembered all of the intensive work, teaching Ryan words with flashcards that most toddlers picked up on their own. The early language delays and therapies had resulted in a young man who loved word puzzles, double entendres, and jokes. The puzzle books supplied to him by everyone who cared about him had been preparing him for this real-world chance to show he was capable of solving complex codes created by a neuro-typical adult. Ryan the codebreaker. Allie shook her head, proud of her little brother and in awe of the mastery of the design of the universe.

"Can I get you anything, Ryan?" she asked.

"Strawberry milk!"

"How in the world did he crack it?" Charlie was now

sitting in the same chair Ryan had sat in for several hours while working on the code in the notebook. Ryan was outside humming and flapping, proud of himself for solving the "puzzle."

"Trial and error," Allie said simply. "He tried several different formulas and combinations, and finally came up with one that turned the code into names and dates."

"And what a list it is…" Charlie said quietly, looking at Ryan's handwriting and at the names on the list. Names that all had quite a motive for killing Ty. "This means we have to go back and look at all of these people as strong suspects. Question them again, and really dig into their alibis to see if they hold up."

"I figured that."

"I'm wondering if you would be willing to help some more…"

"Okay… What are you thinking?"

"Obviously, the Sheriff's Department will need to do some official questioning, but I'm wondering if you could do some of your own. You may get different answers to similar questions just because of who you are. Do you get where I'm going with this?"

"You want me to be a mole."

"Yes. Use what you know of these people, approach them obliquely, and see if they won't open up to you a bit."

"You realize that has long-term implications for me," she said quietly. "These people may never trust me again if they find out I'm using my relationships with them to feed you information."

"I realize that. The question you have to ask yourself is, 'Am I comfortable working and living in close proximity to someone who has killed another human being?'"

She thought briefly of Ty's broken body on the ground and imagined what could happen to Ryan if anything happened to her. Nothing good came to mind.

"Good point. Still, not all of them are killers, and I will have to continue working and living in close proximity to them if and when this case is all over."

"Point taken," Charlie admitted.

Allie thought about how often in her life she had been the new kid, and how difficult it was to form lasting relationships with people. She just didn't make friends easily, and it was hard enough being Ryan's everything without any support. She was risking alienating just about every adult she dealt with on a daily basis. This was no small risk.

"Kat Matthews found me at the park yesterday, Charlie. It wasn't a very pleasant conversation."

"She what? What did she say to you?"

"She made it quite plain that she thinks my involvement is a danger to the case. She doesn't want me near it. She even implied someone could call CPS on my 'neglect' of Ryan in pursuit of the killer."

Charlie was stunned into silence. "Huh," he managed. "She and I have argued about involving consultants in the past, but she has never gone so far as to approach one personally. Something about you or about this situation is really under her skin…"

Intrigued, Allie said, "I wonder if she's the one who is involved in this too much somehow…"

Charlie gave her a hard look. "Kat Matthews is not one you want to mess with on purpose."

"Okay, but I think there are some layers here… I really *would* like to solve this, Charlie," she said wistfully.

"I think I can handle Kat Matthews for you. And we'll work really hard to make sure that even if you find something out, and we have to question someone about it, they wouldn't automatically think it came from you. How does that sound?"

"I guess it's a risk I'll have to take," Allie said. "The contents of this little book are our best bet of finding out who killed Ty."

"Exactly. Thanks, Allie. Hopefully, something will come from the risk you're taking. I understand it's no small thing. But don't forget that whatever happens, you still have me and Sheila to lean on."

"Thanks, Charlie. That means a lot. You both have been so great to us."

"It's the least we can do." Charlie smiled and patted her on the back. "Okay, so do you have a copy of this? You know who to get close to and what we need from each of these people?"

"I have a copy and a general idea. Looks like I'll be getting cozy with some of my co-workers this week."

"And we'll look into the phone here," he said, dropping it into his pocket. "Call me when you find out anything useful. And tell Ryan he gets double helpings of lasagna and extra puzzle books next time he comes over."

"Will do."

CHAPTER TWENTY-THREE

On Sunday afternoon, Allie coaxed Ryan out of the trailer with a promise of lunch and a milkshake at one of his favorites, Cook Out, and a visit to feed some ducks. They grabbed some quick oats from the cupboard, put them into a baggie, and hopped into the pickup.

She headed east on I-70 and enjoyed the scenic drive to New Bern while Ryan played his handheld game system. This stretch was one of the only places in the area where she could drive as fast as she had been used to up north, and for a good portion, there was nothing on either side of them for miles but tall, skinny pine trees. As they neared New Bern, the freeway began to look more like the area around the tri-cities—well-manicured and able to accommodate a much larger population. She took the exit for the bridge that would take them across the mouth of the Trent River and enjoyed the sight of the glittering water, tall sailboats, and red brick buildings of the quaint downtown area. They parked and Allie turned to Ryan to explain the schedule for the day.

"First, we stop at a few shops that sell really old things, and we have to be careful not to flap too much so we don't break anything. Then we will go to Union Point Park to feed some oats to the ducks. Then we can go to Cook Out for lunch and a milkshake, Okay?"

"Okay," Ryan said, smiling and bouncing a little in his seat.

They walked to Middle Street toward a couple of antique shops Allie had scoped out online. She pushed the door open to the first one, and Allie whispered a reminder to Ryan about being careful.

"Hello! Welcome!" the shopkeeper was saying.

"Thank you!" Allie said, smiling. "We are looking for a small figurine, something for our aunt's birthday. Maybe something with some sparkle. Do you have anything like that?"

"Aunt Cheryl?" Ryan asked, looking bewildered for a moment.

"Yes, Ryan. Look at the old boats!" Allie said, trying to distract him.

"Hm... Well, I can show you where we keep our smaller collectibles," the shopkeeper said, coming out from behind the counter. Having shown them the cases, she yelled, "Harold? Can you come out here for a minute?"

Harold appeared a few moments later with his bifocals pushed up on his forehead and wisps of silvery hair framing his ears. "What?" he asked.

"This young lady is looking for a figurine for her aunt, maybe something with some sparkle. Do we have anything in the back that might interest her?"

Harold thought for a moment. "No, I can't say as I do,"

he said, scratching his head. "Sorry," he said simply and tottered back to where he had come from.

Allie looked again in the cases the shopkeeper had shown her, but saw nothing that matched Mr. Leicester's descriptions of the missing figurines. She glanced around the shop and realized there was nothing more here to help her.

"Well, thank you for your help. We may be back!" she said as they went out the door.

When they hit the sidewalk, Ryan flapped a little, after not being able to in the cramped shop.

"Two more stops," Allie said, trying not to get too discouraged.

The next was almost exactly like the first, except that the man was named "Curtis" at this one, and had wisps of silvery hair *in* his ears. Allie let loose a stifled giggle as they left the second shop and headed for the final possibility of the day.

The last shop was on Pollock Street, and it sold fine art in addition to antiques. Allie didn't know if that made her chances of finding the stolen pieces better or worse, but it was worth checking out anyway. They stepped inside to the tinkle of wind chimes attached to the back of the door. She repeated her story when greeted and was shown to the collectibles. The shopkeeper here did not call out to anyone this time, however.

"Are you here alone?"

"Yep, I'm the sole owner and operator," the woman said proudly.

"Wow, that's great!" Allie said, looking over the

figurines. "Do you have anything with real diamonds? Aunt Cheryl adores them."

"You know, I have a piece on consignment that I was going to repair before putting on the sales floor. It's missing a few diamonds from their settings, but I can show it to you if you'd like," the woman offered.

"That would be lovely!" Allie said, heart suddenly beating faster. For a moment, she watched Ryan, who was absorbed in a display of old kitchen utensils for the moment, while the owner went to retrieve the figurine.

When she came back, she held a small black bulldog in the palm of her hand. "He's missing some diamonds here." She pointed. "But once these are re-fitted, you'll have a wonderful little buddy worth some money on your hands."

"Oh my gosh! My aunt has a bulldog, too—she would absolutely love this! Where did you get it?" Allie gushed to hide the question.

"Aunt Cheryl doesn't have a bulldog," Ryan was saying in the background.

The shopkeeper looked at Ryan briefly and said, "Oh, a very nice lady brought him in a few days ago. Said her grandmother had passed away and she was left with a few items. She needed the money for her daughter's surgery, so I helped her out as much as I could."

"Would you mind showing me the other items she brought in? It seems like her grandmother and my aunt may have similar tastes! I wonder if she has more to sell."

"Well, I'm sure I have her info somewhere, but I'm not sure she'd want me to share it…"

"Do you remember what she looked like?"

"Well, I... uh... She was blonde, middle-aged. That's about all I can remember. I'll show you those other pieces," she said as she wandered toward the back. She returned with the mouse figurine, and the unmistakable bas-relief.

I can't believe I found them! Allie thought, and she promised the shop owner that they would be back. She took Ryan's arm in hers and they went back to the truck so they could get to the park to feed the ducks, and Allie could call Charlie.

"Aunt Cheryl doesn't have a bulldog, Allie," Ryan corrected her again.

CHAPTER TWENTY-FOUR

After dropping Ryan off at the young adult dinner party hosted by the Crystal Coast chapter of the Autism Society, Allie realized she had a couple of hours to herself and no plans for supper. She arrived at the trailer and had just dumped her purse into one of the kitchen chairs when she heard her phone chime to let her know she had received a text. She grabbed her phone and found a spot on the sofa.

Her pulse quickened when she saw it was Mike who had texted her, and she smiled at herself for getting a thrill like a middle school girl.

What're you doing? Mike texted.

Just got back from dropping Ryan at a party, she answered.

I'm cooking supper for my dad. Wanna join us?

I'd be honored!

She got the address from Mike, checked the mirror in the bathroom to make sure she was presentable, and hopped in the truck. When she pulled up to the apartment building, she made sure she had the right number and knocked softly on the door.

"Hey, Allie!" Mike said, pulling the door open. "Come on in!"

Allie stepped into a small one-bedroom apartment that was fairly nondescript and sparsely furnished. Mike brushed her arm as he closed the door behind her, and her skin thrilled at the contact. He was so close she could smell his aftershave again, and she felt her body temperature rising. She saw an older version of Mike sitting at the square kitchen table and gave him a wave.

"Hello," she said.

"Allie, this is my dad, Louis. Dad, this is Allie, the friend I was telling you about from work." Mike guided her into the room with a light hand at the small of her back. She flushed at his touch and tried not to melt into a puddle before their eyes.

"Hello," Louis said with a smile and looked back at Mike. "What's for dinner, Mike?"

"I've started to pan-fry us up some fish, Pop. How does that sound?"

"Oh, good. I like fish. What kind did you get?"

"I got some grouper. Will that work?"

"That sounds great."

"Have a seat, Allie. I'll get everything ready. It won't take long."

"Okay. Are you sure I can't help?" she asked.

"I'm sure. Dad, tell Allie about the time you worked on the shrimper in the Pamlico," Mike suggested.

"Oh, you worked on the Pamlico River? That's an area I'm not as familiar with," Allie said.

"Shrimpin' is life up there. It was fairly boring, routine work, but sometimes we caught a bull shark or something in our nets. Nasty fish. One time, we put out our nets and trawled for forty-five minutes when some dolphins untied our nets and we lost the whole load of shrimp. Rascals," he said, smiling.

"Sounds like hard work," Allie offered.

"It is, but there's quite a bit of downtime, too. There are worse ways to make a living," Louis said. "What do you do, dear?"

Unsure of whether he had forgotten that she worked with Mike, or just wanted a more detailed description, she hesitated. "I'm the Office Manager for Guthrie's Marine, so I kind of take care of everything over there," she said.

"So you get to tell Mike what to do?" he said, winking.

"Sometimes," she said, winking back.

"Sounds like fun," he said. "Did you always do that?"

"Well, no. When I lived up north, I worked as an investigator for one of the credit bureaus."

"Catching bad guys, huh? Sounds exciting!"

"It was. Every day was something new," she said.

"Kind of like having Alzheimer's," Louis said with a snort.

Allie looked at Mike who was bringing in the food.

"Dad," Mike said.

"It was a joke," Louis said. "Lighten up."

They continued the chat through the tasty fish dinner Mike had cooked. Mike and his dad cracked jokes and told stories, and Allie found herself laughing more than she had in months. Mike's dad was engaging and fun. She could see why Mike was so protective of him.

"You have a nice place here, Louis," Allie said.

"It's lovely. Everything is within reach and in a calming shade of brown so I don't get too upset, and there is a back door here where the staff can let themselves in if they haven't seen me in a few days. Of course, they'd be able to smell me before too long." Louis laughed at his own dark humor.

"That's awful!" Allie said laughing with him.

When the laughter subsided, it got quiet for a moment, and she noticed Louis seemed suddenly changed somehow. He began to focus on his food, and only give her occasional glances that were fearful.

"Dad, you okay?" Mike asked, picking up on the change, too.

"Sure," Louis said. "Fine."

"Dad, this is Allie. I work with her. She's a friend."

"Okay," his dad said, clearly confused and not wanting to draw too much attention to the fact.

"Are you just about done? Let's clear your plate, okay?" Mike said, speaking gently to Louis. He stood and gathered plates slowly, and took them to the kitchen. Surprising herself, Allie reached out and held Louis's hand in hers.

"It'll be okay, Louis. Hang in there," she said softly.

Louis gave her a weak smile and seemed to calm a bit at her words, although he clearly still had no idea who she was.

"Okay, Dad. Do you want to go lie down and rest? Maybe watch a little TV in your room?" Mike asked.

"Sure," Louis said. He gave Allie another weak smile and let Mike lead him into the bedroom. When Mike had closed the bedroom door and returned to the kitchen, he looked weary and pained.

"He can be fine one minute and not have a clue what's going on the next. It's so painful to see him like that," he said, leaning back against the counter and folding his arms in front of his body.

"I can only imagine how hard that must be," she said, putting an arm out to pat his shoulder awkwardly.

"He was such a force to be reckoned with when I was growing up. Such a personality. Everyone knew him and liked him. He always had a story to tell or a new joke," he said. "Part of the reason I moved him down here was so people up there didn't see him like this. This isn't who he was. It's not him all the time anymore. It's this scared old man. But I don't need to complain to you. You deal with a lot at home, too," he said, shaking himself.

"I can empathize," Allie said. "And it's okay to lean on me, too. You don't have to bear it all on your own."

He couldn't look at her, and his chin quivered as he fought to keep the tears at bay.

"Just remember, he is the same person, even if his memories have left him and he seems lost. You are so patient with him. You're doing a good job, Mike," she said, putting a hand to his arm in reassurance.

She gave him a moment and then retrieved a water glass from the table, offering it to Mike, who gladly accepted and downed what was left in one gulp.

"Did you at least like the fish?" he said, searching her eyes. "I'm kinda well known for my grouper."

She laughed. "It was great! A man who can cook is a rare find these days!"

He reached around her to put the glass on the counter and let his arm linger around her waist for a few moments.

"I have to go pick up Ryan, but I'm looking forward to Wednesday night," she said, suddenly warm and knowing he could feel her heart racing. He smiled, released her, and said, "Yeah, me too."

After they had said their goodbyes, Allie mentally shook herself as she walked to her truck. *It's been quite a while since a man has made my temperature go up by so many degrees. But I'm not really single anymore—I have Ryan to think about, too. Besides, maybe it's cynical, but Mike seems too good to be true.* She headed to pick up Ryan, arguing with herself the whole time.

AFTER MAKING sure Ryan was asleep, Allie went to the other end of the trailer and turned the knob on the door to her parents' bedroom. She felt her way around the bed to her father's side and carefully found the button to turn on the small lamp on the bedside table. It cast a circle of warm light in the area, and she instantly felt a little less anxious. She looked around the understated room. Still not wanting to invade the space, she avoided sitting on the bed and went to the closet. She knew where her mom and dad had always kept the family photos, up on the shelf in their closet.

Pulling down the small green suitcase where they were stored, she then found a spot on the floor, closer to the lamp lighting the space. Allie leaned up against the wall, set the suitcase in front of her, and popped both latches. A pang of grief overtook her when she saw her parents' faces smiling up at her from the top of the pile. She pulled the picture out from the pile and brought it closer to her face so she could study it. It was taken in the fall, outside, and it was both of her parents with a young Ryan. They must have had someone take them, maybe a friend who knew a thing or two about photography. Her mom had her arms folded around Ryan's shoulders, her dad had his hands on her mom's shoulders, and Ryan was, amazingly, looking at the camera with a semi-natural smile. They were all dressed in shades of brown. It was a wonderful picture, and she had never seen it before. How much had she missed when she was gone? Allie knew herself enough to realize that she had left for Chicago in an effort to escape them all in a sense, and she desperately wished every day that she hadn't. Her friends insisted that she had done what was right for her at the time, but she had missed all of that time with her parents, and now they were gone. She could never get that back.

And then there was Ryan. When he was young and first diagnosed, she had felt like the extra child, often having to fend for herself and make do because her parents just didn't have enough energy or attention to spare. She knew why, but it hadn't hurt any less, always having to be strong and self-sufficient. And she supposed she resented Ryan for it, at the time.

She didn't anymore. Heaven knew why it took her the deaths of her parents to force her to realize how much Ryan needed her in his life, but she knew now. She just hoped it wouldn't be too difficult to get to know her brother again. With his communication issues, it wasn't the easiest thing in the world, and she often found herself wishing she could get a glimpse inside his mind. She was learning, though, that he had his own ways of letting her in, through his drawings and other special interests. She felt a surge of love for her little brother and brought the picture back up to her face. She should have been there for it then, and she couldn't go back and change that, but she was here now.

Putting the picture aside with a mental note to find a frame for it, maybe for her desk at work, she began to look through the others. It was an emotional process, and more than once, she had to tiptoe to the bathroom to grab new tissues. There were many of Ryan's drawings that her parents had saved over the years, and she was fascinated by the progression of his skills, and the insight into his thought processes they provided. Every so often, she would remind herself to keep an eye out for pictures that might show the Guthries, as well.

When she got to the bottom of the suitcase, she realized that there wasn't a single picture of the Guthries in the entire lot. That meant that the split with the Guthries had been pretty serious, even though she hadn't consciously realized at the time. She reminded herself that she was just a kid and couldn't possibly know her parents' feelings about everything back then. Parents just don't share that stuff with their kids. But with the perspective she now had as an adult, she realized that when someone, probably her dad, had gone through all of the pictures to remove every trace of any memories the families had made together, it was the act of someone who felt a deep betrayal.

Maybe when her parents died, Neil had felt remorse. Maybe he felt it all along, and her move down here had provided the opportunity to make amends. By offering her a job, she guessed he had offered an olive branch to the memory of her dad. Or it was an attempt to pay Ryan back for the hundreds of thousands he had cheated from his family? In either case, it smacked of pity, and all of a sudden, working for the Guthries left a bad taste in her mouth. Was she betraying her parents' memory by working for the very people who had hurt them the most? And by the apparent number of red files in Neil's file cabinet, they had taken advantage of plenty of other families, as well. She would need some time to really process all of this.

She looked up from her spot on the floor and realized she had been sitting there for quite a while. She figured this was about all she was up for tonight, and she was proud of herself for taking the first step. She wasn't ready to move in yet, but with time, maybe she'd get there. She stood up and stretched, then put the green suitcase back in its place, gently picked up the photo she had set aside, turned the light off, and with one backward glance, shut the door.

CHAPTER TWENTY-FIVE

A llie was surprised to see both Neil's and Vicky's vehicles in the lot when she pulled into Guthrie's Marine on Monday morning. If they planned to stay for the day, she would have to be very careful about talking to some of the suspects during working hours. But she was glad Vicky was here. She was one of the first entries in Ty's little black book.

Allie got settled at her desk. She popped her head into Neil's office and said hello, and headed for the kitchen under the pretense of getting some coffee going. She pushed the door open slightly and found Vicky working on the coffee herself.

"Hey, Vicky."

"Hey, Allie."

"How are you doing?"

"As good as can be expected, I guess. We're kind of in limbo, as the medical examiner's office hasn't released the body yet."

"Wow, really?"

"Yes, and we'd really just like to get this behind us. Of course, we'd like to find out who did this to Ty, but Neil thinks he and I might head South this winter and let y'all handle the yard."

"I think that would be really good for you two," Allie said, taking the cup Vicky offered and holding it in both hands. She leaned against the counter and crossed her legs, effectively blocking Vicky's exit from the kitchen area.

"Vicky, can I ask you something?"

"Sure, honey."

"How long had Ty been blackmailing you?"

Vicky went still and gave Allie a long, hard look. Finally, she raised her cup to her lips and took a sip, her hands shaking. "A long time."

"How did Ty find out?"

"I could ask you the same thing."

"Ty left records."

She snorted. "Of course, he did. I reckon he found out a lot of information about people from the various people he slept with."

"How long did the affair last?"

"Not long. Maybe six months or so."

"But it was after you and Neil had married."

"Yes, it was. When I met Neil, it was romantic and perfect. After Zack was born, the luster seemed to wear off, and I was no longer the focus of his attention. I never did get that back. I was hurt and lonely, so I did what all hurt and lonely wives do. Doesn't make it right, but it's not like it's all that uncommon."

"And Ty found out and cornered you. Pay him or he

would tell Neil."

"Yes."

"If he had told Neil, what would have happened?"

"Neil probably would have left me and I would have had to raise Zack on my own with no money." She paused and sipped her coffee. "I mean, I was cleaning hotel rooms when I met Neil."

"So you paid for Ty's silence. That had to be a special kind of betrayal."

"Resentment isn't a strong enough word. And Neil knew nothing and acted like his boy was God's gift to the world."

"You couldn't even tell Neil that he wasn't."

"He was the last person I could tell. His darling boy could never be such a monster, and his trophy wife wasn't such a trophy," Vicky said.

Allie tried to stifle the thoughts that bubbled up about the letters from Neil's "kitten" in those red files. This was not the time to start feeling sympathetic toward suspects.

"Did Zack know Ty was blackmailing you?"

"I think he had his suspicions. Just never had the focus to do anything about it."

"What happens now?"

"I guess I can either tell Neil the truth, or hope the Sheriff's Department doesn't make all of its findings known. I'll have to think about it." Vicky eyed Allie. "You're not going to say anything, are you?"

"I have no reason to hurt you," Allie said. Vicky looked relieved.

"Thanks, Allie. You've always seemed like a good girl," Vicky said.

"Have you ever heard of anyone with the nickname of Rose?"

"Can't say as I have. Not a name you hear every day," Vicky said. "I better get back into Neil's office."

"Okay," Allie said and stood up straight to let Vicky pass.

"Motive, and possibly opportunity…" Allie whispered into her mug when Vicky had left.

"Allie!" Neil thundered from his office.

She hopped up with a legal pad and pen in hand, a habit she had picked up in her first week at Guthrie's Marine. When Neil yelled for you, you had better be ready.

He didn't wait for her to get settled. "It has come to my attention that there is plenty going on around here about which I have no idea." He paused to see what effect that had on her, and when she only responded by taking notes, he continued. "It seems we have been lax in our security precautions both inside and out."

When Allie raised her eyebrows slightly, he explained. "Key cards, Allie. We have no idea who had them, and no one was keeping track. Someone was able to get onto our property after hours, steal from our clients, and murder my son."

Allie knew better than to say anything when he was like this.

"I had thought when I hired you that your background might mean you were a bit more capable of handling issues like this, but I guess I need to take it into my own hands. I am having a camera system installed, both in the office and in the yard. I wanted to make you aware of the new layer of security, and I need you to draft a memo to all employees making them aware of it, too. I don't think I need to explain that I will be the only one with access to the feed, either."

"Yes, sir," she said. "Is that all?"

"For now, Allie. Make this a priority. I want the staff to get the memo before lunch today."

"Can I ask when the cameras will be installed?"

"That's not something I'm willing to share with you," he said coldly.

NEIL AND VICKY left for lunch, as did Mike and Sammy. Allie did a quick search for *Guthrie Restoration* on the Secretary of State website to see why she had never seen it on the books here at Guthrie's Marine Center, and found out it had stopped operations in 2009. *Maybe it had been absorbed into the other operations here. Or maybe it was "off the books."* When Charlie called, Allie told him about Neil's renewed interest in security.

"It's probably all for show," Charlie said. "And he probably suspects you're working with me. In other news, the phone you found was a burner phone. Ty probably purchased them on a regular basis so that if anyone ever tried to prove he'd been blackmailing them, the number couldn't be traced back to him."

"I wondered if that was the case," she said.

"Everything you'd expect was on it, though. Phone

numbers for all of his victims and text messages between them. Phone numbers for all of his little girlfriends, too. Many on the list you gave me from his Facebook profile. We're cataloging it all now."

"Was Holly's number on it?" Allie asked.

"Sure was," Charlie said.

"Had he messaged her recently?"

"I can check. Why?"

"Just want to check her story. She said they broke up about a month ago. Any texts between them after that would indicate maybe that wasn't the truth, or at least not the whole truth," she said.

"I'll find out and let you know," he said.

"Any unidentified numbers?"

"A few. And there is one labeled as Rose."

"Did you call it?" she asked.

"There was no answer, but it hadn't been disconnected, at least. We may be able to track her down with this number. I'll keep you posted on that," he said.

"You mean with a Wolfhound or something?" Allie asked, showing off her background a bit. Law enforcement she had worked with in Chicago used them to listen in on private phone conversations.

"If we had one of those, I wouldn't be telling you about it and getting civilians all riled up about their rights to privacy!" He chuckled. "Some surprising findings in the QuickBooks file, too."

"Such as?"

"Barbie would be disappointed to know how much Ty was making, at least on the books," Charlie said.

"Really? Maybe that was why Ty felt he needed to make some cash on the side," Allie offered.

"And cash is the operative word. Can't be traced, wouldn't declare it as income, and wouldn't have to include it in the alimony formula," Charlie said.

"I wonder if Barbie knew more than she let on about Ty's blackmailing activities," Allie said.

"And I wonder what he was saving up for. There were a lot of searches in his search engine history about Costa Rica," Charlie said. "Maybe planning a trip?"

"Really?" Allie asked. "I wonder if he planned to go alone."

"Now there's a thought. Something to ask all of these girlfriends he seemed to have," Charlie said.

"And maybe one in particular," Allie said, wondering if she had eliminated Holly as a suspect too soon.

CHAPTER TWENTY-SIX

"Uh-oh…" Allie said, looking at the computer screen.

"Do what?" Holly said, a worried look on her face.

"That invest we've been watching has turned into a tropical storm in the islands. It's intensifying, and it's possible it might be coming our way," Allie said.

"Oh, crap," Holly said, putting the nail polish away and flapping her hands in the air. "I guess we have work to do."

"Let me go tell Mike, and then I'll be back in to help," Allie said, jumping up and crossing quickly to the door. As she stepped outside, she noted that it was a beautiful dry day with a light breeze, and no indication of what might come their way. She scanned the yard and spotted Mike and Sammy working on a forty-footer called the *Swingtime III* in the far side of the yard. As she headed their way, Mike realized what she was doing and crossed over to the ladder so he could meet her on the ground.

"What's up, Allie?"

"You know that invest that was threatening the Caribbean Islands this weekend? Well, it is now Tropical Storm Grady and getting stronger. Some of the models are projecting it heading our way," she said.

"Great," Mike said, wiping the back of his neck with a rag. He looked up at the sky and sighed. "On top of everything else."

"We'll keep a close eye on it, and keep hoping it heads out to sea," she said. "But I thought you should know. Holly and I are gearing up to do our part in the office, just in case."

"Thanks for the update, Allie. We'll need all hands on deck if we need to do a haul-out, so could you call Neil and give him a heads up? He may even want Zack to be here."

"Sure, I was going to do that anyway. I'll keep you posted," she said, shading her eyes to look up into his face.

"Thanks, Allie. You're the best." He smiled at her. She blushed and went back to the office.

ALLIE LEFT work and decided to head down 101 straight into downtown Beaufort. She had one more suspect to speak to today.

After parking the Dakota on Turner Street, she crossed over to the Royal James, patted the old basset hound tied to the bench outside, and pulled the door open. The radio was a little too loud, the crowd a little too rowdy, but the beer was cold, and they had pool tables.

She went to the bar, got herself a beer, and scanned the growing crowd for Sammy.

He was chalking up a cue at the table in the middle, and she walked toward the table, sipping her beer as he made his shot. He was in the middle of a run, so she waited until he missed to get his attention.

"Hey, Sammy," she said.

"Allie!" he said, eyeing her. "What are you doing here?"

"Just thought I'd come out to where the locals go to hang out for a bit after work."

"Good choice. I come here a lot. Play a little pool, drink a few beers before I head home."

"Helps to shrug off the work day, huh?" She smiled.

"I reckon," he said, unsmiling. He paused and lowered his head. "It was a shame what happened to Ty."

"Yes, it's sad when someone dies before their time."

He looked up and held out his hands. "I didn't really mean what I said the other day. No one deserves to be murdered. That's what they're saying now, isn't it? That he was murdered?" There was an unmistakable edge to his voice now.

"That's what they're saying."

"Listen, I know a lot of people had reason, but who would do that?" His face hardened and his brows knitted together. "Maybe it happens in the big city all the time, but people around here…"

"Well, it looks like somebody did," Allie said. She took a sip from her beer. "So you have a sister, Sammy?"

He cleared his throat at the change of subject, and then his voice dropped. "Yes. Younger sister. Gemma."

"And she lives around here?"

"Yes, she lives here in Beaufort," he said, eyeing her again.

"And Ty had a relationship with her?"

Sammy snorted. "You could call it that. Hang on. I gotta take my shot."

Allie watched him shoot and miss, wondering if the talk about Gemma was rattling him.

Sammy returned and took a drag on his beer. "Yeah, he was screwing her for a while." His lips flattened into two thin lines.

Allie paused before asking, "How did she feel about him?"

"I think she fell hard for him. Older man with some money, respected family. I think she really believed he was going to lift her up and out and that they were in love."

"Ty led her on?"

"Oh, yeah. You can ask anyone. That's how he operated with women." He sneered and took a swig of his beer. "He was going to leave Barbie for every single one and marry each of them. Or so they thought."

"So Gemma was upset when it ended."

"She cried for weeks." He lowered his head again and traced the linoleum with the toe of his boot.

"And you got mad."

His head snapped up and his eyes blazed. "You sure are asking a lot of questions," he said and flexed his fists. "Of course, I did. She's my little sister. I'm supposed to protect her from guys like that. I had no idea until it was too late, though."

"Did he bring it up at work?"

"All the freakin' time." He shoved his hands into his pockets. "He thought it was hilarious to get me riled up, ready to fight him. There were plenty of times I threw down my tools and started at him. Mike always stopped me."

"What happened?"

Sammy looked away and took another sip of beer. "One day, I finally realized he was never going to change, and that he was the one that deserved to be made fun of. If I ignored him, maybe he'd stop. It was really, really hard to do. But I got in the habit of walking away. If he questioned where I was going, I just came up with some work-related answer or told him I was going to the bathroom. After a while, the game wasn't fun for him anymore and he gradually stopped."

Allie paused. "How is Gemma now?"

He took a deep breath and crossed his arms. "Better. She's seeing someone else who treats her right, so we'll see."

"You're a good big brother."

"Well, I try," he said and grimaced.

She put her empty bottle on the bar, and said, "Well, I wish you luck on your game, Sammy. Thanks for talking with me. I've got to get back home to Ryan."

He stepped in her way for a moment, grabbing her arm, and said, "Allie, I really didn't do it. I probably hated him more than anyone, and I can't say I'm not glad I don't have to worry about him anymore. But I wouldn't ever go that far."

"Okay, Sammy. I hear you," she said softly. "I'm going to head home, now, okay?"

He stepped back out of her way, releasing her arm and bowing slightly to her as she passed him. When she reached the sidewalk outside, she took a deep breath and peered back in the windows of the Royal James. Sammy was watching her as he took another deep pull on his beer. Unnerved to see him following her with his eyes, she hustled across the street to her truck.

CHAPTER TWENTY-SEVEN

C harlie Bishop came in early again on Tuesday.
"I see Neil and Vicky aren't here yet?"

"No, I don't think they're coming in today," Allie said.

"Good. I need to use Neil's office again. Zack's coming in about ten minutes. I thought it would be better to question him here than at the station. Fewer ruffled feathers."

"Good idea. Leave the door open, and I'll listen to see if I can pick up anything."

Zack came in a short while later. Allie was surprised to see him up so early.

"Hey, Zack," Charlie said when he entered the office.

"Chief Detective Bishop," he said.

"So I have to ask you a couple questions, okay?"

"I figured."

"Have a seat."

"Thanks." Allie heard the chair creak as she assumed Zack leaned back.

"No one can verify your whereabouts after you left the Backstreet Pub, is that correct?"

"Not that I know of. I was pretty out of it."

"You were last seen there around one a.m., and you left alone. Is that how you remember it?"

"Like I said, I don't really remember, but I know Loreli was pissed because I left her there, so I guess I was alone." Allie caught the whine in his voice.

"Do you remember anything else after that?"

"I know I didn't drive. I left the truck keys with Loreli. So I s'pose I walked."

"You were walking up 101 when you were picked up," Charlie pointed out.

"Not sure where I was headed. The only thing up 101 is this place. I don't even think I have keys to the office."

"Do you have a key card to get into the yard?"

"Yeah, but that's in my truck."

"Hmm. Okay." A chair creaked, and Allie thought Charlie had leaned back, ready to change tactics. "How did you and Ty get along?"

"We were brothers. He always kinda resented me, and I always kinda resented him, but at the end of the day, we were family. I'd never kill him. Get in a fight, maybe, but kill him? Nope. Wouldn't happen, even if I was messed up." Zack's voice had risen with this answer, Allie noted. He was anxious now.

"You're sure about that? Maybe it started as a fight, and Ty went overboard accidentally?"

"Nah. I was in no shape to do anything to anybody."

"Maybe so. All right, Zack. You're free to go, but don't leave town. We may have more questions for you." Allie heard the sound of chairs being pushed back as the men stood.

"Yeah," he said and left.

Allie went into Neil's office. "He has no idea where he was?"

"None at all."

"Well, I don't know if I really buy this 'brother' line he was feeding us. From what I've heard already, there was no love lost between any members of that family. And just because Zack's name wasn't mentioned in that little black book, it doesn't mean Ty wasn't holding something over him. Plus, Zack may have known about him blackmailing Vicky and wanted to get him back for that little piece of nasty business."

"Yes, very true." Charlie looked at his phone. "I have to take this."

"Okay." Allie went back to her desk and a moment later, Charlie came out of the office, his characteristic smile nowhere in sight.

"Something's come up. I have to head into the office. I may be back a little later," he said.

"Sure thing. See you later!" she said as she watched him leave the office.

———

ALLIE CAME out of the bathroom and saw Sammy leaned over Holly's desk. They had been whispering but were now talking in a slightly louder-than-normal volume about the weather and their evacuation plans for Tropical Storm Grady.

Nice save. Allie pretended she hadn't seen them whispering and heading back to her desk. *Wonder what was so important y'all had to whisper.*

As she sat down, Sammy quickly uttered his goodbyes, and Allie returned his nervous smile with a sunny one, expertly masking her curiosity. "See you later!" she called as headed out to the yard. She would have to figure out a way to get some answers out of Holly about the nature of her relationship with Sammy without raising her suspicions. She had never seen the two speak more than pleasantries to each other, and had pretty much ruled Holly out as a suspect, but what had she interrupted here? Had she been too quick to assume Holly wasn't smart enough to have pulled off a theft or even a murder? And why had Holly and Sammy hidden the connection between them, whatever it was? The questions buzzed around her brain, distracting her all afternoon, but she knew she had to play it cool, or Holly and Sammy would become suspicious.

CHAPTER TWENTY-EIGHT

A t lunch, she decided to visit a couple of people she hadn't spoken with yet. She rode by Zack's house and saw Loreli's car in the driveway. *All she can do is shut the door in my face*, Allie thought as she pulled in.

The house itself hadn't been cheap. Even though it was several blocks outside of what was considered "downtown Beaufort," anything in that area was valued in the hundreds of thousands, and Allie knew that a waitress and a usually unemployed kid with substance abuse issues couldn't afford anything close to it. She assumed the Guthries had paid for it, and Zack and Loreli weren't taking care of it very well. Weeds sprouted everywhere, and a partially fallen gutter hung down against the carport. Allie stepped over a hose that had never been put away and knocked on the door.

"Oh, hey, Allie," Loreli said when she finally came to the door in a slouchy pair of shorts and a tank top. Allie had clearly woken her up, which she supposed wasn't too unusual for a waitress who worked nights.

"Hey, Loreli. I was driving by and thought I would drop off a copy of Zack's work schedule while I was in the neighborhood."

"Okay," Loreli said as Allie handed her the schedule.

"Can I talk to you about Zack and Ty?" Allie asked.

Confused, Loreli held the screen door open, and said, "Uh, sure. Come on in."

Once inside, they sat in two of the kitchen chairs close by. Loreli offered Allie something to drink.

"No thanks. Listen, what do you remember about the night Ty was killed?"

"Oh, this again? You can't tell me that the Sheriff's Department still considers Zack a suspect."

"Well, they are trying to narrow their focus, but it would be nice if I could help cross Zack off their list with had something definitive. He left you at the Backstreet Pub in Beaufort?"

"Yes, he left me but made sure I had the keys."

"And this was about one a.m.?"

"That's right."

"Where did you think he was going?"

"I was so mad, I really didn't care. In the back of my mind, I wondered if he was going to go sleep it off at a friend or former girlfriend's house, but I refused to worry about it."

"Does Zack do this a lot?"

"He just doesn't think. He's like a little kid in so many ways. He needs someone to take care of him, and for some reason, I'm always there to pick up the pieces."

"How did you two meet?"

"Through some mutual friends. I'm not going to lie,

we both like to party, and we've been a part of that scene for a long time. But we're getting older now, and I find myself wanting more out of this life. I don't want to be that girl who dates a guy for twelve years and never gets a ring, never moves to that next step."

"And how does Zack feel about all this?"

"He knows he's not a kid anymore, but he seems like he can't help himself. He's going to turn into that older guy who just doesn't know when to hang it up. He's going to embarrass himself before too long. And me."

"Sounds like you've had this discussion before."

"Too many times. He needs to start acting like he comes from money."

"Tell me about Zack and Ty."

"Typical half-sibling relationship, I guess. They both resented each other. It didn't help that they were so far apart in age. They never really had anything in common except their father's genes. Both stubborn as hell, and addictive personalities. Ty was addicted to women, and Zack's addicted to everything else."

"So they didn't get along?"

"You could say that. Ty was a hard worker and therefore got most of his dad's attention. Zack resented that, and rather than encourage him to work harder, it encouraged him in the opposite direction."

"Has Zack been in trouble with the law before?"

"Can't the Sheriff's Department tell you that?"

"Yes, but I'm asking you."

Loreli picked at some fuzz on her shorts. "Yes, he's been caught shoplifting. He's been picked up for DUI, some petty stuff, but nothing major."

"How long ago was that?"

"Before he met me, I can tell you that." She sat straighter in her chair and crossed her arms. "I may like to party, but I don't put up with that crap. I work too hard to be paying out bail money all the time."

"So he cleaned up his act when he started dating you?"

"More or less. He knew I'd walk if he didn't. That's why I was so pissed when he got wasted that night. We deserve a better life but we'll never get there with him pulling this crap."

"This is kind of a touchy question, but has he been faithful to you?"

"Yes. That was a major difference between him and Ty."

"How do you know?"

"Listen, I have lots and lots of girlfriends across this county. Comes from waitressing all over the place. I would have heard about it as soon as he had done it."

"And he's been true to you, huh?"

"Yes, he has. That's one thing I can say for the little bugger. He's been faithful."

"So, in your opinion, Zack could not have murdered Ty, even in the state he was in on Monday night?"

"Especially in the state he was in. He couldn't have tied his shoes, let alone lured Ty onto that boat and shoved him off. He would have been the one on the ground."

"Okay, thanks, Loreli. You've been a big help."

"Anytime, Allie."

ON THE WAY back to the office, Allie thought she had time for one more stop. Allie hoped Gemma still had her job at Burger King and pulled in. Luckily, Gemma was on the register, and Allie asked if she could speak to her a minute. Like a sulky child, she asked her manager if she could take a break, and when given the go-ahead, she led Allie to an empty table in the corner.

"Gemma, thanks so much for talking with me."

"You're welcome. I just can't believe what happened to Ty. I can't believe someone murdered him!" Gemma said in a hushed voice, leaning forward and looking to see if anyone could overhear.

"Yes, it looks like someone lured him to the boat and somehow tossed him over the side. Nasty stuff," Allie said, adjusting to that rolling, Down East accent again, although it was softer coming from Gemma's mouth.

"Yeah," Gemma said, smoothing her hands out on the legs of her work pants.

"Did your brother tell you about Ty?"

"Yes, he said Ty had it coming, but of course Sammy didn't do it. He said some people would probably come by to ask questions, and just to tell the truth."

"Did you believe him? I mean about the not doing it part?"

"Of course. My brother has always been a little over-protective, but he has never seriously hurt anyone."

"You said seriously. Does he have a history of hurting others?"

"He's a hot-head, and everyone knows it. He hangs out at the Royal James, and every once in a while, he'll get into it with someone. They usually throw a few punches and that's the end of it. No one ends up in the hospital, and no one goes home with more than a bloody nose or a few teeth knocked out."

"So you think he's more of a spur-of-the-moment kind of guy, rather than a planner?"

"Yeah, I guess so."

"Tell me about your relationship with Ty."

"Relationship is a strong word." She sat back and laughed. "Anyone who knows Ty knows that that word wasn't in his vocabulary. But he was certainly a charmer. Could make any woman believe she was the only one. At least for a little while."

"What happened, exactly?"

"Well, at the beginning, he would come over every night. We would do fun things together, and it felt like love. We liked to spend time together. But gradually, he distanced himself. He would come over every other night, or he would be somewhere else the whole time he was with me. It wasn't as much fun anymore. And then he stopped coming altogether. He ghosted me."

"As in, no phone call, no explanation, just stopped coming over?"

"Yep. You got it. I wasn't even worth a phone call to him." Gemma leaned back and folded her arms.

"Did you try to reach him?"

"Yes, but he never responded to texts or phone calls. I'm not stupid. I got the picture."

"You felt used," Allie surmised, trying to look Gemma in the eye.

"Yes, to say the least. My brother saw me tore up, and

from that day to this, he has hated Ty with a passion." Gemma finally looked at Allie.

"But you don't think he would do something like this, even with a hatred as deep as that?"

"No," she said, worry in her eyes.

"How has Sammy been since you got the news about Ty?"

"Calmer. Happier. He laughs more."

"What do you think about that?"

"Look, how the hell do I know? Maybe you should be asking Sammy these questions."

"I'm just looking for your perspective, Gemma. No one probably knows your brother better than you. We just want to be able to rule him out as a suspect, but we can't because he has this little thing called motive, and his motive was you. He also didn't have an alibi."

"I see," she said, paler now. Allie guessed she hadn't realized the seriousness of the situation.

"Do you have any information that could help us?"

"I don't think I do. I wish I did. I'm sure Sammy had nothing to do with this at all. Please give him the benefit of the doubt. He wouldn't ever do anything as nasty as all this."

"I'm doing what I can, Gemma. Will you give me a call if you think of anything else?"

"I will, I promise."

"One more thing before I go, Gemma," Allie said as she stood.

"Sure," Gemma said.

"How does your brother know Holly Mason?"

"Oh…" Gemma said, shifting her eyes away from Allie

momentarily. "You know everyone Down East knows everyone else. Lots of our families have been friends for generations. Knowing everyone else is just a normal thing, Down East."

"Ah, okay," Allie said, acting as if that satisfied the questions that had been swirling in her brain since she had caught Holly and Sammy whispering in the office. "Thanks, Gemma," she said, but the momentary look of wariness in her eyes and the pause before answering meant there was more to this story. And if everyone was hiding something about these two, it must be something worth hiding.

CHAPTER TWENTY-NINE

Back in the office that afternoon, Allie watched Charlie's cruiser roll back into the lot. Charlie stepped out of the vehicle and checked his belt for all of his gear, handcuffs, badge, gun, before he went into the office. Something was up.

"I need to know where Mike is," he said tersely.

"Uh, let me see which boat he's working on today," she said as she checked the clipboard. "The big catamaran, *The Lucy May II*," she supplied. Charlie was out the door.

Allie walked over to the window and leaned against the wall so as not to be caught staring. Charlie called out to Mike, and Mike headed down the ladder, wiping his hands on a rag. Words were exchanged, and Mike looked at the office briefly, and then back at the boat. Charlie said something else, and Mike shrugged and followed Charlie to the cruiser. Charlie seated Mike in the back, and he looked one more time in her direction before ducking his head to get in. Charlie, too, paused to look in her direction with an unreadable expression on his face. He got in, and the cruiser drove away. She turned, putting her back to the wall.

What the hell?

A COUPLE OF HOURS LATER, Charlie called. "I'm sorry I had to do that, Allie."

"Sorry to me? Why? Mike and I are friends, but I understand the nature of law enforcement."

"Well, I'd like to fill you in. You going to be there a while?"

"I'm here until four today."

"I'll be there in a bit."

When Charlie arrived, he checked to make sure they were alone in the office and pulled Holly's chair over to Allie's desk.

"I feel like I have to explain things to you. I know you're closer to Mike than you'll admit."

"I... it's not like that..." she started to explain.

"No, you don't need to do that. But I need to tell you what's happened. Mike is now one of our prime suspects."

"What?" Her hands pressed onto the surface of her desk as a knot formed in her throat.

"Listen. Mike isn't even his real name. Yes, he grew up in Pamlico County, but as Spencer Michael Gillikin."

"Okay, so he's using his middle name. Lots of people do that."

"Yes, but he needed to make sure the name Spencer wasn't attached to him because he has a criminal record, as well."

"What?" She shook her head to clear it.

"He stole a car and did a little time for it. When he got out, he started going by the name Mike, and that's when he went to get his marine mechanic degree. He also doesn't have an alibi for the night of the murder. He said he was at home, but some of his neighbors said that his truck was definitely not in front of his apartment that night."

"So what did he say when you questioned him?"

"He said he was young and stupid, and just because he went joyriding in a car as a teenager doesn't make him a killer."

"A valid point."

"He said he was taking care of his dad who has early-onset Alzheimer's, and staying at his place that night. He said he lied to protect him. Didn't want his dad to go through the stress of questioning."

"Noble."

"There's one more thing, Allie. Mike threatened Ty's life in the yard. There are witnesses."

"When was this?"

"A few years ago. Shortly after Mike started here, actually."

She crossed her arms. "That was eight years ago, Charlie! This is all so thin, and you know it."

"His name was in the black book," Charlie reminded her.

"Only his name. No dates, no notes, no money."

They sat staring at each other for a minute.

"I think you might be a little too emotionally attached to this suspect."

"I think you are grasping at straws."

"Well, we've released him, but he has been told not to leave town."

"Is Kat Matthews behind this?"

"The evidence is behind this."

She sat up. "Thanks for the update, Charlie."

He cleared his throat, got up, and returned Holly's chair. "We'll talk in the morning."

"Great," she said, and Charlie left quickly.

HER PHONE RANG JUST as she was putting the key into the lock to close up the office for the night. She rummaged for it while she put her keys in their place.

"Hello?"

"Allie, it's Mike."

She paused for a second. "Hey," she said, quieter.

"Hey." He paused. "I'm not sure what to say. I'm sure you have a million things running through your mind, and none of them good. All I ask is that you give me a chance to explain."

She stopped still. "You didn't admit to the murder, did you?"

"No! No, that's... no. This is all such a mess. I lied, okay, I lied about where I was that night. But not for any reasons you might assume, and I didn't hurt anyone. You know I couldn't do that."

"Okay... okay. Listen, I will talk to you in the morning. They've released you, right?"

"Yes, but they told me not to leave town," Mike said, and she could hear the nervous laugh he was holding back.

"Then I will see you in the morning, and maybe we can talk then?"

"I'd like that more than anything."

"Okay. See you tomorrow," she said.

"All right. Thank you, Allie."

———

ALLIE WAS STILL LOST in thought as she picked Ryan up and drove to the trailer park. *I hope I haven't pissed Charlie off, but what they have on Mike is incredibly thin, isn't it? I couldn't have judged his character so incorrectly, could I? No, Mike is a good guy. What the Sheriff's Department has on Mike is really no more than they have on anyone else. This just isn't right.*

She glanced at Ryan next to her, playing on his game system. He looked so much like an adult, but was still a kid in so many ways. She had to be careful and protect him from anyone who might hurt him. *Mike would never hurt Ryan, though.*

Allie pulled in in front of the trailer, and as they were gathering their things and walking to the front door, her phone rang again. Normally, she didn't answer an unknown number, but it was local and she thought it might have something to do with the case. She shifted her belongings to her left arm and managed to answer the phone.

"Hello?"

"Stay out of it, Allie!" a manipulated voice screamed out of the phone.

"What?"

"Leave it alone, or Ryan's next!" and the line was dead.

As the full impact of the call hit her, she dropped everything she was carrying in shock. Her hands were shaking, she noticed, and her breathing ragged. Ryan, normally oblivious to anything she was experiencing, curiously doubled back and put his hand on her arm.

"Allie?" he asked.

She looked at him and managed to get her breathing under control. "I'm fine, buddy. Let's get our stuff inside." As she bent to pick up everything she had dropped, Peg's screen door slammed open.

"Allie!" she called. "You okay?" She was hustling over the small patch of grass between their trailers.

"Fine," Allie replied. But Peg noticed her shaking hands.

"Fine, my ass," she said under her breath, shooting Allie a dark look. "Let's get everything inside, Ryan," she said, craning her neck toward the road, looking for suspicious activity.

Once inside, Peg made sure Ryan was settled in his room, quietly shut the door, and came back out to the living room. She settled Allie on the couch with a blanket, and quickly made some tea.

"Spill it," she said as she brought the tea in. Allie looked at her, hesitating. She didn't want to burden Peg. What good would it do? But she knew she wasn't going to come up with a story that would satisfy Peg, either. She sighed.

"Just got a phone call threatening to hurt Ryan if I didn't stop helping with the investigation."

"Oh my God," Peg said, wrapping her hands around

her own mug. "You should tell Charlie Bishop and let him look into it. And maybe you should just let it go."

"I can't, Peg. Mike is their prime suspect now, and I know he didn't do it." Once the words were out of her mouth, she knew she believed he was innocent.

"Is it worth the risk? Maybe this call wasn't a bluff."

"Do you really think someone could hurt Ryan? He's always supervised. I think whoever it is is just trying to scare me."

"Seems like they're doing a good job, judging by the way your hands were shaking," Peg said. She gave her a look as she sipped from her mug.

"I'll mention it to Charlie, see if they can up the patrols in the area. But I will see this through. I need to make sure they don't pin this all on the wrong guy."

"Oh, to be in my twenties again," Peg said. "So full of conviction and foolhardiness. Well, you know if you need me, I'll be there."

CHAPTER THIRTY

When Allie pulled into the parking lot in front of the yard Wednesday morning, Mike was there already, leaning against his truck with arms folded, waiting for her. She took her time gathering her things in the car before getting out, her heart racing the whole time.

"Listen, Allie, I need to explain to you," Mike said when she closed the door to her truck.

"No, you don't. You don't owe me anything. We're friends, Mike. We're friends. That's it. Whatever secrets you have are yours to keep, and they're none of my business," Allie said.

"I don't know what it is about you, Allie, but I felt like... Hell, I don't know. I haven't ever been able to talk to a girl like I talk to you. You just seem to get me like no one else does, and I... I think I screwed it up, didn't I?" He made a movement as if to reach out and touch her arm but stopped himself.

She thought about what to say and wished for a

moment that she was more like Barbie, with a quick comeback just at the right time. But that was not her way. She often didn't say anything and then couldn't remember half the conversation later.

"Mike, friends tell each other the truth and don't keep secrets. If you needed to hide things, that's fine, but then you can't expect people to trust you," she said, her voice softening. "And I have to be able to trust you if… if we're friends," she said.

He looked at his boots and scuffed the sandy earth of the yard. "I was afraid. And I'm sorry I didn't tell you the truth. It's not something you bring up in everyday conversation, and let's face it, you and I haven't had a chance to have much of anything deeper," he said. Watching her brows knit, he said, "But I'm not making excuses. You are absolutely right, and I can't expect you to trust me if I keep secrets from you."

"At least we're clear on that," she said.

"Can you understand my perspective, though?" he asked. "'Hi, my name's not actually Mike, and I'm an ex-con. Nice to meet you!'" He mimicked, trying to make her smile.

"Yeah, I can see your point," she said, allowing herself a tentative smile.

"Not sure I'd have ever even gotten your trust if I'd led with that line," he said.

"Okay, so what was this all about?" she asked, dropping her smile.

"I was young and stupid and stole a car to go joyriding. But I got caught, and they used me as an example. I served a couple of years. When I got out, everyone in

Pamlico County knew I had a record, and there was no way I was going to find a job up there. And what skills did I have? I went to Florida, where no one knew me, took my middle name as my first, and went to school. My dad's health started to get bad, so when I got my certification, I had to come back. But I moved him to Carteret County so I might have a chance of starting over, and the Guthries turned a blind eye to my record, maybe on account of Zack and his troubles. I don't know. But I'm grateful, even if Neil is a jerk sometimes, and Ty was a jerk all the time."

"Okay," she said. "So you were a stupid kid. Was that so hard to tell me?" she asked, but smiled.

"I guess not," he said. "It's not like I killed anybody!"

As soon as it was out of his mouth, they looked at each other.

"But now they think you did," she said softly.

"But I didn't," he said, this time cupping her upper arm in his big hand, his eyes pleading with her.

"I know," she said.

Mike exhaled. "I'm so glad you said that. It means so much to me."

"We just have to find out who really did kill Ty."

ONCE SHE HAD SETTLED into the office that morning, Charlie called. "Hey, Allie. I wanted to let you know, we've upped the patrols around the park, and I'm not taking this threat against Ryan lightly," he said.

"Thank you, Charlie. We're lucky to have you in our corner."

"I also wanted to let you know I had some guys follow up on your tip about Mr. Briggs being a bit too concerned about law enforcement. They did some research, and it seems he's not always been the fine, upstanding citizen we know today," Charlie said.

"Oh?" Allie said.

"Shocking, I know. In jolly old England, he's had several run-ins with the law, dating back to when he was a teenager, selling counterfeit handbags. From there, he developed quite a few unsavory skills. It appears he cleaned up his act about ten years ago, strangely coinciding with a sudden increase in assets and his marriage to Donna," Charlie said.

"Do you think he really went straight?" Allie asked.

"Not for one hot second," Charlie said. "In my experience, people don't change. I think he probably just got better at hiding it."

"Interesting. How do you think this relates to the case at hand?" Allie asked.

"It bears looking into. It's quite possible that Briggs isn't quite the innocent victim, here, at least in the theft."

"You think he was involved? Maybe an insurance scam?" Allie said.

"He could have been. We'll definitely be asking some more questions and will be considering him a person of interest."

"He'll love that," Allie said, thinking about how pleasant he was when he *wasn't* being investigated. "What does this mean for Mike?"

"It's an active investigation, Allie, with many layers, like you said. I haven't hung my hat on Mike, as much as

DA Matthews would like me to, but he remains our prime suspect. I still have to investigate all of the evidence."

"Fair enough," she said.

"Doubt we can get a search warrant for the Briggs' condo in Beaufort, but it might be worthwhile to search the boat again, now that we know a little more about the owners. And might you have contact numbers for the crew that was aboard when she arrived?"

"I sure do. I'll email them to you," Allie said. "Is there anything you want me to do?"

"If they come in, don't let on that you know any of this, but if you can find a way to steer the topic toward the theft and what was stolen, maybe they'll let something slip that we can use," Charlie said.

"Now that you mention it, whatever happened with the stolen stuff at the antique shop?"

"It's Craven County up there, so they have a team on it. Of course, we're working with them, but they have to take the lead which slows everything down."

"That's helpful. I'll see if I can lead the conversation in that direction," Allie said.

"And let me know the next time they've come and gone, and we'll get over there to do another search of the boat after they leave. No point in letting on that we know more than we did," Charlie said.

"Okay, I'll keep you posted," Allie said. "Is there any reason to include Donna in your suspicions?"

"She didn't have any record in the UK," Charlie said. "But that doesn't mean she's innocent, either. It would be great if we could find some character witnesses. The information we have on her is pretty thin. Maybe the crew will know more," Charlie said.

"Well, the Briggs have been in town since the spring. Maybe there are some people in Beaufort who have caught a thing or two," Allie suggested.

"You wanna poke around a bit?" Charlie asked.

"I could," she said. "See where they hang out, see if anyone has overheard anything."

"Just be discreet," Charlie said. "I really don't want to show my hand with them just yet."

"Of course," Allie said.

ALLIE WENT OUT to the yard to find Mike. She found him on the *Swingtime III* again and waved him down. Her eyes couldn't help but rove over his muscular arms and perfect butt as he climbed down the ladder, and she blushed when he turned to face her.

"What's up?" Mike asked.

"A couple of things. We've been tracking that storm in the islands, and it's now a CAT 2, with more of the models showing it heading this way, including the European model which has been correct more often than not. Also, after Holly and I have done all the prep work in the office for haul-out, I'm going to run into town to do a couple of errands, and Holly is going to hold down the fort while I'm gone," Allie said.

"You sure I can't come?" he asked, glancing in the direction of the office before grabbing her hand and trailing his thumb over her forefinger.

"I'm sure," she said, stifling a giggle.

"Okay. I started prepping on Monday, so we're ready out here to start haul-out. We'll get it taken care of," Mike said. "Have fun with your errands!" He smiled and climbed back up the ladder.

ALLIE PULLED into a spot on Queen St. and walked the half block to the Front Street Grocery. She ordered her usual, a chicken salad on sourdough, from the deli counter in the back of the store and while she waited, she struck up a conversation with Jenny, the girl behind the counter.

"Still getting a pretty steady tourist business?" she asked.

"Oh, yeah. It doesn't really slow down until October," Jenny said as she constructed the sandwich. "Of course, we get a lot of business from the yacht owners that stop here on their way down to Florida or the Bahamas, or whatever."

"Ah, so you have some regulars, then, too," Allie said, grabbing a medium cup and heading to the drink machine to fill it with ice and then sweet tea.

"Some. We get all kinds here." Jenny laughed.

"And from lots of different countries, too, I expect," Allie added.

"You're right about that! We hear all kinds of languages and accents in here."

"Languages and dialects have always fascinated me," Allie said carefully after filling her cup with sweet tea. "I've caught quite a few from Britain lately."

"Oh yeah! Me too! We have one couple that comes in several times a week, and they must be from England because they sound like Jason Statham—that actor from those action movies," Jenny said. She looked around before saying, "And the man is a big as a house, too! Not your typical yacht owners, I'd say."

"What makes you say that?" Allie said, hoping it came out as casually as she had hoped.

"Well, the things you overhear them say to each other. Or rather, the things they *don't* say. Most yacht owners are talking about their 'puppies' or their businesses, or the menu for their next party, and they want everyone to hear it. Ya know? They want everyone to know they have money. But lately these two haven't been talking much, and if they do, they're whispering. It's all just… not typical." She finished wrapping Allie's sandwich. "Is that going to be all for you today?" Jenny asked, glancing at the long line forming to place orders.

"Yes, that's it. Thank you!" Allie said cheerfully, realizing she wouldn't get any more from Jenny. "It was nice talking to you!"

"You too. Have a great day!"

ALLIE SAT on one of the benches along the waterfront to eat her lunch and think about what Jenny had told her. The boardwalk ran a few blocks between the town docks and the shops along Front Street. Across Taylor's Creek, the scruffy beaches and vegetation of Carrot Island were visible, and tourists dotted the boardwalk, craning their necks to spot a wild horse over there. They were out of luck—none were visible today. Jenny hadn't told her much of anything, really. She already knew the Briggs weren't your typical large boat owners. *They were both from the poorer parts of London, so how did they end up here? And just because they aren't what you would expect, does that mean they were involved in any of this somehow? They've been in town about four months. Donna is rarely without Keith, and since Donna is the target of my little investigation today, where might she go without Keith?*

"The salon," Allie said out loud. The seagull on the boardwalk that had been eyeing her sandwich cocked its head when she spoke. "None for you, buddy. I know how this works," she said to him.

She needed to find out where Donna went to get her hair and nails done. That was where women told almost perfect strangers about their lives, and the one place Keith was sure not to tag along. Luckily, there weren't that many salons in Beaufort, and Allie was pretty sure Donna would not skimp on these services, considering how much she had to have spent on her plastic surgery. *Appearances are important to her.* She finished her lunch and headed to Jack's.

A DELICIOUS SMELL of expensive shampoos and conditioners wafted Allie's way when she opened the salon door. "Hello," she said as she approached the counter. "I need to make an appointment for a manicure." She leaned over the counter slightly as the girl looked at her appointment book. She had hoped that appointments would be written in a book by hand, and that the handwriting wouldn't be too hard to read upside down. If they were, she'd have to come up with a story.

"When would you like to come in?" the girl asked.

Allie was in luck. The girl had a pen in hand, and a peek at the book on the desk revealed she had very large script writing. Just then, the phone rang.

"Excuse me for a moment," the receptionist said to her and answered, giving Allie plenty of time to peruse the appointment book from her vantage point. It looked like Donna had been in on Monday and had seen a woman named "Missy" to have her nails done. She looked at today's schedule and found luck was on her side again as Missy was just finishing up another appointment and had an opening.

The receptionist hung up the receiver and asked, "How can I help you?"

"I was going to make an appointment, but I was wondering if Missy might be able to take me now?"

"Let me check," the receptionist said. "It looks like she is available. Why don't you pick out a color and have a seat?"

A FEW MINUTES in the waiting area allowed Allie to come up with a story. She would pose as a personal assistant to Donna, and try to work the "fellow working girl" angle to get Missy to open up about what, if anything, Donna had told her about her personal life.

When Missy called her name and began the manicure routine, Allie struck up an easy conversation with the girl, first about the weather, then about their similar backgrounds, and finally about her employment with Donna Briggs.

"Oh, Mrs. Briggs comes to me for her nails!" Missy said.

"Yes, she was the one who recommended you to me. Not that I can afford it all the time like she can," she added.

"Oh my gosh, that woman has some money, doesn't she?" Missy said, waggling her eyebrows.

"I think it *is* possible to have too much of a good thing!" Allie giggled.

"What's she like to you?" Missy asked carefully.

"She has her days…" Allie said, looking around to be sure she wasn't overheard.

Missy took the cue and leaned in. "She is quite full of herself, isn't she?"

"You have no idea," Allie said knowingly.

"And it sounds like she wasn't always so well-off…"

"Not quite," Allie said carefully.

"She talks a lot about the love of her life who was clearly not her husband, and how they had to break it off, as he had to 'go away' for a long while," Missy said, using air quotes.

"You and I both know what that means," Allie said.

"That's what mamas tell their kids when their daddies are going to jail." Missy laughed.

"You know, I've heard about this boyfriend before, but she never dropped a name. Did she mention it to you?"

"I know the last name was Graves because it was so creepy, and I know the first name started with R because she showed me an inscription on the inside of one of her rings that she said she got from him," Missy said, scrunching up her face. "Robbie, maybe?"

"Does she ever talk about Mr. Briggs? Have you ever seen him?" Allie asked.

"She complains about him, but I've never seen him, why?"

"Just curious. He's not really the loverboy type," Allie said. "He's quite... round."

"Ew," Missy said. "No, she doesn't talk about him too much. But there is this other guy she mentioned once or twice."

Allie's ears perked up. "Oh, yeah?"

"Yeah, this was a few months ago, but it sounded like she was getting hot and heavy on the side with this guy. She would say something and then make a big deal out of it like she shouldn't have. Like she wanted everyone to know she had a boy toy, but that it was a huge secret," Missy said, relishing in her gossip.

"Wow, any ideas who that could have been?" Allie asked.

"Someone local, I'm pretty sure. But like I said, she played like it was this big secret, so I have no idea who," Missy said.

"Well, she definitely shares more with you than she does with me." Allie laughed.

Missy then looked around, bent down a bit, and lowered her voice. "But when she was here Monday, she got a phone call right in the middle of her manicure, so she asked me to pull it out of her pocketbook for her. When I did and showed her the screen, I thought she would faint!"

"No!" Allie replied.

"Yes! After she took a few gulps of air, she asked me to

decline the call and put the phone back in her pocketbook," Missy said, eyes round.

"Did the screen identify the caller?" Allie asked, holding her breath.

"The screen said, 'The Gardener,' and it about scared her to death."

"Isn't that something," Allie commented, shaking her head for emphasis.

Missy finished up the manicure, and Allie promised to stop in again for more gossip. She made sure to leave a good tip and waited until she got back to the truck to call Charlie with the new info.

CHAPTER THIRTY-ONE

"A women's size seven, men's size eleven, and whatever he is," Allie said to the teenager at the counter, gesturing to Mike.

"An eleven also," he supplied.

They grabbed the shoes and met Ryan at their lane. She watched Mike as he took his boots off and put the bowling shoes on.

"You didn't get those just from being a boat mechanic," she ventured, gesturing to her own biceps.

"What, these? I do a little cross training. You?"

"Boxing for me."

"Boxing?"

"Yeah, girls box too," she said with a laugh. "My dad taught me. Right when I turned twelve and he realized girls turn into women who need to be able to protect themselves when their daddies aren't around."

"Smart man," Mike said. "You have a signature move?"

"I have a mean right hook. We should spar some time so you can find out for yourself."

He laughed. "You make me laugh, you're super smart, and you're beautiful."

Before he could see her blush, she turned toward the ball return, grabbed her ball, and said, "And you haven't even seen me bowl yet!"

When they had finished the game, Allie put some money on a card for Ryan to use in the arcade, and she and Mike found a relatively quiet table where they could talk while keeping an eye on Ryan.

"So you're still the prime suspect," she began.

"I figured. They told me not to leave town, so I knew it was pretty serious." He looked at her. "They don't have anything on me, though."

"I know. I told Charlie he was grasping at straws." She took a sip of her Coke. "I think you tick most of their boxes, but I don't think Charlie's convinced of your guilt, either."

"You're sure I didn't have anything to do with it, then?"

"Would we be here if I did?"

"Good point. What now?"

"Now we have to find out who really did do it."

"You've been working with Charlie up until now, right?"

"Yes. It wasn't really a secret, but we didn't broadcast it either."

"Why you?"

"My position in the company. Insider but not really. Plus, my background in investigation, even though it was online fraud—completely different."

They sat quietly for a moment.

"I'm not sure Charlie's going to be so open with me anymore, though."

"Why not?"

"Well, he's looking at you, for one. I told him he was wrong. He said I was too attached to you."

"Are you?" he asked quietly, covering her hand with his on the table.

"Probably." She blushed. "But I also know what he has on you is incredibly weak."

Mike smiled at her but said nothing.

"Secondly, he's probably not going to put me in the thick of things after the threat I got yesterday."

"Wait, what?"

"I got a phone call right when we got home. The voice had been altered, but the person told me to back off or they'd hurt Ryan."

Mike wasn't very good at hiding his emotions, and the color in his face was visibly rising now. He gripped her hand. "They threatened Ryan?"

"Yes. But he's supervised at every hour of the day. They were just trying to scare me."

"Okay. But you are no longer doing this alone, got it?"

"Don't you forget, Mike Gillikin, that I am a grown woman and I can take care of myself," she bristled back at him, snatching her hand back from his grip.

That shocked him out of his protective-man fog. "Of course, you are. I'm sorry. I didn't mean to treat you like a child," he said, apologetic. "But you still need to be careful. I'd like to help you, if you'll let me." He gave her a lopsided grin.

"Sure," she said and smiled back at him in a truce.

"Can I ask you something personal?"

"Uh, sure," she said.

"Were you and Ty ever…?" He let the question hang in the air, unfinished.

"Hell no!" Allie said, whacking his arm with the back of her hand. "Why would you think that?"

"Well, he seemed to treat you differently. He wasn't an ass to you, and he was to just about everyone else. Also, why would you be so interested in his murder?"

"I was kind of like a kid sister to him, plus I just learned that I looked a lot like his mom did. Weird, huh?"

"A little."

"He was a nice guy to me when I was a young girl with few friends and too much going on at home. I guess I'm interested because no one deserves to be killed, and no one deserves to get away with it."

"A woman who likes to see justice served. I like it," he said with a smile, picking up her hand again.

"Yep, and you're not exactly off the hook for hiding things from me either, Mr. Gillikin."

"I should have told you everything a long time ago, but I have a lot to protect, just like you do." He gestured to Ryan, bouncing in front of the Frogger game.

"Do you trust me now?" she asked softly.

"I sure do," he said, taking her other hand in his.

"Can I ask you something?" she said.

"Anything," he said.

"That fight in the yard between you and Ty all those years ago… What was it about?"

"He somehow found out my secrets and threatened to

blackmail me. I didn't back down. You see, I knew a little something about him, too. I know a girl that he used and got pregnant who actually had his child. His family still doesn't know. After that fight, he pretty much left me alone."

"Damn," she said, her mind racing to keep up. "Can I ask you one more thing?"

"Anything," he said.

"This girl you knew that Ty knocked up. Was there something between you two?" she asked, suddenly curious about the type of girl Mike had dated in the past.

"No! Just a girl I knew from school. We had been friends since middle school and had kept in touch over the years," he explained.

Allie paused for a moment to think about his answer, decided he was telling the truth, and asked, "What was her name?"

"Erica," he said. "Erica Mason."

Again, Allie paused. "Did you say Mason?"

"Yeah, Mason. I think she's related to Holly somehow," he said. "Everyone's related in this part of the state, anyway," he said.

Allie tucked that little tidbit away for now and asked, "So you weren't threatening his life, you were threatening to reveal his secret."

"Yep."

"Did you tell Charlie any of this?"

"He didn't ask."

"Well, Mr. Gillikin. It is a school night. Let's see if we can round up Ryan and head home. Okay?"

"Sounds good." They stood. "Thank you, Allie."

"For what?"

"For not believing I could murder someone."

"A girl's gotta trust her gut," she said, smiling. "Let's go."

CHAPTER THIRTY-TWO

Thursday morning, the governor had recommended evacuations, but true to form, traffic was no heavier than usual. Locals just didn't leave for a hurricane like this. Most had generators, and unless they couldn't live without the internet for a day or two, hunkering down was what most were preparing to do. Allie was sure the shelves of the grocery store were bare of bread, milk, and beer by now, but that was about it.

Mike stopped in to fill out his timecard, and he glanced back at Holly, clearly wanting to say something to Allie, but not wanting to be overheard. The phone rang, and Holly answered it.

"Have you ever heard about what the Guthries did to Sammy's family's business?"

"No, I haven't. What can you tell me?"

"Stop and see me at lunch, and I'll tell you the story," he said, handing his timecard back to her and heading out the door with a wave for Holly.

DONNA AND KEITH BRIGGS pushed the office door open with a bang and stormed inside.

"They've recommended we evacuate, but we're not leaving town until we're sure the incompetent numbskulls that work out there have *The Sunset Lady* secured for this blasted hurricane," Keith Briggs bellowed.

Allie had forgotten the British pronunciation of "hurricane" lacked the long "a" sound, and mused on that momentarily before answering, "I believe *The Sunset Lady* will be secured early this morning." She consulted a clipboard on her desk, which only contained invoices for boat remodel materials like decking, vinyl sheeting for seat covers, wood polish, and paint stripping chemicals. "Yes, it says right here she will be secured at roughly eleven this morning." She looked up, smiling sweetly. She ignored Holly in the background, who was stifling a giggle at Allie's use of the prop.

"All right then. If anything happens to her, I'm blaming it all on you," he said, pointing a chubby finger directly at her. "And I will file suit against you individually *and* the yard. Don't think for a second I won't, eh?" he added with a smirk and a quick look at his wife. "Let's go," he growled and walked out the door.

"We will be staying at the Umstead Hotel and Spa in Raleigh if you need to reach us for some reason," Donna said, briefly inspecting her manicure. "I hope you two are leaving town, soon," she added.

Allie and Holly were surprised again by the almost-human moment. "We'll stay here as long as the boys are working in the yard. Hopefully, haul-out will get finished soon," Allie said.

"Well, be safe, ladies. We don't need any more dead bodies around here," Donna said, starting for the door. As she did so, her phone rang. She stopped to pull it out and look at the screen, clearly annoyed at the interruption. When saw who it was, she seemed to lose her balance momentarily, and Allie half rose in reaction, expecting her to fall to the floor.

"Are you all right?" she asked.

"Uh, yeah… Yes, I'm fine," Donna said, recovering herself and turning to push the door open a bit more gently this time.

ALLIE CLIMBED the ladder to *The Lucy May II* and handed a can of soda to Mike. "All right, tell me a story," she said, finding a seat.

"So, Sammy's family used to own a shrimp boat. That's how they made their living. But it's a hard way to live—no guaranteed paycheck. After a couple of cold winters and bad seasons, they couldn't afford the insurance on the boat anymore and were behind on lots of bills. By then, Sammy was working here to help out the family, and the Guthries caught wind of their troubles. They offered to help. They said they would buy the boat, as it was in pretty good condition, and they run a boatyard, after all. Sammy's family should have gotten two, maybe three hundred thousand dollars for it, but Guthrie offered $100,000 cash. What could they do? They had to accept.

The money just barely helped them out of their debt, but then what? They still had new bills to pay and no way to make money."

"They've taken advantage of so many people around here. It's a wonder Neil wasn't the victim," Allie said.

"The Guthries may have money, but they treat people like trash."

"Seems like they like power and like to hold it over people, as well," Allie said. "I never knew that about Sammy's family."

"Yeah, I think he'd be gone pretty quick if he could find something else, too," Mike said. "He has a fierce hatred for the Guthries."

"He's got a lot to be angry about," Allie said.

As she came back into the office, she realized she should look in Neil's files to see if the story about Sammy's family checked out. Holly had left for lunch, and Allie took advantage by heading directly to Neil's file cabinet where she had found the files about Neil's private business dealings before. Curiously, the file cabinet had been locked. Allie stood for a moment, heart beating a bit faster, and wondered if Neil had somehow known she had snooped before. Had he already had the cameras installed? Her mind raced through possibilities and rejected them all, becoming more and more certain it was just a coincidence. Luckily, she had picked a lock or two in her life and was able to open the bottom drawer full of red files fairly quickly. After twenty minutes of flipping through the files labeled *contracts*, she found a handwritten receipt on a torn piece of notebook paper that attested to the fact that Neil Guthrie had purchased a 1995 shrimp trawler from one Bernard Piner of Harkers Island for $100,000 cash on April 17, 2008. She replaced the receipt and the file, pushed the lock back in on the file cabinet, and returned to her desk. The story checked out. Just how much did Sammy hate the Guthries?

CHAPTER THIRTY-THREE

On the way to pick up Ryan after work, Allie's cell phone rang, instantly putting her on high alert. She didn't get too many phone calls and immediately suspected something was wrong with Ryan.

"Hello?" she answered quickly.

"Allie? It's Peg. Ryan's okay," she said, obviously knowing that would be her first concern. "But something weird has happened. He's here at the trailer."

"What?" Her heart was in suddenly in her throat.

"Like I said, he's okay. But he's pacing and humming. I can't get a word out of him, and he's here. So, come home quickly."

"On my way," she said and hung up. She tried not to break too many traffic laws but raced toward the trailer park.

She pulled in and saw Peg sitting on the porch, keeping an eye on Ryan while he processed. Feigning calm, Allie said, "Hey, buddy! How was your day?"

He stopped and hugged her tightly, then took her hand

and led her into the trailer, Peg following behind. They sat on the couch and Ryan began to rock back and forth slightly, biting the nails of his right hand.

"How did you get home, bud?" Allie asked gently.

No verbal response, but his eyes flickered to Peg and then away.

"You're not in trouble, Ryan. We just want to figure this out. You didn't do anything wrong," she said, patting his hand, still entwined with hers.

She reached for her phone and called the Station Club and asked to speak to a supervisor.

"Hello, Ms. Tracey, this is Allie Fox. I'm sitting here at home with Ryan and wondering how he got here. I was supposed to pick him up today like I do every day."

"Ryan was picked up by a woman named Peg Thompson. She's your neighbor, I think? She was listed on your emergency contact form, so when she came to pick him up saying you couldn't be there today, we released him to her."

Allie said to Peg, "They're saying you picked him up."

"I most certainly did not! I've been here all day. About a half hour ago, I noticed Ryan outside pacing. That's when I called you!"

"Ms. Tracey, the woman who picked Ryan up was definitely not Peg Thompson. Did she show you an ID?"

"Yes, she did. We require that any time an emergency contact comes to pick one of our young adults up."

"Okay. Could you please ask your staff never to release Ryan to that woman again, and please get whoever was working to come up with a description of her? My next call will be to the Morehead City Police Department to report an attempted kidnapping."

"Oh my! Yes, Miss Fox. I'm so sorry about this. This has never happened before!"

"I'm sure. Thank you, Ms. Tracey."

As soon as she put the phone down, it rang. "Hello?" Allie answered.

"See how easy it was?" the nasty altered voice cackled. "This was a warning, Allie. Back off!" and the line went dead.

Her hands were shaking as she replaced the phone on the table.

"Was that them?" Peg asked, her voice pitched unnaturally high.

"Yes," Allie replied, her mind racing furiously.

"I'm calling Charlie right now."

WHEN THE YOUNG officer who had taken her report left the trailer, Allie called Charlie back.

"I have already gotten with the Police Chief in Morehead to ensure that this is looked into immediately, Allie. The sketch of the kidnapper is a woman with big blonde hair and a pretty average face. No one I recognized right off the bat. Do you want me to come over?"

"No, I think Ryan has had enough confusion and excitement for one day. We're going to take it easy tonight. But would you be able to request some extra patrols here in the park?"

"Already done. And I'll ride through there myself a

time or two, as well. Even DA Matthews asked after you. Is there anything else you need, Allie?"

"Not right now. I wouldn't put it past Ms. Matthews to be the mastermind behind this, but thank you, Charlie."

"You're welcome. Tell Ryan I said hey."

"Will do."

"Oh, I almost forgot. Looks like Ty and Holly did text back and forth a few times in the past few weeks."

"You know, I'm starting to think there is more to Holly Mason than meets the eye," Allie said. "Thanks again, Charlie."

"Take care of yourself, kiddo," he said.

She hung up and put the phone on the table. Peg, who had been by her side since she had arrived after work, put her hand on Allie's arm.

"I'm going to check with some of the older neighbors here in the park to see if they saw an unfamiliar vehicle about the time Ryan was dropped off. You'd be surprised how much they see." When Allie didn't respond, she asked, "Have you thought about supper, honey?"

"No. Let me check on Ryan, and I'll be right back."

She went down the hall and knocked lightly on Ryan's door. She heard him pause his game, and then entered, knowing he wouldn't ask her to.

"Hey, buddy. How are you doing?"

Ryan came over and gave her a brief hug, and then sat on the bed again, biting his nails on his right hand again. She sat next to him.

"So today was a bit weird, huh? Had you seen the lady who picked you up before?"

His eyes flicked to her, and then back down again. He began to rock back and forth.

"Not sure, huh? Well, that's okay. I don't want you to worry about it, okay?"

He jumped off the bed and began to pace, hands and arms beginning to flail.

"It's okay, Ryan," she began to repeat. She got up and tried to get close to him to squeeze his arms or provide some sort of sensory pressure, but he shrugged off her touch and began to cry and wail, throwing things around the room. All she could do was stand back and watch helplessly, and keep repeating reassuring things to him.

When he finally returned to the bed, he curled up in a fetal position but continued to cry. She sat down next to him. She hugged him tightly and didn't let go for a long while. Finally, his breathing much more even, he grabbed her hand with his left hand, but still said nothing.

"I am here. You are safe. I love you," she said to him, reaching up to brush his bangs up from his face. "Charlie will be looking out for you, and so will Peg. We'll figure this out, okay?"

"Okay," he said. His hand left hers and he rolled over to reach for his game controller.

"Are you hungry?"

His eyes flicked to hers again. "Not yet," he said. This meant he was but wasn't ready to abandon his game to eat yet.

"Let me see what we can scrounge up, okay?"

"Okay," he said, and she left the room.

She walked back down the narrow hallway to find that

Peg had found a spot on the couch and had turned the TV on.

"He okay?" she asked as she saw Allie enter the room.

"He's anxious, but he'll be okay. I'm sure he has no idea what's going on."

"Well, I guess that's okay. Do you want me to fix you something for supper? I know you have to be tired."

"You don't need to do that," Allie said, but she was tired. "I have an idea," she said.

HEADLIGHTS SWUNG across the wall of the trailer about a half hour later. Peg looked up. "Are you expecting someone?" she asked, a worried look on her face.

"Yes," Allie said and smiled.

She went to open the door, and Mike swept in with a Little Caesar's pizza box in his arms.

"Ryan! Pizza's here!" she called. They heard the heavy footsteps as Ryan heeded the call quickly.

"Pizza!" he said, smiling at Mike.

"Yep, pizza just for you, buddy!" Mike said, laughing.

All four of them settled with plates, and Allie introduced Mike to Peg.

"Ah, this is the one who is Charlie's prime suspect, huh?" Peg asked, unapologetic.

"Yes, that's me," Mike said with a smile.

"Stole a car?"

"The mistakes of youth," he said.

"Lied about your name?"

"Just to protect my family and to be able to get a job.

Neil actually knew about my record and hired me anyway, so there's that," he said.

"And you think you can trust him?" Peg whispered to Allie.

She laughed. "He wouldn't be here if I didn't," she said, echoing her sentiment from the other night.

"Mike, you know how I got a phone call the other day threatening Ryan?" she said, glancing nervously at Ryan, a bit worried how he might react to being talked about like this.

"Yes," he said, sitting up straighter in his seat.

"Well, today, someone picked up Ryan at the Station Club and brought him here. They told them she was Peg, but she wasn't, and she even showed them a fake ID."

"What? Someone kidnapped him?" Color was flushing up from his neck to his face. "Why would someone do that?"

"To show me that it could be done. To scare me."

"And *now* are you taking this seriously?" He stood abruptly and began to pace.

"Um… yes, I guess I am."

"Is Ryan okay?" He seemed to remember Ryan was sitting right there and addressed him instead. "Are you okay, buddy?"

Ryan gave him a nervous smile and continued eating his pizza.

"He's okay, although a little rattled," Allie said. "I think he thought he had done something wrong," she said, patting Ryan's hand as she said this. "But you didn't, bud. You didn't do anything wrong."

"I'll be honest, Allie. I'm beyond pissed right now. This

makes me want to go out there, get to the bottom of this, and take care of this joker right now." He flexed his hands into fists.

"I understand. I feel the same way."

"So what do we do?"

Allie looked at Peg. "Well… Peg and I have been theorizing about this whole thing from the beginning, and I think it's a good idea if we share it all with you. See what you think."

Mike looked from Peg to Allie. "Well, I'm honored, ladies. You sure you should do this with the prime suspect?"

"Yeah, are you sure?" Peg asked, looking at Allie.

"I'm sure," she said, laughing. Ryan picked up on her laughter and started giggling. They were all laughing after a few moments.

Peg stood. "Okay, let me clear all this away, and we can get started."

As Peg cleared the table, Ryan took his leave to watch *Pirates of the Caribbean* on his portable DVD player, and Mike and Allie looked at each other.

"You don't have to do this," he said.

"I know. But you said I could lean on you, so I'm going to, okay?"

"Okay," he said, grabbing her hand briefly before Peg came back in.

———

AFTER PEG HAD LEFT for her trailer with a quick raise of her eyebrows at the fact that Mike was not leaving as well,

Allie showed Mike the shed behind the trailer where her bag was.

"Impressive," he remarked, checking out the rigging above.

"Dad wasn't playing around. I trained in the garage at the old house before I moved up north, and he set it up here when they downsized," she explained.

"Do you want to move it out of the way and spar for a bit?" he asked.

Allie hesitated. This was her sanctuary, and she wasn't sure if she was ready to allow anyone else in. "Can we discuss the case while we do? Sometimes, the physical activity spurs my thought process."

"Great idea," he said, and they set to work making space.

"How much experience do you have with this?" Allie asked, trying to sound casual.

"I know some basics, but it's been a long while since I've done anything with it," Mike admitted.

"Okay, we'll stick to body shots, and I'll stick to defense... mostly," she said with a mischievous smile. "Can you take instructions from a girl?"

"I think I already know you could kick my ass in a boxing ring. But I do have strength on my side," he said.

"That's why we're going to take it easy on each other," she said. "Ding!"

They began to circle each other in the relatively small space of the shed.

"So we know the 'kidnapper,' for lack of a better term, was a woman with blonde hair. Did you get any more of a description?" Mike asked as he threw a combination of jabs.

"Not really. The woman at check-out looked to make sure the picture on the ID looked like the woman, but couldn't really describe any noticeable facial features. She was of average build and height, the woman said. I guess all witnesses say that when they can't remember details," Allie said, deftly blocking all of Mike's punches.

"Have you thought about who it could be?" he asked, changing his direction.

"With a description like that, it could be anyone," she said, throwing a combination of her own and tagging Mike in the process.

"I know, but think about it. It's obviously either the killer or an accomplice, right? And they know about me and about Ryan, so it's someone who works in the yard, or knows someone who does," he said, seeming surprised by her punch.

"That's a pretty wide web," Allie said, leaning in.

"Let's try to sort it out by suspect. Let's say Zack is the killer. Who are the blondes in his life?" he asked, trying a few more jabs.

"His girlfriend, Loreli is blonde, and his mom Vicky is also blonde," she supplied, leaning back to avoid his hits.

"Okay, so they could both have tried to take Ryan. Does Loreli know about Ryan?" he asked, changing direction again.

"Probably vaguely, but I don't really see Zack being a mastermind behind all of that, do you?" she asked.

"Probably not. And he probably wouldn't be able to get

Vicky to do it for him, either," he said, landing a punch to her right flank.

"Oof," she grunted. "Unless Vicky was the killer herself," she said, landing her own left jab.

"Good point. She had access, motive, opportunity... Does Vicky know Ryan?" Mike asked, popping back to avoid her tag.

"Yes, she does. Not well, but from when he was little," Allie said, moving laterally to pick up the pace.

"There you go. Your first suspect," he said, pausing and popping his gloves together for emphasis.

"I suppose so," she said, testing a right shovel hook to his side.

"Ow. Okay, Sammy?" Mike asked, again surprised by her punch.

"Sammy's sister Gemma is blonde," she said.

"The one who had a thing with Ty?" he asked, dropping his guard momentarily.

"The very same," she said after delivering a combination and a hit to his stomach.

"Oof! Take it easy!" He laughed. "So she could have taken Ryan. She probably didn't know Ryan, though, right?" He threw a longer series of jabs.

"No, although Sammy could have told her I had a brother," she said, blocking all of his shots once again. "He probably knew about Ryan, and about him working at the Station Club."

"Okay, so another possible suspect," he said, dipping down to throw a jab-shovel hook combination of his own. "Who have we got left?"

"Well, Barbie is a blonde, but again, she would be

rolling around on her little scooter, so I think she can be ruled out," she said, seeing the combo coming a mile away and popping out to avoid it.

"Right. Anyone else?" Mike asked, continuing to move laterally to look for an opening.

"We haven't thought about this before, but you know the owners with active projects may have key cards, as well. Like Donna Briggs," she said, waiting for him to decide on what to throw.

"And she's blonde. Would she know about Ryan?" he asked, deciding on a left-right-left hook to the body.

"I don't think so, but I don't think she had a motive to kill Ty, either. They may have had a fling, but that doesn't equate to murder. I suppose we can't rule her out." Allie blocked all of his shots and stepped out of range.

"Sounds like Vicky may be your best guess, right now," he said, sounding a bit winded.

"Except that I know she was being blackmailed by Ty, and she asked me to keep it quiet. If anything happened to Ryan, and I found out it was her, what would prevent me from telling the world her secrets?" She paused to allow him a minute to catch his breath.

"Maybe she doesn't intend to either let you know it was her, or she doesn't intend to leave you or Ryan alive," he said, hands on his knees.

Allie was stunned into silence, finally realizing how serious this all was. Someone may really have the intent to kill her and harm Ryan.

"Vicky? Really?"

"It's pretty rare when a killer is caught and everyone who knows the person says, 'Yeah, I could see that coming.' Most sociopaths are good actors," he said, nodding to show her he was ready to continue.

"Huh," she said, lifting her gloves to her defensive stance.

"You okay?" he asked, dropping his gloves and standing up straight.

"Pretty creeped out, actually. Not sure if I'll be able to sleep tonight, but glad we worked this out. Now I'm more confused than ever," she said.

Mike laughed. "Of course, there's always the possibility of a wig, too." He paused to catch his breath. "I think it's been three minutes. Let's talk about something else. Anything else. Between Charlie and me, we're not going to let anything happen to you or to Ryan. Let's head inside and see what dire predictions the Weather Channel has about Grady for us, okay?"

"Okay," she said, trying to calm her fears. It was nice to have someone in her corner.

He held the door to the shed open for her and yanked on the string to cut the light off. As soon as it was dark, Mike suddenly pulled Allie toward him and enveloped her in his arms. She could smell his sweat from the workout, but it wasn't a bad smell, especially combined with the clean scent of his shampoo. She felt the heat of his face near hers and heard him ask, "Can I kiss you, Allie?"

Her eyes adjusted to the little light from the moon reaching them in the doorway to the shed as he tucked a stray hair behind her ear. She realized her heart was beating faster than she had ever thought physically possible, and that he was waiting for her answer.

"Yes," she whispered, closing her eyes. His hand found

the back of her head, and he bent down to brush his lips against hers. Finding her ready, he kissed her, lingering for only a moment before releasing his hold on her. She immediately longed for more kisses and to be wrapped in his arms again, and said, "No, don't stop," surprising herself.

"Yes, ma'am," he said, and she could hear the smile on his lips as he held her tightly and kissed her harder and longer this time. Her back arching involuntarily, Allie returned his kiss hungrily and wrapped her arms around his neck as he stumbled backward against the doorframe of the shed with the intensity of the embrace. Their lips seemed to fit perfectly together, and she was amazed that the meeting of flesh could spark such an intense flame within her, igniting somewhere south of her belly button and spreading instantly upward to her scalp. Stars burst behind her closed eyelids and she broke off, surprised by the intensity of her reaction. She looked up at him in shock and saw the concern in his deep blue eyes, likely worried that he had done something wrong.

"Allie?" Ryan's voice came from outside the shed.

They recoiled from each other as if touched by hot pokers, realizing he had come looking for her. They both took a moment to straighten their clothes, and as Mike found and squeezed her hand lightly, they giggled softly before exiting the shed to collect Ryan.

Allie smiled as Mike whispered, "To be continued," into her hair, their hands clasped as they greeted Ryan and headed inside.

CHAPTER THIRTY-FOUR

Allie was surprised to get a call from Charlie as soon as she arrived at work Friday morning.

"I thought I'd call and let you know that we found a witness who saw Ty with a woman who may have been his mystery lover."

"Oh, really? The one he mentioned on Facebook?"

"It may be. We're making arrangements to have that person come down to sit with a sketch artist and meet with a sergeant so we can get a description and an idea of what she may look like."

"Are you thinking this person may have been the one who took Ryan home?"

"We're looking at all possibilities, but I have to say I really want to know who did that to you and Ryan. It's got me a little shaken up."

"We're all a little shaken by it. I thought no one could get to Ryan, but someone has gone to great lengths to do so. Luckily, he wasn't hurt."

"This time," Charlie supplied.

"You're right. But have you thought that maybe they've ramped it up because we are looking in the right direction?"

"Yes, I think somehow we're getting closer, and I have to admit that maybe Mike's not who we should be focusing on."

"Oh?"

"It doesn't make sense for someone to threaten you and Ryan over Mike. You didn't believe he was a good suspect anyway."

"Someone else we've questioned about the black book, then?"

"Possibly. I'll let you know when we get more concrete details from this witness." Charlie paused. "One more thing. We followed up on this Robbie Graves person you think Donna may have been involved with... Turns out he was sent to prison in the eighties for bank robbery, and Scotland Yard never recovered all of the money. I'll have one of the deputies send you the report, but if Donna Briggs was involved with that in any way, we are looking at a very unsavory couple in our midst here. We'll keep looking into this, but just so you know, they remain persons of interest."

"Okay. Thanks for still keeping me in the loop, Charlie."

"It helps me keep an eye on you and Ryan by extension. I don't want anything happening to the two of you."

"Me neither," she said, wondering if she really could protect her brother.

. . .

LATER THAT DAY, Sammy came in from the yard. "Is Neil here?"

"Not today," Allie said.

"How 'bout Holly?"

"Nope, she went home to pack so she can head out of town tomorrow."

"Good," Sammy growled.

A chill ran through Allie's body. "Good?"

"Yeah, I've got a bone to pick with you." Sammy put his hands against the front edge of her desk and leaned in. She cautiously pulled her phone out of her purse in case she needed to call someone in a hurry.

"And what would that be?" she asked.

"You have been spying for Charlie Bishop, and somehow you got it in that pretty little head of yours that I killed Ty Guthrie," he sneered.

"Uh…"

"There's no use denying you're a narc. They've been to my place *twice* now to question me, and my neighbors saw all the cop cars, and now everyone thinks I'm a killer!" he finished, punching the desktop for emphasis and leaving a vibrating sound echoing in the small office.

"Sammy…" Allie held up her hands and inched her chair back, startled by the violence.

"Oh, just shut up. You've done enough, haven't you?" He stood, then, ran a hand through his hair and pointed a finger in her face. "Just watch your back, Allie Fox. This ain't over by a long shot!" He turned to leave, and shouted over his shoulder, "And tell Neil Guthrie that *I quit*!"

She flinched when he slammed the door behind him and let out a breath she didn't know she'd been holding.

After he left, Allie went out to the yard to find Mike. "Mike, Sammy just quit."

"Do what?"

"He just came in, threatened me for ratting him out, quit, and walked out!"

"He can't do that! We're in the midst of hurricane prep! We need him!" Agitated, Mike seemed to refocus, and now with eyes blazing, he said, "Wait, he threatened you?"

"He told me to watch my back," she said.

Mike couldn't speak and was seething with anger.

"Well, I figured he hadn't said anything to you so I came to let you know. Did something happen out here today?"

"Nothing at all! What the hell?"

"Is there anything you'd like me to do?"

"Call Zack and tell him to get his ass here ASAP. He's going to have to step in and fill Sammy's shoes right quick."

"Will do."

"And call Charlie. Before I go after Sammy's ass for threatening you."

ZACK CAME IN A WHILE LATER, all business. He checked in at the office and went to the yard, getting right to work. Holly had returned from her lunch hour and she and Allie were making their own preparations for the hurricane that was coming their way, notifying customers and cross-checking all haul-out and hurricane insurance paperwork. At about 1:15 p.m., they heard an awful, loud crunching noise from the yard. They both jumped out of their seats and ran outside. Zack was on the ground, half under a lift that had toppled sideways. The boat that had been on the lift was now a pile of rubble on the ground, and Zack was screaming in pain.

"Holly, call 911," Allie said breathlessly, running toward Zack.

She noticed in her peripheral vision that Mike was running in the same direction, and they reached Zack at about the same time. Allie gripped his hand and tried to calm him, while Mike tried to move the lift.

"It's okay, Zack. We're here and help is on the way. Try to breathe," Allie said softly.

It looked like his left leg was broken, possibly crushed under the weight of the lift, and his right leg was bent at an awkward angle. Mike couldn't budge the lift and went to see if any of the other equipment in the yard could be used to move the lift. Mike waffled between one of the cranes or another lift.

Allie shouted, "Which one is closer?"

"The lift," Mike said, and he ran to get it started up and headed toward Zack.

"Don't let it roll on top of him this way!" she said.

"I know, Allie. I got this," Mike said calmly.

"If he can get the lift bars under your lift and get it off of you, it'll hurt like hell, okay? All the blood will rush into your leg, so be prepared for that, okay, Zack?" she murmured.

Mike did his best to get the lift bars where they needed to be and then slowly started to raise the arms of the lift. The damaged lift wobbled, and Mike immediately stopped. Everyone held their breath until it steadied, and then Mike continued to raise the arms.

Mike said, "Allie, I'm not going to be able to raise it all the way off the ground, so when I tell you, you're going to have to pull Zack out from under the busted lift, okay?"

"Okay," she said, scooting around behind Zack's head and looping her arms underneath his arms. In another two minutes, Mike yelled, "Okay!" and Allie scrambled to pull Zack backward, out of harm's way. She heaved on him for another twenty seconds that seemed like an eternity, and he was free, but moaning and screaming in pain. *Another half a minute, and he might pass out,* she thought. Mike eased the damaged lift back down and they huddled around Zack, saying, "It's okay, buddy. Not too much longer. You're all right now."

Finally, the ambulance came and the paramedics took over. When they had transported Zack out of the yard, Mike and Allie turned to each other. "What the hell happened?" Allie asked.

"I couldn't tell you. I didn't see it, did you?" Mike asked.

"Was it an accident?" Allie asked.

"I guess so, but lifts don't often fall on their sides like that. Did the boat's weight make it topple?" Mike wondered aloud.

Charlie was suddenly beside them, asking questions that none of them could answer.

"Could it have been tampered with?" he asked Mike.

"I suppose it could have. Do you think someone did this on purpose?"

"It's always a possibility, especially in such close proximity to where Ty was killed. I don't like coincidences."

"Well, it was supposed to be Sammy on the lift, right?" Allie pointed out.

"Where is Sammy, anyway?" Charlie asked.

"He quit today," she said.

"And threatened Allie, too," Mike said.

"Interesting," he said, his lips tensing and turning into white lines. "Well, we'll get some techs out here to see if this is a crime scene or not. I know you have a lot of work to do with the hurricane coming, but take it easy out here today, and keep your eyes peeled."

"Yes, sir," they replied. He walked off to his cruiser, and the two of them went into the office to clean up and take a moment.

"Is Zack okay?" Holly asked when they opened the door.

"I think he'll be okay," Allie said. "He's in a lot of pain, but I doubt his injuries are life-threatening. Although it could have been much worse," she added, looking at Mike.

"He was pretty lucky," Mike agreed. "I hate to think that was an attempt on someone's life, but I guess we can't rule it out, can we?"

"I'm with Charlie. I don't like coincidences," Allie said.

"Now we're short a person again. More work for me," Mike said. "I'll clean up a bit and get back at it. I don't want to be here all night, especially if someone is out there trying to pick us off," he added.

Allie said, "Lovely thought. I'm staying until you're done."

"Okay," Mike said and smiled.

. . .

WHEN IT STARTED to get dark, Mike finished up what he could do for the day and headed back to the office. He looked exhausted but satisfied that he had done the best he could shorthanded.

"Any word on Zack?" Mike asked.

"They took him to Vidant Hospital in Greenville."

"Because you know they can't handle any more than an appendectomy at Carteret General," Mike said with an eyeroll.

"He's in surgery now. He actually wasn't as badly injured as he could have been, although he has compound fractures in his left leg and some torn ligaments in his right. He won't be working for a while."

"That could have been much worse."

"Yes, it could have," she agreed.

"I'm slam wore out, but wired for some reason, too," Mike said.

"Adrenaline," she said. "Peg's keeping an eye on Ryan. I called her to let her know I was going to stay a little later tonight. Do you want to head downtown for a bite to eat?"

"That sounds fantastic. I'm starving," Mike said.

"Great. Let's go."

THE WAITRESS BROUGHT her shrimp basket and Mike's clams. "Good thing you came in tonight. We're boarding up the windows and closing up tomorrow. The surfers had fun today, but Grady's already off the coast of South

Carolina," she said, pausing to look south into the darkness and then retreating to the kitchen. It was a warm, breezy night, and the porch at the Dock House was a relaxing place to be that night, but the wind was picking up. The live music drifted upstairs, and they ate in relative peace, both hungry and tired.

"Do you think someone really tampered with the lift somehow?"

"I'm not sure. I don't see how, but it would be a hell of a coincidence, wouldn't it?"

Allie agreed. "So this all started with a theft, or at least it was made to look like it, but maybe Ty was the real target and the theft was an afterthought? Ty could have been targeted because of his blackmailing attempts, or his philandering. But the fact remains that someone most likely had a key card to get into the yard in the first place, and they know about my brother, so it means someone who works for or had worked for Guthrie's Marine. Is that all logical?"

"Sounds like it to me, although someone could have hid in the yard during the day rather than get in with a key card after hours," Mike said, sipping his beer.

"Wouldn't we have noticed someone in the yard?"

"I'd like to think so," he said.

"It sure would be nice to find that key card and wrap up that loose end," Allie said.

"What are you thinking?" Mike said, eyeing her.

"Are you too tired to go back to the yard and see if we can find anything on the Trumpy?"

"Why not? I don't think I've had enough excitement for the day," he said, laughing.

CHAPTER THIRTY-FIVE

Mike turned his headlights off as his truck crept toward Guthrie's Marine. They parked in the lot across the street from the yard and Mike cut the engine off. They watched to see if there was any movement or sign of life in the office or yard. After a couple of minutes of surveillance and hearing nothing but the wind whistling by the truck, Mike asked, "You got the flashlight?"

"Yep," Allie said, wondering if she was only imagining the wind getting louder.

"Don't turn it on until we get aboard unless you have to. That will reduce the chance of us being seen."

"This isn't my first rodeo, cowboy," she said and he chuckled.

They climbed out of the truck and shut the doors quietly. Her hand warmed in his as they navigated the dark, crossing the road and into the gravel lot of Guthrie's.

"Oh, shit," Allie said.

"What?" Mike said, turning to her.

"The camera system Neil said he was installing. It'll record our every move!"

"Were they installed? I haven't seen anyone in the yard."

"I haven't either. And I haven't seen an invoice for installation, either," Allie said.

"Then it was probably just another threat from Neil." Mike put a hand to her shoulder.

"I think you're right. We're probably good to go, then," she said.

Mike waved his key under the reader and the chain link gate began to creak open. They both stepped back into the shadows, watching again for movement or any sign of life spurred by the noise of the gate opening. After a couple of breathless minutes, Mike pulled Allie into the darkened yard and towards *The Sunset Lady*. The gate closed behind them.

They climbed the stairs and entered the pilot house. Allie turned on the small flashlight and pointed it at the ground.

"So we're looking for a key card and anything else?" Mike whispered.

"Maybe a possible murder weapon? Ty was hit in the chest with incredible force. But I doubt the killer brought a baseball bat or a golf club with them. Maybe they used something already on board?" she ventured. "It's doubtful the scene techs missed anything, but they don't know boats, either."

"All right, let's split up. You start on the staff end of the quarters and I'll start on the other. We'll meet in the middle and compare notes."

"Okay," she said and they headed downstairs. She took a right turn at the bottom and Mike turned left, toward the bow. She began to search each room methodically, removing the contents of each storage space and then replacing them carefully when nothing out of the ordinary turned up. Getting on her hands and knees, she checked less obvious locations and even tapped lightly here and there in case there were hidden compartments like she had found on the *Barbara Jean*.

After searching the Captain's quarters, the crew quarters, and the crew bathroom, she had turned up nothing. In fact, it had looked like nothing had been disturbed since the captain and crew had left the vessel in the spring. She headed down the hallway to see where Mike was and to help him search. She found him in the master bunk room.

"Hey," she whispered.

Mike whirled around, automatically landing in a fighting stance with arms out. He relaxed when he saw her and laughed quietly. "You scared me!"

"Sorry." She started to laugh with him but suddenly swallowed it as they both caught the faint sound of a voice outside. Allie grabbed Mike's arm reflexively, making sure he had heard, and clicked the small flashlight off. They both attempted to squeeze in between the bed and the porthole so they could try to hear what was said. There were two voices, but the wind was carrying some of the conversation away. Allie reached for her phone in her back pocket, raised it to the porthole, and set it to record. She hoped it would be able to pick up some of what they were hearing.

One voice was clearly a woman's, but the other was not so definite. She heard the words *plan*, *deal*, and *stolen*, and then she and Mike both stiffened when they heard *dead* and *murder*. They looked at each other in the dark, and he pulled her closer. She couldn't help but think about how good it felt to be held close. And even though he had worked so hard all day in the yard, Mike still managed to smell good. Really good. How did he do that?

Focus, Allie. You both could be in mortal danger. But by that time, the conversation had faded to imperceptibility and Mike straightened toward the porthole to see if he could see anything outside. Just as he did, a set of headlights swung his way as a vehicle pealed out of the gravel parking lot. He ducked just in time to see another set of headlights swing around the small space. Whoever it was out there had left in two separate vehicles. Mike and Allie looked at each other and let out a big breath. Mike straightened, shaking out his hands, and they both laughed at the tension.

"Wow. That was pretty close," Mike said.

"I know. I kept wondering where we could hide if they boarded *The Sunset Lady*."

He put his arms around her, hugged her tightly, and kissed her lightly on the forehead. "I've wanted to do that since last night," he said. "Are you okay?"

"Just a little ramped up. That's a jolt of adrenaline, huh?"

"You could say that."

He squeezed her again. "And that was just because you smell so good." He didn't quite let her go this time and she found she didn't mind at all. He tilted her chin up and kissed her tenderly. They held each other for a moment longer and then stepped back from each other.

"Do you think your phone picked up any of that?"

"I have no idea. I'll have a listen when I get home and let you know. Have you found anything?"

"No, and I was just about done in here."

They went up on deck to look around a bit before calling it a night.

"I don't see anything here, do you?"

"No. I think there's a possibility there are some accomplices involved here and they have access to the yard. Maybe someone came back after the scene techs and wiped it clean."

"It's very likely," he said. "It sounds like at least one woman is involved, but of course we knew that based on the attempted kidnapping of Ryan."

"And the lack of any kind of weapon could mean that the killer himself was the weapon. Some sort of lethal strike to the chest," she mused. "Did you check the little kitchen area?"

"No, I hadn't gotten there yet," Mike said.

"Let's look real quick, and then we can get out of here," she suggested.

"Okay, lead the way," he said.

"I'm thinking Ty was chased from below deck up to the main cabin. Saw something from the *Barbara Jean*, came to investigate. The attacker surprised him downstairs and chased him up."

"Then it would be likely the killer lost the card in the chase," Mike surmised.

Allie slowly descended the stairs, absorbing minute details of the relatively small space. When she reached the bottom, she noticed the granite countertops again, and the brand-name appliances that were downsized to fit a tiny galley kitchen.

Slipping the flashlight from her back pocket, she turned it on and held it over her head. She aimed it into the nooks and crannies between cabinets and appliances, craning her head this way and that to try to make sense of what she was seeing and not seeing. She got down on the floor, laid the flashlight next to her, and tried to pry the toe-kicks off the cabinets to see if any were loose and hiding any goodies. No luck. Next, she tried to pry the base grill off the compact refrigerator, but saw that it was secured with screws.

"You don't have a screwdriver with you, do you? A Phillips head?" she asked.

"I've got a small multi-tool on my keychain. Hang on a minute," Mike said, unlatching his keys from his belt loop.

Allie shined the flashlight through the grate and thought she saw something angular that was out of place. She tried not to get her hopes up.

Mike handed her the multi-tool with a tiny Phillips head screwdriver extended. She unscrewed the grate and shined the flashlight where she thought she had seen something. Sure enough, there was a dusty key card lying about two inches past the front edge of the base of the refrigerator.

"Mike, we got it," she said calmly.

"All right. We should take it with us in case anyone wants to revisit *The Sunset Lady* to retrieve it. I'll look around for a bag," he said, running up the stairs and returning quite quickly with a waterproof map bag from the boat's steering area. They switched spots so Mike could retrieve the card with the bag.

"You are some kind of lucky," Mike said in wonderment, holding the bag with the card up for her to see.

"I'm not lucky, I'm good," she said with a wink.

"Don't know how the scene techs missed it before," Mike said.

"Well, it's possible they didn't, you know," she said, reminding him that the scene hadn't been secured for the better part of the week. "That's why Charlie won't really be able to use it as evidence. But the suspects don't know that."

"Good point," he said. "Weather's getting a little bad. We should get going," Mike said. "I'll drive you back to your truck at the Dock House."

"Okay," she said, suddenly a little shy. She didn't want the night to end, even though their activities couldn't rightly be called a date.

"Weirdly enough, I enjoyed myself tonight," he said smiling, echoing her thoughts.

"I was thinking the same thing," she said. "But I'm not going to say 'Let's do it again sometime.'" She laughed. "I don't think I've ever held my breath so long!"

Mike laughed. "Agreed," he said. "Can I take you somewhere nice soon?"

"I'd really like that," she said and blushed.

He leaned in for a lingering kiss that turned her insides to molten lava, then took her hand and led her back up the stairs.

CHAPTER THIRTY-SIX

I t was late when Allie got home, and she was ready to crash on the couch until Peg reminded her that she was evacuating early in the morning. She filled her in as best she could about what had happened.

"Allie, you're taking big risks, and I'm worried about you. When are you and Ryan evacuating?"

"Probably tomorrow afternoon," Allie said.

"So late. Why don't you call off work and come with me in the morning?"

"I can't. I've got to finish up at the yard. We're short-handed as it is. We'll be fine," she promised.

When Peg saw that she couldn't persuade Allie, she hugged her, asked her to let her know when she was safe, and then left.

Allie remembered the recording she had attempted to make and pulled her phone from her purse. After messing with the app a bit, she got it to a volume where she could make out some words. It wasn't as clear as what she and

Mike had heard, but you could definitely hear that two people were having a conversation.

She had thought Ryan was asleep, but he wandered out in his pajamas and sat next to her on the couch. He pointed to her phone, and she said, "This is important stuff I've recorded here, bud. I can't let you have it because I need to make sure we don't lose it, okay?"

"Play," he said.

"Okay, I'll play it again."

Ryan listened. "Again," he said when she had finished. This happened a few more times, and Allie finally said, "Why don't I send you a copy to your iPad so you can listen as many times as you want?"

Ryan smiled and bounced down the hall to get it. When he returned, they made sure the file had transferred, and then Allie sent him to bed. She set her alarm and rolled over on the couch, too tired to change into pajamas.

SATURDAY MORNING, she woke up on time, albeit tired, and started to get ready. She wasn't used to working weekends, but knew they had to get all the prep done today—Hurricane Grady didn't care if it *was* Saturday. That meant Ryan was coming with her to work today, too, as Peg had already evacuated. She heard some noises coming from Ryan's room and ventured down the hall, knocking lightly on the door before entering. He was sitting on the bed, listening to the recording from the previous night. When he saw her, he smiled.

"Like Jack Sparrow!"

"What?"

"Like Jack Sparrow!" He pointed to the iPad.

"The voice sounds like Jack Sparrow?" Allie asked.

Ryan nodded. He kept repeating, "Like Jack Sparrow!" with a wide grin on his face. Allie listened and could kind of make out some sort of accent on the deeper voice.

"You think it sounds like a pirate?"

"Like Jack Sparrow!" Ryan said, agreeing.

"Huh," Allie said. "But who talks like a pirate?" she asked herself. To Ryan, she said, "Good job, buddy! I didn't catch that! We'll have to figure that one out!"

They continued to get ready for the day and went out to the truck. The forecast didn't look good, and today should be their last day of work this week. The wind was blowing pretty good, making driving a little difficult, so Allie didn't catch what Ryan said at first.

"What did you say, Ryan?"

"Like Fake Peg, too," he said.

"Fake Peg?" she asked and her heart dropped into her stomach. "You mean the lady who brought you home the other day?"

"Fake Peg," he repeated softly.

"So one voice is Jack Sparrow, and the other is Fake Peg?" she asked.

"Jack Sparrow and Fake Peg," he said and beamed at her.

Allie knew they were very, very close.

ALLIE STOPPED at the Sheriff's Department to drop the key card off for Charlie and decided to wait for him to contact her. She wasn't too excited to tell Charlie about last night's adventure. He would probably frown upon their activities, but they *had* found the key card, even if they weren't sure when or how it had gotten there. Ryan's theory that one of the people they overheard was the one who had attempted to kidnap him and that the other sounded like a pirate wasn't a whole lot to go on, but it was something. She texted him and asked him to stop by the office.

Allie installed Ryan in Neil's office and made sure all of his electronics and chargers were close at hand. "You all set, here?" she asked.

Ryan nodded, and she said, "Okay. I'm going to shut the door. Stay in here for a bit, and when it's time to go, I'll come get you." He nodded again, and she closed the door and got to work.

When Holly came in and started to talk, something twigged in Allie's brain. Maybe the Down East accent was what Ryan was talking about, sounding like a pirate. The Down East accent was rooted in Old English, which was basically what pirates spoke back in the day. As she listened to Holly chatter, she began to see the logic in what Ryan had said. This was a possibility. So who was from Down East? Holly, obviously, and Sammy. They both had pretty thick accents that it took Allie a while to get used to and understand. Was that what he had meant? Holly's voice wasn't very deep, but what about Sammy? He had quit yesterday, had a huge beef with Ty, and had access to the yard. *And* he had threatened her. She decided to talk to Mike about her theory.

When he came in, they decided the three of them

would get a quick lunch together later and talk about it then. He had to finish the haul-out today because it looked like Grady was going to hit tonight, and that was top priority in the yard. He had a lot of work to do.

At lunchtime, they went to the deserted boardwalk and picked a random bench while Ryan paced and flapped around them. There was little chance of being overheard, even here, as most of the businesses had sandbagged and boarded up. Allie told Mike about Ryan's revelations about the recording.

"So whoever brought him home was the female voice on the recording," Mike said.

"Sounds like it," Allie said. "Ryan would know."

"And the other voice, which could be a man or a woman, sounds like a pirate to Ryan."

"Which means it had an accent of some kind. I was thinking maybe a Down East accent?"

"That would make sense! Old English and all that," Mike said.

"Holly has a Down East accent, and so does Sammy. Can you think of any other suspect who has one?"

"No. Unless she was disguising her voice, Holly's is too high, which leaves Sammy."

"Do you think it was him?" Allie asked.

"It could have been, but this isn't much to go on. Would he need to steal from the boat? Would he even know what was valuable on it? Would he know where to offload it?"

"I should have had Ryan listen to Holly while we were at the office. And I feel like we're forgetting some small detail," Allie said. "But Sammy was pretty threatening with me when he quit."

"And he did have a motive. He was still really pissed at Ty over his sister. I don't think he ever got over that."

"He told me that Ty eventually stopped harassing him about it, but I don't believe it," she said. "*And* he had opportunity. If the theft was just a ruse to get Ty on the boat…"

"Maybe it's time to call Charlie and suggest they search his house," Mike suggested.

"Do you think it's enough for a search warrant?"

"Well, with him quitting yesterday, too, yeah, I think they could probably get one."

"Okay, I'll call Charlie when we get back."

"You're heading inland tonight, right? You shouldn't have stayed, Allie. Grady looks to be a mean storm," he said, the corners of his mouth tightening into a frown. He put his arm around her as she scooted closer to him on the seat.

"That's the plan," she said.

"I wish I could go with you," he said, carefully tucking her hair behind her ear with his free hand, and nuzzling her neck.

"Me too," she said, distracted and suddenly super-heated. This man had magic powers over her internal thermostat. They both jumped when a strong gust raced past them with a shrill whistle. "We'd best get back so we can finish up," she said reluctantly.

"It's getting dangerous out here," Mike agreed.

HOLLY BEGAN to pack up her things and hesitated as she headed toward the door. "Allie, I…" she began.

"Be safe, Holly. Get going," Allie said.

"No, it's not that. I feel like I need to tell you something."

"Okay," Allie said carefully. "What is it?"

"Sammy's family and mine have been friends since before the Park Service kicked people off Shackleford Banks," Holly began. "I know he's been so angry and hasn't really handled all of this well,"

Allie waited for her to continue.

"But I need you to know he has an alibi for Ty's murder."

"Then why hasn't he shared it with Charlie?" Allie asked.

"He's afraid it isn't strong enough, and will only seem like he had even more motive," Holly said.

"Is this what you two were whispering about the other day?"

"Yes," Holly sighed. "I was trying to get him to tell someone, but he refused."

"And what is his alibi?"

"He's been seeing a girl and was with her," Holly said. "She's my cousin Erica. She had Ty's baby."

"Ah," Allie said. "Yes, that does complicate things, doesn't it?"

"I just thought I needed to say something before he gets charged with murder," Holly said. "I don't know if it was the right thing to do, but it's the truth."

"You did the right thing, Holly," Allie said gently. "Can I ask you something personal?"

"Sure," Holly said.

"Why did you date Ty if he had treated your cousin so poorly?"

"I didn't know he was Erica's baby's father until after. Didn't even know they had been a thing. What a mess," Holly said, shaking her head.

"Get going, and be safe," she added.

Holly left, and Allie pondered what Holly had said. Maybe Sammy did have an alibi. Or maybe Sammy and Erica Mason were lying about having been together when Ty was murdered. He was right that it did give him quite a motive to harm Ty. She didn't have time to consult Mike about this new information, but she would text Charlie, even though she knew he was up to his eyeballs with Grady sure to hit land tonight.

As soon as she hit *send* on the text, the phone rang...

"THANKS FOR THE UPDATE, honey. You doin' okay? Are you going to finally get out of town today?" Charlie asked.

"Yeah, we're going to head inland tonight, I think."

"Good, good. I know you had to stay and help with haul-out at the yard, but you should have left on Thursday. It's going to blow a gale, I think. Ryan thought this person sounded like a pirate, huh?"

"Yep. He loves language."

"He's pretty clever. I'm not too happy about you risking your neck, poking around that boat like that, but at least you took Mike. And you *did* find the key card."

"Don't forget, Charlie, that my dad taught me how to take care of myself."

"True, but you don't know who you're up against yet, either."

"I'll be careful," she promised.

"You're all that boy's got," he reminded her.

"I know."

"The techs have processed the scene of Zack's accident. Do you want to hear what they've found?"

"Sure!"

"How good were you in physics?"

"Huh?"

Charlie laughed. "There are several ways a forklift can be caused to tip over. We have to determine which of these ways was the cause in Zack's case, based on the evidence, since no one saw it happen. Once that is determined, we try to figure out if the cause could have been manufactured by someone else. We'll assume that because he had a boat on the lift at the time, the center of gravity was either toward the front or the side of the lift, and not the rear. If it was near the front, the cause could have included the boat being too heavy, the mast tipping forward, the lift stopping abruptly, the lift quickly accelerating in reverse, or the lift driving up a ramp. If the center of gravity was on the side, it could have been due to an unbalanced load, a pothole, or a sloped surface. The lift could have tipped forward and then on its side on top of Zack's leg, or it could have gone straight over on its side."

"Okay, so could the techs tell which it was?"

"They examined the ground and did not see any deep indentations which would be caused by the front bumper of the lift smashing into the ground, and it's more likely that the lift toppled over directly onto its side on top of Zack."

"And did they find evidence of a pothole? Because he wasn't on a sloped surface, as I remember."

"No, there was no pothole. Therefore, they think it was just an unbalanced load."

"That very well could be. Zack doesn't have a ton of experience on the lift and was probably rushing to get everything done for haul-out."

"So, at this time, we're thinking this was just an accident."

"Would you say this is definitive?"

"I wouldn't rule out foul play, but it's not the most likely scenario. The lift could have tipped forward first, which leaves a lot more possibility for causes involving tampering, and then fallen to the side when the boat became unbalanced. This wouldn't necessarily leave an indentation in the ground."

"But…"

"But it's not very probable, and you know Occam's Razor…"

"The hypothesis with the fewest assumptions is the most likely."

"Correct."

"So that's what we're running with?"

"That's what we're running with," he said. "Oh, and it looks like the partials on the key card belonged to Sammy and Barbie," Charlie reported.

"Barbie, I understand because she issued it, but it must have been Sammy's card," Allie said.

"Yep, that's added to plenty of other evidence we have

pointing in that direction."

"It may have been dropped there at another time, remember," Allie cautioned.

"I know that. But it may have been dropped the night Ty was murdered, too."

"All right, well, they've served the search warrant on Sammy's place, and they're going through evidence now. I'll keep you posted if and when they find anything."

"Not sure if you know this, but Holly just told me that Sammy is seeing Erica Mason, a young woman who apparently had a baby by Ty. He says he was with her the night of the murder."

"We had caught a rumor of that, and we'll definitely be questioning Sammy again," Charlie said. "One more thing. They processed the black smudges on Ty's clothing. Burnt cork."

"Huh. Not what I was expecting. Does that mean anything to you?"

"Not yet. We'll have to see how that ties in. We'll keep digging into it," Charlie promised.

"Okay. I guess I'll talk to you soon," Allie said.

"Yep, bye."

ALLIE HEARD the crunch of gravel as someone pulled in outside the office. *Who in the world would be coming here with the hurricane so close?* She craned her neck to see out the window and had a sinking feeling in the pit of her stomach as soon as she saw the familiar black SUV parked there. *I sure hope Ryan stays in Neil's office.* Kat Matthews hopped out with her huge sunglasses hiding half her face again. She quickly strode to the door and opened it. "Allie. Just who I was hoping to see. Got a minute?"

Trapped by the constraints of her employment, Allie could do nothing but nod and gesture for Kat to pull up Holly's chair.

"I just stopped by on my way home to Eastman's Creek. The county offices and courthouse have closed up for the hurricane. Seems you and I need to have another little chat," Kat said, removing her sunglasses and lowering her chin to give Allie a hard stare, meant to intimidate her prey. "As I told you before, Neil Guthrie is an old friend, and now he has one son in a casket and another in a hospital bed, no thanks to you. Your involvement has weakened the focus of this investigation. I don't like it when citizens such as yourself"—here she paused to look Allie up and down—"take it upon themselves to go rogue and impede an investigation. Luckily for you, I believe we have identified the perpetrator and are about to wrap this up." She paused and stood. "I just wanted to make clear to you that if it weren't for Charlie Bishop, you may have been brought up on obstruction charges, and believe me, honey, when I say you'd be in a jail cell in a heartbeat. And then where would that leave poor Ryan?" She pouted for full effect, then stood, looking down on Allie.

Matching Kat's stare, Allie slowly got to her feet and said calmly, "I suggest you have a seat because I have a few things to say to you, as well."

After a moment, Kat sat back down carefully.

"From the beginning, you've had an irrational need to get me away from this case, and I couldn't figure it out.

But then I found something that helped explain your nervousness about my involvement. You're supposed to recuse yourself when you have personal involvement with the victim or suspect, Kat. You know better than that," Allie said coyly.

"It's a small county, and everyone knows everyone around here, especially in the upper echelons of society. I've been upfront about being old friends with Neil and it has had no bearing on this case," Kat said defensively, fiddling with her watch.

"But you were more than friends with Neil, Kat," Allie said. "Or should I call you Kitten?"

Kat Matthews turned a bright shade of pink and sat stock still, staring at Allie with her mouth slightly open. Allie let her process that for a minute and continued. "What would happen if an affair between you and Neil Guthrie got out? Would your Good Ol' Boy Club continue to back you, or would they leave you to the whims of the media and the voting public? Probably hard to predict, huh? That's why you've been so nervous. You knew my background in investigations and knew it was only a matter of time before I sussed it out."

Kat Matthews closed her mouth and swallowed carefully. "What do you intend to do?"

"Me?" Allie asked innocently. "Nothing. I'm not convinced you have the right suspect in your sights, but I don't think your involvement with Neil has put anyone in jeopardy. Yet." Allie paused and said, "But I will ask you to leave me and my brother alone."

Kat Matthews nodded slowly, stood, and returned her

sunglasses to her face before turning and making her way carefully back to her SUV.

"Somehow, I doubt that's the end of that," Allie said to herself.

AFTER A FEW MINUTES, Neil breezed into the office. "How's Mike doing? Is he almost finished with haul-out?" Neil asked.

"Yes, he should finish up within the hour. He's been working his tail off. How's Zack?"

"Okay. He won't be on his feet for a while. So much for motivating him to step up and fill Ty's shoes. I hope he doesn't get too used to the pain meds, either. What the hell happened with the lift?"

"I didn't see it and I don't think Mike saw it either."

"Was it an accident?"

"The Sheriff's Department has ruled it an accident," she reported.

"Okay. Well as soon as he's done, there's no need to stick around. You both can get the hell out of there. I'll call you on your cell after it's over to let you know when to come back in. I'm going to check on Mike before I leave."

"Okay. Be safe, Neil."

"Yep," he said gruffly and left.

When Mike had secured the last boat, he came inside. The wind was starting to howl, screaming as it whipped around the corners of the building.

"Neil said we can go when you're finished," she told him.

"Good, let's get the hell out of here," Mike said.

"Be safe on the way to the hotel, Allie," Mike said, reaching out for her and pulling her into his arms.

"Are you going to your dad's?"

"Yes," he said.

"Okay. I'll be safe. I'll call you when we get to the hotel."

"Okay."

They paused for just a moment, hesitant to go their separate ways. Then Mike put his finger under her chin, tilting it up so could kiss her fully and deeply with all of the frustration he had to be feeling at the moment. She smiled at him, sure he could hear her heart humming, and watched him walk to his truck before getting Ryan ready to go.

WHEN THEY RETURNED to the trailer, Allie started to prepare to leave for the hotel in Raleigh to avoid the hurricane, but watched Ryan bounce to his room and come back with one of his drawings.

"Oh, you've been working on this one for a while," she said. "Is it all done? Can you show it to me now?"

"All done," he said, beaming. He handed her the drawing.

"What is this big building here, Ryan?" she asked patiently.

"Dad," he said, ignoring her question and pointing to one of the windows in the large building. Sure enough, she could see a man in a bed in the room he was pointing to. Trying to remember when her dad may have been in a situation like that, she repeated, "Where is this, bud?"

He pointed to a panel-type truck in front of the building, and it clicked. That was an ambulance, and Ryan had drawn their dad when he was in the hospital for foot surgery about five years ago.

Funny, Allie thought. *Why would he draw this now?*

And at that moment, all of the pieces suddenly snapped into place, and she saw it all clearly. She knew who had killed Ty. Then the phone rang.

"Hello?"

"I told you to drop it, Allie. Now Ryan will pay," the altered voice threatened.

"No, listen. I know who you are. I have proof you did it. But I'll turn it over to you if you promise to leave my brother alone." The words were out of her mouth before she knew what she was saying. She noticed her hands were shaking again.

The line was silent for a moment, then, "Meet me on *The Sunset Lady* in a half hour. I don't need to tell you to come alone."

The line went dead.

She looked at Ryan. "Change of plans, bud."

SHE PULLED up at Mike's dad's apartment twenty minutes later. She knew he'd be there with his dad. He was surprised to see her with Ryan in tow at the door.

Allie grabbed Ryan and hugged him hard before letting him head inside and find Mike's TV. "I need to take care of something, and I didn't want to leave Ryan alone in the trailer with the hurricane and all. Peg has already gone to her sister's in Raleigh. I hope you don't mind. I shouldn't be long."

"What is this, Allie?"

"Can you keep an eye on him, please?" Her voice was pinched and anxious.

"I'll go with you."

"You can't. Someone needs to be here with your dad and Ryan."

He hesitated. She could see that he realized her plan was logical, but he didn't like it. "Can I call Charlie?" he asked.

"He'll be crazy busy with the storm," she said. "I'll tell you what. Call him in an hour, okay? If I'm not back?"

"What do you mean if you're not back??"

"Just… Please?"

"I don't like this, Allie," he said, anguished. "Please, please be careful," he said finally. "And I've got this. Don't worry," he added, squeezing her hand.

"Thanks!" she said, giving him a quick kiss and running back to her truck.

CHAPTER THIRTY-SEVEN

A llie rolled the truck, headlights off, into the spot where she and Mike had parked the night before. She looked and tried to listen for anyone out there in the darkness, but the wind was just too powerful to hear anything. She stashed her phone and her small flashlight in her pockets and slipped out of the truck, pushing the door closed behind her. Keeping to the shadows, she crossed the road and onto the property of the marine yard. She peeked through the chain link to see if she could see any movement but couldn't beside the leaves and branches blowing by in the steady wind. She waved her key card under the reader and then stepped back into the shadows to wait for it to open. When the gate creaked open, she thought she saw something move on *The Sunset Lady*. *The killer must already be here*, she thought, tensing. She took a slow deep breath and slipped into the yard, the gate closing slowly behind her.

She walked over to *The Sunset Lady* and climbed the metal stairs to the deck, slowing as she neared the top.

She didn't want to have her head blown off as soon as it appeared above board. She heard a voice from the pilot house say, "It's all right, Allie. I don't have any weapons."

"You didn't when you killed Ty, either. Just your own body and the element of surprise. It probably didn't hurt that he'd had a few beers, either," she surmised.

"He always drank too much. You don't seem surprised to see me."

"Like I said on the phone. I knew it was you, Barbie. Plenty of mistakes gave you away."

"And those were?"

"The first was the hospital. You said you went to Carteret General for your surgery, but they don't do specialized surgeries there. You would have had to go to Greenville for that. Ryan figured that one out."

Barbie laughed as lightning struck nearby and a crack of thunder boomed. "Not a single person thought to look into that. They all just took my word for it! I guess the scooter was all the proof they needed."

"And your physical therapy? Why would you need to go to Jacksonville for that? It didn't make sense. But if you never had surgery, what were you going to Jacksonville for? Unless it was martial arts training that you couldn't get here in Carteret County. You trained in something special to make your body your weapon." Allie could feel drops of rain driving into her skin from all angles.

"Yes, I did. Muay Thai, and a special kick that can stop a heart. And I surprised the hell out of Ty," Barbie said, a glint in her eye and a wicked smile on her face.

"He didn't know it was you at first."

289

"No, he didn't know, really, until he snatched my hat off and saw my hair."

"You used burnt cork to darken your face. The cork from the one wine bottle in your kitchen without one."

"How did you put that together?" Barbie asked, seeming interested now.

"There were traces of burnt cork on Ty's sleeves. Did you get that idea from Pinterest, too?" Allie smirked.

"Okay, I think I've had just about enough of you. I don't see anything in your hands. You didn't bring me any proof like you said you would, did you?"

"Now, why would I do that? So you could get away with all of this? The theft, the murder, the threats against my brother?" Another lightning flash and a louder rumble of thunder.

"The theft wasn't just my idea, you know."

"Oh, I know. This all started with an insurance fraud scheme between you and Donna Briggs, didn't it?"

"You're no fun. Yes, you're right clever, Allie. Donna was the one who told me it was a bigger payout to stay married, and I knew I'd get screwed if I went for alimony. But please tell me more," Barbie mocked.

"Donna didn't know you were going to murder Ty, did she?"

"No. Why would I tell her that?"

"So that's why she wanted to meet you here last night. She was pissed you made everything so complicated, wasn't she?"

"Are we done here? I'd like to kick your ass now," Barbie said, smile disappearing.

"Did you know she was screwing Ty behind your back the whole time? I think they call it shagging in the UK."

Barbie stood stock still, absorbing the news. A flash of lightning illuminated the dumbfounded look on her face.

"He called her Rose, as in his English Rose, and she called him The Gardner," Allie explained, thunder rolling all around them.

As the sky let loose and rain pelted them both, Barbie shrieked and sprang toward Allie in a rage.

Allie dodged to the side, and Barbie almost slipped and went over the edge, but caught herself and instead turned around backward in a 360 kick move aimed at Allie's head. Ducking, Allie put her hands up in defense. When Barbie resettled, she too, had her hands up, battle ready.

"No more threats, Allie. Now it's you who will have to be eliminated. I did warn you."

"Yes, you did," Allie said, backing toward the deck of the bow with careful steps on the slick surface. She threw a few punches at Barbie's head but failed to connect with anything other than elbows. When she threw another punch, Barbie deflected with one elbow and came around with the other to land a hit to Allie's jaw. She hadn't seen that coming. Barbie wasn't just boxing with her. This was something else entirely.

Allie saw Barbie's kick in a flash of lightning before it landed. She spun out of the way and threw some punches to Barbie's torso, careful to distance herself from Barbie's elbows, too. She was quickly being maneuvered to the same spot where Ty had fallen overboard. She saw Barbie spin backward and ducked low as her foot sailed over her head. Before Barbie recovered, Allie started throwing a flurry of punches, not even caring where she connected. She began to gain ground, and when she stopped, she realized Barbie was stunned by her speed and agility. She took the opportunity and put everything she had behind her right hook. It connected with the side of Barbie's head, and she crumpled to the deck.

Allie stepped back out of range of a sweeper kick and kept her hand fists up in defense, in case Barbie wasn't really knocked out cold. She waited a moment, and when the prone form on the deck in front of her didn't move, she dropped her fists and shook out her body briefly before stooping to check Barbie's pulse. She was alive. Allie pulled some zip ties from her back pocket, secured Barbie's hands behind her, bound her feet, and called Charlie.

CHAPTER THIRTY-EIGHT

Sunday was a gorgeous day, and Allie, Mike, and Ryan were outside, working on repairs to the trailer. Everyone in the park had the same idea, and the mood in the air was one of goodwill and hard work. Mike was on his way over, and Allie was ready to set the place to rights.

Her phone rang, and she hesitated then answered it. "She's aiming for a plea deal and told us everything," Charlie said. "More than we needed to know, really. I thought you might want to watch the recording of her interrogation."

"You know what? I'm good. She pretty much told me everything, I think," Allie said, gingerly touching her jaw where a big purple bruise marked the impact of Barbie's kick.

"She was the one who went to pick up Ryan," Charlie said. "Through her contacts at the Muay Thai dojo in Jacksonville, she was able to get a fake ID pretty quickly that said she was Peg Thompson. And she was able to get a couple of burner phones to call you and threaten you."

"What was she charged with?"

"Barbie's being charged with first-degree murder. She could get life in prison or even the death penalty, but she was cooperative, so we'll see."

"And Donna Briggs?"

"Donna is looking at felony theft and breaking-and-entering, maybe more. Plus, Scotland Yard is pursuing an investigation regarding the money from Robbie Graves's bank robbery."

"Do you think Barbie would have hurt Ryan?" Allie asked him.

"Who knows, Allie? I think murdering her husband proves she's not exactly stable."

"I'm sure glad we caught her, Charlie."

"You caught her, kiddo. With a little help from Ryan." He laughed.

"Thanks for giving me a chance to help, Charlie."

"Hey, we're a small department and can always use help. You are a smart girl with a talent for investigation. Tell me this hasn't been a little fun for you."

"Are you offering me a job?" Allie laughed.

"Hey, you never know." He chuckled.

"Closing this case... It's definitely the best feeling I've had since I heard about my parents."

"Something to think about," Charlie said.

ALLIE WALKED across the space between the trailers and knocked on Peg's door, knowing she had returned the night before.

"Hello, honey!" Peg said when she opened the door.

She gave Allie a big hug and said, "Not too much damage to the trailer, I hope."

"No, not too much. A few patches of shingles blown off, and some siding down, but I think we were lucky that Grady died off so quickly when he hit land," Allie said.

"Yes, we were! What are you up to?"

"Just checking on you. Making sure you're okay. Mike is coming over later in case you need anything done."

Peg pulled her into a hug. "If you're okay, I'm okay," she said. Allie hugged Peg extra tight and even kissed her hair before saying she'd check on her later. She walked back across to the trailer and went down the hall to Ryan's room.

"Hey, buddy. You doin' okay?"

He looked up from his iPad and smiled at her.

"You are amazing, you know that?" she asked him.

"Yes," he said simply.

She tousled his hair and leaned in to give him a kiss on the cheek, which he immediately wiped off with the back of his hand.

"I love you, kiddo."

"Love you, too," he said.

MIKE WAS GETTING Ryan into it by asking him to retrieve certain tools from the toolbox on his truck.

"Now I need the Phillips head screwdriver. It has a blue handle and looks like an X on the pointy end. It will be on the driver's side, in the toolbelt at the bottom of the box."

Ryan bounced off to the driver's side of Mike's truck,

reached into the open toolbox, and rooted around until he found the correct screwdriver, and walked it back to Mike.

"Thanks, buddy. You are a big help," Mike said.

Allie smiled, watching them. There weren't too many guys who would be so patient with Ryan, and she appreciated Mike that much more for it.

Her phone rang and she retrieved it from her back pocket. "Hello?"

"Hey, Allie. It's Neil. We'll be opening up again tomorrow, so we'll need you back in at your normal time. Also, since you helped so much finding Ty's killer, and running the place in our absence, I want to offer you a bit of a raise. We can discuss it when you come in tomorrow."

"Uh, Neil? I'm sorry to do this, but I have to give you my two weeks' notice," she said, voice quivering. "Listen, I know you undercut my dad. I just don't think it's in my best interests to work for you anymore. I've decided that I need to move on and do my own thing."

Mike walked up behind her and put his arms around her waist, knowing what was going on.

"Do what? You can't do this! We need you here!" Neil was snarling now.

"I'm actually going to start a new career as a private investigator. If you need me, I'll be there, but I can only stay for two weeks."

"Fine," Neil said and hung up.

"Well, that was awkward," she said, putting her phone back in her pocket.

"Had to be done, though," Mike said, kissing her hair.

"You only have one life, and you need to be doing what makes you happy,"

"I'm so glad I've got you in my corner," she said, turning so she could see him.

"And you do. For as long as you'll have me," he said, smiling. "Let's get Ryan and go get some ice cream."

"Sounds like a plan," she said.

NOTE FROM THE AUTHOR

Thank you for reading *Diamonds, Teak, and Murder*! If you enjoyed it, please consider telling your mystery-loving friends or posting a short review. It would mean a lot to me. For a free mystery novelette entitled *Death at Sunset Pines*, and to be the first to know about the next release in the Crystal Coast Case series, take a moment to sign up for my newsletter.

Thanks again!

Connect with A.M. Ialacci:
www.amialacci.com
www.facebook.com/AMIalacci
www.instagram.com/amialacciauthor
www.twitter.com/AMIalacci
www.bookbub.com/profile/a-m-ialacci
www.goodreads.com/author/show/18931413.A_M_Ialacci

ACKNOWLEDGMENTS

I'd like to thank my parents and my son for their unwavering support, and for believing I could get this, the first novel I ever wrote, into actual print.

I'd like to thank the friends who read it and gave me feedback: Linda Ialacci, Colette Barth, Midge Silver, Lissa Johnston, Amanda Rebello, and Julie Strier.

I'd like to thank Amabel Daniels, Kiersten Modglin, and Laura Hidalgo for their **amazing** skills in editing, formatting, and cover design, respectively.

I'd like to thank NaNoWriMo for existing. Without it, this book would never have been written.

I'd like to thank my sensitivity reader, Joel Francis, for giving me an honest perspective on my character with autism. Don't tell anybody, but we moms don't know everything.

Made in United States
Orlando, FL
22 July 2023